# THE LAST
# SHADOW
# WARRIOR

# THE LAST
# SHADOW
# WARRIOR

## BY SAM SUBITY

SCHOLASTIC INC.

This book was originally published in hardcover by Scholastic Press in 2021.

All rights reserved. Published by Scholastic Inc., *Publishers since 1920*. SCHOLASTIC and associated logos are trademarks and/or registered trademarks of Scholastic Inc.

ISBN 978-1-338-63608-6

10 9 8 7 6 5 4 3 2 1     21 22 23 24 25

Printed in the U.S.A.  40
This edition first printing 2021

Book design by Baily Crawford

FOR REBECCA, FOREVER MY VIKING QUEEN

# CHAPTER 1

# THE SHADOW
# DARKER THAN NIGHT

Most people spend their lives collecting secrets.

Me? I was *born* into my secrets. Well, one *huge* secret really.
And the one person I'd ever been able to fully share it with—the
only person who really got it—was gone.

*"Eeeeyaaah!"*

I swung my battle-ax into Ivar's neck. Torso. Knees. Each blow
reverberated all the way up my arms and rattled my teeth, but I
didn't stop. Couldn't stop. Not if I was ever going to live up to the
legacy she'd left behind. And the promise I'd made.

"WHOA! WHOA! WHOA!"

I spun around. Dad stood at the bottom of the basement steps,
one eyebrow raised as his gaze shifted from the training dummy
to the ax in my hand. "It's a good thing that's made of wood, or
Ivar the Boneless here would be *head*less too." He smiled.

It took a few seconds for his words to register as I stood there
with my chest heaving. Then I scowled at the weapon clenched in
my fist. "I've been practicing for years with this thing. When do

I get to use the real stuff? I think I'm ready." With a final look of derision, I tossed the ax to the floor, where it landed with a clatter.

My dad stepped toward the wall and adjusted a gleaming Viking broadsword that hung among a collection of axes, knives, and other wicked-looking battle gear. Not exactly what you'd expect to find in the basement of most suburban homes. But then, we weren't a normal family. Not by a long shot.

"Abby, we've talked about this before. Warrior training starts at fourteen. Not my rule. That comes directly from the Grey Council." He slid his arm around the dummy's shoulders. "What do you think, Ivar?" Then, dropping his voice an octave, he pretended to speak for the dummy. "I vote we wait till she's thirty."

"Daaaaddddddd . . ." I turned away to hide the slight upturn at the corner of my mouth. I wasn't ready to be out of my funk yet.

"Oh, there it is. Daaaaddddd. Exactly the way every father dreams of being greeted by his adoring daughter." He stopped and waited, maybe expecting a reply.

My bangs were plastered against my forehead and poked into my eyes. I grabbed a towel off a nearby hook and swept it across my face with an angry grunt.

"Anyway," he said. "I didn't come down here to annoy you. Really. Just wanted to let you know I'm going to run down to the store and pick up a couple things. I could get you something. Maybe some cookie dough ice cream? The kind you like with the fudge in the middle?"

I only sighed in response as I knelt and started gathering up the training manuals that lay strewn on the floor in a semicircle around me.

Dad squatted in front of me, trying to catch my eyes. "Look, I get it. This day is hard for me too. Really hard. Your mom . . ." He sucked in a sharp breath and let it out slowly before continuing. "I just wish she was here to help you with this stuff. All of it. Because I'm clearly clueless."

The mention of Mom finally pierced through my anger, and I could almost feel it fall away like a discarded cloak. "Me too," I said quietly. "But not because you're clueless. Well, you are. Sometimes. Not about everything. But . . ."

He held up his hands and laughed. "Okay, okay, I get it. No need to kick a guy when he's down."

I slid one foot across and nudged him with my toe.

"Hey," he said as he stood, "we're still doing our usual thing in her memory tonight, right? A batch of my famous banana chocolate chip pancakes. Then watch *The Princess Bride* for, what is it, the three hundred ninety-fifth time?"

I smiled and nodded. "Twenty-third. And, you know, if you just happened to find some of that ice cream you mentioned, that wouldn't be a bad thing."

"The one thing my daughter learns from me is drowning her problems in copious amounts of sugar." He laughed and glanced down at his watch. "Okay, ice cream it is. I'd better get going, then. Shouldn't be more than twenty . . . twenty-five minutes. You okay here by yourself?"

"Dad, I'm twelve, not two. I'll be fine."

"I know. Miss Independent. Roger that." He started up the stairs, then poked his head back into view. "Abby?"

I turned and looked up at him. "Yeah?"

"Love you."

"Love you too, Dad."

I listened as he walked the rest of the way up the stairs, including the one that squeaked every time. He kept trying to fix it but said it remained hopelessly incorrigible. His footsteps echoed down the hall, then the front door opened and closed.

I shut my eyes and focused on my breathing. In through the nose. Out through the mouth. Push out with the senses. The feel of the rough coolness of the basement floor on the bare skin of my feet. The rich scents of wood and leather that filled the room. Even the familiar *rattle-hum* of our air conditioner doing battle with the unseasonably warm North Carolina October afternoon.

It had been four years since my mom died, but it still felt like yesterday. When I opened my eyes, my gaze fell on the scarred oak surface of a workbench in the corner of the basement. Crossing toward it, I slid my training manuals into the gap on a small shelf above the tools, right beside a thick leather-bound volume where she'd meticulously recorded her life's work.

My hand automatically strayed under the desk's surface, probing among the thick knots for a tiny latch.

*Click.*

A hidden drawer popped open in the lower left of the workbench.

Mom and I had always used it to send secret messages to each other.

I extracted the last thing I ever gave her—a yellowed piece of notebook paper—from the drawer and unfolded it, pressing its corners flat on the desk's surface. On it a crayon drawing showed stick figures of Mom and me battling a giant green monster with sharp, pointy teeth. "My little Grendel hunter" was written in one corner in Mom's neat handwriting.

I traced the letters with the tip of my finger. "I'll finish what you started, Mom." My whispered words felt small, quickly swallowed up in the settling gloom. Was it because I wasn't sure I could keep that promise? I was already sort of past the expiration date when most Aesir kids start to show signs of special abilities. And with each passing year, it became less likely . . .

*THUMP.*

My pulse leapt. I twisted my head to stare up at the ceiling. What was that? Probably just the wind banging a tree branch . . .

*SMASH!*

The sound of glass shattering.

Okay, there's no way that was the wind. My eyes flicked toward my wooden ax on the floor, then to the weapons hanging on the wall. Sure, I wasn't supposed to use them. But if there was someone upstairs, I was totally not going up there with a toy ax. Dad would understand.

I crossed to the wall and selected a short one-handed sword. Better for fighting in close quarters. Then I turned toward the stairs. At the bottom step, I paused and listened.

Nothing. Silence.

At the top of the stairs, the door stood open like Dad had left it. But at my angle, I couldn't see anything except the light fixture over our kitchen table. It was off, the shadows of late afternoon stretching toward it across the ceiling. My hand was trembling so badly, I thought I might drop the sword. Some warrior I was.

I could always call the police, right? With a groan, I pictured my cell phone charging on the kitchen counter. A lot of good that did me down here. But then, I could always wait for Dad to come home. He'd said he wouldn't be gone very long.

No. I needed to show him I wasn't just some little girl anymore. I could take care of myself. And maybe he'd already come back and was in trouble.

I forced myself up one step, then another, placing my foot carefully each time, starting with the balls of my feet and then silently rolling my heel downward like Mom had trained me. About midway up, I remembered the squeaky step. Which one was it again? The fourth from the top. I think. Or was it the fifth? Ugh. I couldn't remember. Could I somehow vault over both of them? Likely I'd end up falling down the stairs and making an even bigger racket. Okay: eeny, meeny, miny . . .

*CREEEEEAAAAK!*

Argh! Well, there went my element of surprise. I quickly covered the remaining stairs to the top and pressed my body flat against the wall next to the doorframe. It had been, what, two or three minutes since I'd heard a sound up here? I replayed the noises in my mind. Maybe Dad had forgotten something and come back.

Yeah, that was probably it. Our little suburb of Charlotte wasn't exactly an epicenter of criminal activity. I was probably making a big deal out of nothing.

Still . . .

"Dad?" I called. Nothing. "Dad?" A little louder. No response. Okay, so he probably got whatever he needed and left again. I was just being a big baby who couldn't be at home by herself for twenty minutes. I lowered my sword and stepped out into the kitchen. My overactive imagination . . .

That's when I saw the shattered glass on the floor. The curtain lining the French doors to our back patio stirred gently in the breeze. The door itself stood open, one of its panes smashed out.

I instantly jerked my sword up again, nearly slicing off my own ear. Maybe Dad had a point about waiting to use real weapons. The blade wobbled even worse than before. I was probably more dangerous to myself than to any intruder.

The only sound other than the thudding of my heart in my ears was the ticking of the clock on the living room mantel. I swiveled my head side to side, quickly surveying the room. The dying sun left me in a gray twilight where every shadow and object seemed to loom with sinister intent. In the corner of the dining room, I could just make out Dad's desk. Every drawer stood open, papers, pens, and file folders strewn across the floor. Fortunately, whoever had done it appeared to be long gone. I hoped.

*Bzzzzzzzzzz.*

I about jumped out of my skin. What was that noise? I swept the rooms with my eyes. It seemed to be coming from the kitchen.

I took a tentative step in that direction, then another. At any minute, I half expected a figure to fly out of the shadows. In a few more steps, I stood in the entryway to the kitchen. I tilted my head to the side and listened, trying to pinpoint the source of the noise.

*BZZZZZZZZZZZZZ.*

Then I saw it. A small object in the middle of the kitchen floor, obscured by shadows thrown from the dim light of the range hood. Everything about this screamed, *Wrong. Get out now.* But I stepped into the kitchen anyway and in two quick strides reached the source of the noise. I crouched down to get a better look at it. What?

There in the middle of our kitchen floor, an old windup toy Viking ship lay vibrating. I recognized it as one my mom had given me when I was probably four or five. But I hadn't seen it in forever. When I picked it up, the tiny oars on the sides of the ship whirred into motion, no longer obstructed by the floor. I pinched the windup mechanism and spun it forward. The oars spun wildly for a few seconds and then stopped. Where had this come from?

A faint glow caught the edge of my vision, and I turned toward it. In the center of the dark glass of the oven door burned a strange red glow. Was the oven on? It took me a few seconds to realize I was looking at a reflection. My head jerked downward to my chest. The runestone my mom had given me years ago seemed to smolder with an angry red light where it hung on a leather cord. I snatched the stone in my hand and pulled it closer to my face. The Norse rune Algiz—protection, life—in the shape of a trident shone in crimson against the coal-black surface. But it was upside down. What did that mean?

I could guess: danger. Death.

As I squatted there inspecting the stone, a tiny tickle at the base of my skull warned of a presence behind me. I whirled, dropping the toy ship and bringing my sword up in the same motion. My heart hammered as my eyes searched the darkness. There. Framed by the entrance to the hallway. A shapeless form even blacker than the night around it. Was that . . . ? My sword bounced uselessly in my trembling hand as the stench of decay seemed to flow around me like a grasping claw.

"Hello, Abby," came an ancient, raspy voice.

I screamed.

# CHAPTER 2

# AN ORDINARY GIRL

"Abby!"

Someone was calling my name. But I couldn't answer. Frozen. So cold.

"ABBY!" Louder this time. "Can you hear me?"

Suddenly my eyes snapped open. I blinked and Dad's face swam into focus. The headphones of his ancient Walkman radio hung loose around his neck. His forehead glistened with sweat.

"Dad! Wh-what happened?!" I squinted and turned my face away from the harsh glare of the overhead fluorescents. A toy Viking ship lay on the floor near my feet where I sat huddled in a corner of the kitchen, my knees hugged tightly to my chest.

The ship. The voice. It all came rushing back to me.

"There was . . . I saw . . . Is it gone?" My words tumbled over themselves as I swung my head side to side wildly, at the same time pressing closer into Dad for protection. It was only then that I realized I was shaking violently.

"Whoa, slow down a minute, honey. You're okay. Tell me what happened." He gently pried the sword from my white-knuckled grip and set it aside next to a grocery bag with a pint of ice cream spilling out, its sides already beading with moisture.

My whole body shook, and I was having trouble forming coherent thoughts. But I didn't miss that he hadn't answered my question: *Is it gone?* "The door," I said. "I heard a noise and thought maybe you were in trouble . . ."

Dad glanced in the direction of the back door, then at his desk, which looked like it had been hit by a mini hurricane. "I ran down to the store like I said. When I was just getting home, I heard you scream, then rushed in and found you huddled here on the kitchen floor."

"So you didn't see . . . anything else?" I asked.

A flicker of fear crossed his eyes and then was gone. "No . . . Abby, what happened here?" His tone was scary intense. Which is saying a lot for a guy who, despite his hulking six-foot-five frame and scruffy beard, is more teddy bear than grizzly. "It's very important that you tell me everything you can remember."

After I'd filled him in on everything from hearing the breaking glass to finding the toy ship and waking up on the kitchen floor, Dad sat back with a stunned look on his face. "No. Not again," he whispered, his gaze going out of focus as he withdrew into some internal landscape. "This can't be happening again. How?"

"Dad? Do you think it was a . . ." Some inner recess of my mind whispered a word: *Grendel*. I winced, remembering the fearless crayon me from the drawing. Then the me from real life, weak and trembling. Finding myself in the face of the nightmare that had haunted my dreams for as long as I could remember, I had merely withered and shrunk away.

Without answering, he suddenly stood and turned, heading down the hall. He pulled open the linen closet and wrestled a pair of suitcases out onto the floor, then started rummaging through the mess on his desk and flinging things into the open luggage.

"Dad?" I said, a wave of panic rising at his strange behavior. "What's going on?"

He pulled out his phone. Thumbed through his list of contacts. "We need to go."

"Go? Go where?"

"I . . . don't know yet," he said, disappearing into the back of the house with his phone to his ear.

Thirty minutes later I stood in the driveway staring into the back of our rusty old Civic hatchback. Crammed into every spare inch of a space roughly the size of a large refrigerator were clothes, books, pictures—all the pieces of us that were portable on short notice.

My shoulder throbbed from three failed attempts to get the hatchback door closed. All I needed was another inch. Two at most. As I built myself up for a final go at it, I glanced around at the looming night. My nerves jangled at the sound of a dog barking in the distance, momentarily breaking the stillness.

I couldn't stop thinking about that thing in our house. Somehow darker even than the night around it. I fought down a panicky feeling remembering the clawlike mist that had reached out for me.

Encircled me. I didn't understand any of this. And Dad had barely said two words since we'd started packing.

I watched a moth beat its wings against the bare bulb over our front porch. The wings made tiny *tink tink* sounds against the glass as the insect continued its fruitless assault on the bulb.

What had Dad meant by *happening again*? I was determined to get some answers. Right after I warmed up a bit. All the heat of the day seemed to have fled with the setting of the sun, leaving behind an unusually frigid night with air that seemed to pierce my lungs like a thousand needles with every breath.

I turned back to the car. "Give it up, you old bucket of rust," I growled, the words escaping like ghosts into the chilly night. Great. Now I was talking to cars. Better get this over with before it started talking back.

I let out a yell and launched myself at the car again, hitting the hatchback door like it was a football blocking sled and shoving for all I was worth. Gritting my teeth and grunting as I leaned into the unyielding steel frame. Finally, there was a small *click*. It was closed.

Feeling a sudden rush of swagger from my little victory, I stepped back and stared defiantly into the night. "I'm not afraid. I'm not—"

*BANG!*

A small explosion came from inside the car, but I was through the front door of our house like a shot, not waiting to see what it was. Probably the bag of potato chips I'd stashed for a late-night snack.

"All packed!" I announced, tossing the keys but missing the bowl on the coffee table in my hurry to cross the living room. Two mismatched chairs huddled around the scarred old table like a life preserver in a sea of shag carpet. Everything in the room was probably older than me.

Dad looked up from the kitchen table. "I don't think it's a good idea for you to be outside alone right now, okay?"

"Sorry . . . I guess I wasn't thinking."

"It's okay. I just want you to be safe." His gaze dropped back to the road map spread out in front of him. I'd tried to get him to use Google Maps, but he was hopelessly old-school with most things. "And I want to get on the road ASAP."

I couldn't help taking a peek over his shoulder at the map. The midwestern United States sprawled across the table, suggesting any of hundreds of potential destinations. Chicago? Cleveland? I shuddered. It was impossible to guess.

My thawing fingers prickled as I tucked the wild wisps of my chronically frizzy red hair under the edge of my blue Tar Heels ball cap. Dad always said he didn't know where I'd gotten the funky-hair gene but that he thought my hair was a reflection of my personality—unique, passionate, strong. *Weird* was more like it.

"Abby?"

I met Dad's gaze in the mirror on the far wall. His eyes were dark, unreadable pools.

I turned toward him, thinking maybe I'd finally get some information. "Yeah?"

One corner of his mouth turned up. "You're blocking the light."

I blinked, then straightened and turned away, deflated.

"Do you need to use the bathroom before we go?"

"Dad. Again. Twelve. Not two."

"Old habits . . ." He trailed off as the screen of his cell phone lit up. He snatched it off the table, but not before I read the first line of the message:

*Hurry. Events in motion.*

He typed a quick reply and then shoved the phone into the pocket of his pullover before turning back to me with a flicker of fear in his eyes. "Time to go."

Then we were on the road, disappearing into the night. I clutched one of Mom's worn flannel shirts that I now wore tighter around me, hoping to draw some of her strength from it. Because she'd been a true warrior. And not just metaphorically speaking, like she was super tough or something. No, she was descended from an actual line of Norse chieftains. Tight-lipped and stoic were sort of in her genes.

But I always knew she loved me. Despite her frequent absences on what she called monster-hunting expeditions, tracking our ancient enemies, the Grendels. Even though there hadn't been any recent confirmed sightings, Mom knew the Grendels were still out there. Somewhere. Maybe in hiding, biding their time until the right moment.

I craned my neck, looking through the car's rear window as if clinging to a lifeline. Our little white house framed in a rectangle of glass like a painting of a safe haven in the wind-tossed sea that was my life. Then we turned the corner and it disappeared out of sight, leaving me with a few cardboard boxes full of my stuff and a secret that would follow me wherever I went.

That I was just an ordinary girl from Charlotte. Who happened to be a Viking.

# CHAPTER 3

# INTO THE STORM

Four a.m. at an all-night Waffle Stop off the interstate in southern Ohio looks about what you'd expect. A tired-looking waitress idly polishing cracked Formica tables while she waits for the end of her shift. In one corner, a solitary guy huddling over greasy eggs, looking like he regretted both the reheated bacon and the strange twists of fate that had brought him to that moment.

I could totally relate to that. If someone had asked me yesterday where I'd be spending my next twenty-four hours, hurtling through darkness toward an unknown destination wouldn't have been remotely near the top of my list. As we exited the restaurant, I earned a sidelong look from my dad when I shoved the door open hard enough to make it rattle against the doorstop.

I shoehorned my five-foot-two frame into the back seat behind oversized cardboard boxes full of books. Because this is the reality of life as the kid of an English teacher. Instead of competing with real siblings, you lose shotgun to old, dead dudes like Shakespeare and the Brontë sisters. It only made me mildly insecure when Dad's immediate reaction whenever he hit the brakes hard was to throw out his arm to protect the books the same way he'd do with his own flesh and blood.

Our tires yelped on the cold pavement as we pulled away from the yellow glow of the Waffle Stop sign. I turned a raised eyebrow to Dad's reflection in the rearview mirror, but he was busy singing along with "Let It Be" on the radio. Mom had been a huge Beatles fan. My name even came from their album *Abbey Road.* So listening to her favorites had become one of our ways of keeping her memory alive, especially when we were going through a tough time.

I've heard that poker players have "tells" that clue you in to their hand. Dad's was singing. He'd never let anyone hear him sing unless something was really bugging him. Right now, outwardly he was doing an Oscar-worthy job of faking it. But I could tell by the way he was really drawing out the notes in the chorus that he was majorly tense. It wasn't the first time we'd pulled our Houdini act, but something about this time was different.

He took the turn onto the freeway on-ramp like we'd just robbed a bank. The sideways momentum threw me against the pile of stuff in the seat next to me, and I winced when the side of my head came into contact with something hard. I extracted a dog-eared *Roget's Thesaurus* from the pile and stuffed it into the footwell.

"Sorry, honey," Dad said with an apologetic look. We merged onto the freeway to join the few other anonymous sets of red taillights momentarily united by our mutual disregard for the waking hours of reasonable people.

I studied his reflection in the rearview mirror. The crease of worry lines on his forehead and frequent checking of the side and rearview mirrors belied his calm exterior. He noticed me watching him and turned down the radio.

"Everything okay back there, kiddo?" He smiled at me, but the smile didn't reach his eyes.

"Yeah, just . . . Don't you think it's time you let me know what the plan is? Where we're going at least?" I shifted positions and immediately started to feel prickles in my numbing leg. Realizing I'd probably sounded a little harsh, I softened my tone. "I mean, we talk about things, you and I." Or was it you and *me*? The kid-of-an-English-teacher thing again. "No secrets between us. Right?"

As I'd gotten older, I'd noticed that adults sometimes put on brave faces thinking they're somehow protecting us. Especially if they think it's better for us that way.

Dad considered this for a long time, then nodded slowly and said, "That's fair. You deserve to be a part of this and not just along for the ride. So what do you want to know?"

I sat forward, a million questions popping into my head all at once. "Well, how about where we're going for starters?"

He nodded again. "They're moving us to Minnesota. To Minneapolis, specifically. It may be temporary. Or not. I don't know. It's just . . . Things are all sort of happening pretty fast right now."

"They?"

"The Grey Council."

So the faceless entity that seemed to pull all the strings in my life from behind the scenes. Where we lived. When and how I could train and study. Sometimes it felt like even how many marshmallows I could have in my Lucky Charms. Great. "But what's the plan, then? We just stay hidden until things blow over?"

"Not exactly. You'll be attending a school there called Vale Hall."

Vale Hall. It sounded like one of those preppy academies for rich kids. Which was . . . definitely not me. My stomach twisted into a knot as I thought of starting over again at yet another new school. Trying to fit in. Making new friends. The thousand-miles-and-a-left-turn-from-cool new home we were being banished to loomed ahead like some frozen, forbidding wasteland.

"It's where your mom went when she was your age."

I leaned forward. "Where . . . Mom went?" I knew she'd grown up somewhere up north but had always been fuzzy on the exact details. This unexpected chance to maybe fill in more pieces of her past suddenly made the whole prospect of moving a little less painful. "Where will we live? What will you be doing? I mean, you sort of had to bail on your old job and all."

Smiling at my new enthusiasm, he said, "Well, my old school has already been gracious enough to grant me an indefinite leave of absence. And I've been offered a teaching position in Vale's English department. The new appointment comes with its own cottage right off the school's campus. Just big enough for the two of us."

I stared out the window into the dark, trying to picture our new life that lay ahead.

After a long pause, he added, "There's just one part you may not be too excited about."

I jerked my head to look at him, alarm bells going off in my mind.

His eyes flicked toward mine, then back to the road. "They sort of didn't have any spots left in the sixth grade. With the school year having started already and all, you know. Except one. So they're bringing you in on a knattleikr scholarship."

The word rattled around in my head like a coin falling into an empty jar.

*Kin-attle-eye-kur.*

When I didn't say anything, he continued, "It's sort of a mash-up of lacrosse and rugby."

I waited for more, but he just studied the road in silence. Maybe he was kidding. Was he kidding? The word sounded like something from Balderdash, that game where you make up definitions of words no one's ever heard of to try to fool your friends. Dad had always been great at that game. *Knattleikr: sort of a mash-up of lacrosse and rugby.*

I decided to call his bluff. "LOL, Dad. You almost got me there."

He shook his head and gave a little shrug. "Not kidding."

"But . . . but," I sputtered. "I've never even *heard* of it before, much less *played* it. Are you sure it's a real sport? Maybe I could kind of, you know, skip that part and no one would notice?"

He laughed. "I'm pretty sure you have to at least go to practices and games or risk forfeiting the scholarship. Anyway, I'm glad your mom isn't around to hear you say that. She loved knattleikr. I guess it's real popular up north where we're going. Sort of like North Carolina's obsession with basketball."

I was just about to reply when the voice of Darth Vader cut in from the GPS suctioned to the dashboard: "Take the ramp ahead, then continue approximately forty miles."

The GPS is Dad's one piece of technology from this century, and even *that's* out of date. I got him the one with the Darth Vader voice for his birthday a few years ago as a joke, but he uses it all the time. Unlike the cereal bowl I made him out of construction paper in second grade. Turns out paper isn't the best at holding milk.

Dad nudged the GPS screen in his direction so he could see the map better. "Any word from Aunt Jess yet?"

I knew he was trying to change the subject, but I dug my phone out of my back pocket anyway. There was only a link to a cat video that one of my friends had sent me. No word from Aunt Jess. She's my mom's younger sister, but I'd only really gotten to know her well since Mom's death. I guess loss and grief sometimes bring people together like that. She lived on the West Coast, so we rarely saw her, but she was an Aesir like my mom. Like I desperately wanted to be.

The Aesir are an elite class of Vikings with one main mission: to protect humanity from Grendels. You know, no big deal or anything. They have what my mom always called "extranormal abilities." Since I've never felt normal at all, being *extra* normal always sounded pretty great, to be honest. It's hard making close friends when you feel like you're constantly hiding a big not-normal part of yourself. But in this case my mom just meant a variety of special abilities. She'd had the most amazing brain and could figure out what seemed like anything. Aunt Jess's talents lay more on the athletic side. Mine were, well, still TBD. Short for "too bad, dude." Because Aesir abilities aren't necessarily passed down genetically. And usually by my age you know if you're one or not. So the needle on my Aesir-o-meter was leaning hard toward "not."

"Nothing from Aunt Jess yet," I said, and slid my phone back into my pocket without watching the cat video. I'd texted her before we left. It wasn't like her to take so long to reply.

"She's probably out on one of her scuba-diving or rock-climbing expeditions," Dad said. "I'm sure she'll have some more exciting stories to regale us with when she gets back to civilization."

"Mmm . . ." I mumbled in reply, not really paying attention. Something about the timing of Aunt Jess's silence set off the paranoia alarm in my brain. Was there some bigger picture I was missing here?

Sometimes having time to think is therapeutic. But too much time can get your brain twisted into more knots than a string of Christmas lights in October. I leaned my head against the cold glass of the car window and chewed my bottom lip in frustration. Eventually the rising sun turned the sky a canvas of gold and orange. Buildings and trees took shape in the gray dawn, and then more cars joined us as rush hour came and went. Exits and overpasses led to more of the same endless gray miles. It's impossible to understand how mind-numbingly long all those inches on a map really are until you drive them. We stopped now and then to gas up and for bathroom breaks. Later, with my stomach comfortably full of waffle fries and a chicken sandwich from lunch, combined with the steady hum of tires on asphalt, I drifted into a drowsy, Zen-like daze.

"Ooh, it's starting to snow!"

I woke with a start at Dad's words and realized I must have drifted off. The sun was hidden behind a canopy of slate-gray clouds. What seemed like the same trees and empty countryside flashed by the window like we were stuck in the most boring infinite loop ever.

We passed a sign that read "Minnesota Welcomes You" as a few solitary white flakes swirled past my window, spinning and dancing wildly in our wake. Some welcome. The snowfall rapidly increased as we drove north and west. I shifted my gaze to the sprawling suburbs sliding past beyond the freeway while the world seemed to turn white. It looked like a thousand little kids had blown soft dandelion-seed wishes that filled the sky and settled to the ground.

I made my own silent wish that I could somehow live up to my mom's legacy and make her proud. Even though I knew by now one of the big secrets about growing up: Wishes don't come true. Not really. They just float to the earth like tiny snowflakes and dissolve into nothing like they were never there. Still, I couldn't completely let go of the hope that maybe I just had to find the right wish.

The snowfall intensified until even to my inexperienced eyes, I'd say we were in the middle of a pretty decent blizzard. The sky had grown prematurely dark from the storm, making the afternoon look more like twilight. Eventually I noticed I hadn't heard anything from the front seat for a while, so I sat up and rubbed my forehead. "You okay, Dad?"

He sat hunched forward and squinting out the windshield, doing barely thirty in the swirl of white all around us. "Yeah, I—" Our car suddenly rocked side to side, buffeted by the wake of another car passing. In weather that would be basically an apocalyptic event back home, Minnesota drivers gunned their engines and cruised by like it was the Minneapolis 500. I turned and looked out the back window as an SUV suddenly emerged from the whiteness behind us. It spotted us at the last minute and careened into another lane to avoid turning us into roadkill.

The swirling flakes obliterated the view beyond maybe five feet in any direction. But as I stared behind us, a single bright headlight materialized out of the snow. I don't know why, but a little chill ran down my spine. The light grew larger and larger until I couldn't imagine what it was attached to. For a second, the wild idea gripped me that we'd horribly lost our way in the storm and driven onto a railroad track where we were about to be crushed by a train. But I realized that was impossible. Right?

Still, the circle of light behind us continued to grow, never wavering despite the wind and snow. Soon the shape of a big black motorcycle materialized. No, not just big. Ginormous. Cars swerved and skidded off the road to get out of its way.

Straddling the motorcycle was a massive figure in wraparound black sunglasses and a thick mustache caked with snow. He looked like he could bench-press our car with his pinkie. Despite the freezing cold, the guy was wearing only a leather vest with his large, muscled arms exposed and leather chaps over black jeans.

As he pulled up alongside us, I craned my neck to stare up at him. At full height, I guessed he was at least eight feet tall. I blinked, thinking maybe the storm was playing tricks on my eyes the way mirages do to people stranded in the desert. But he was still there. And still huge.

Then he turned to me all cool-like. He smiled and tipped his dark glasses down. And I about needed a change of pants.

Mr. Big, Dark, and Scary had no eyes.

# CHAPTER 4

# MR. BIG, DARK, AND SCARY

"D-D-Dad," I sputtered, pawing at his shoulder while my brain froze like it had lost its Wi-Fi signal.

"Abby, what are you . . . ? Can't you see I'm trying to . . . ?" Then the car swerved off course, and I knew he'd seen him too. He gripped the steering wheel so tightly I could hear the plastic creak in protest. "Hold on."

We fishtailed as he punched the gas. The tires struggled to find a grip on the snow-covered freeway. Finally, they caught and we lurched forward, steadily picking up speed.

I watched the needle on the speedometer climb, but the motorcycle guy was right there with us the whole time. Pacing us. Snow flying from his enormous tires like he was cutting through water. He regarded me with chill malevolence, or what I guessed would have looked something like that if he'd had any eyes. Was this the same guy who had been in our home last night? I had the sudden sensation that all the snow from outside had coalesced into an icy ball inside my gut.

"He's still there!" I shouted.

"I *know*!" Dad's voice was tight. "Give me a minute. I'm trying to lose him."

"Who . . . what is he . . . it anyway?"

At first I thought Dad didn't hear me. When he finally spoke, his voice was almost too quiet to hear. Somehow the deathly calm in his voice freaked me out even more. "I'm not sure. But they warned me someone might try to stop us from reaching Vale."

Stop us? Why would someone want to stop us? My quick, shallow breaths started to fog up the window. I wiped the glass with my coat sleeve, which seemed like a mistake as soon as I'd done it. Did I really want to see my own death in full high-def?

As if he'd heard our conversation, the corner of the biker's mouth curled up in a wicked side grin. I slowly reached down and locked my door. Not that it would do any good if he decided he wanted to come in. He looked like he could tear the door right off.

That's when he started inching closer. I noticed nasty-looking spiky things protruding from the hubs of both his tires. Our little Honda was built for fuel economy, not demolition derbies. It was only marginally safer than a tin can on wheels. So I was pretty sure we were toast if he got anywhere near us with those.

"Spiky things! Spiky *thinggggsss*!" I whined. In my blind panic, my mental state had basically reverted to a kindergarten level.

Dad glanced away from the road briefly, then gritted his teeth. "Grab on to something!" But I was already so tightly wedged into all our stuff that I wasn't going anywhere.

A second before Big and Ugly turned us into a kebab, Dad

jerked the wheel to the left, skidded through the snow spray tailing a big rig, and tucked in beside the rig's trailer. He hugged the side of the trailer, trying to keep it between us and the giant motorcycle. From my vantage point, I could just make out the motorcycle's tires from underneath the other side of the rig.

The giant rider leaned forward so his head was below the trailer and stared right at me, then wiggled his fingers at me with a terrifying grin. Then he slowed and disappeared behind the back of the truck.

"He's coming around from the back!" I shouted. "I don't think we're gonna be able to lose him!"

"So close. We're *so* close to Vale," Dad said, banging the steering wheel with the heel of his hand at each syllable.

Then he glanced toward the back of the car before his gaze found mine. By the look in his eyes, I could tell he was trying to make a decision.

Finally he said calmly, "I need you to take the wheel."

"Whoa! What?!" I exploded. "Why? Where are you going? I don't even know how to drive. I . . ." I trailed off, close to hyperventilating.

He reached back and took my hand, the way he used to do when I fell and hurt my knee or had a bad day at school. His eyes flicked from the road to the rearview mirror, catching mine.

"Abby," he said in a calm voice. "I really need your help right now."

"But—"

"I know. I *know*. Your training hasn't covered anything like this. But it was as much about handling yourself in danger as it was about any specific combat skills. This *is* what you trained for. You can do it."

I took a deep breath. Nodded my head. I couldn't let him down.

"Here's all you need to know," he said. "Steering wheel. Gas on the right. Brake on the left. No big deal." He smiled at me reassuringly.

Normally he would never dream of even letting me back the car out of the driveway. And believe me, I've tried. But this time we weren't just cruising the neighborhood to pick up milk and eggs either.

"Where will *you* be?" I asked again.

"Just keep us on the road. I have an idea."

I leaned forward and grabbed the wheel with both hands. He slid under my arms toward the passenger seat while keeping his foot on the gas, and I awkwardly catapulted my body into the driver's seat. It reminded me of a game of Twister, except we were doing eighty and the consequence of losing was a fiery death.

I flexed my fingers on the steering wheel. Keep us on the road. That didn't seem so . . .

The car wobbled nauseatingly on the icy asphalt like an over-sized, out-of-control snowboard as I jammed my foot on the gas pedal. Dad disappeared over the back seat. His head and arms came back into view as he reached forward and yanked open a box in the front seat. The familiar smell of old books filled the car.

"What are you gonna do?" I asked. "Hit him with the *Oxford Shakespeare*?"

He grunted and dug through the box, scooping things out haphazardly into the footwell like he was trying to get to something on the bottom. Finally, with a cry of triumph, he sat back, hauling out something that I couldn't see from the corner of my eye.

I flicked my eyes to the rearview mirror to see what he was doing. At the same moment, the motorcycle's headlight blazed through our rear window as it rounded the back of the tractor trailer, silhouetting Dad holding what looked like a giant crossbow.

"Where did you get *that*?" I cried out in surprise. Sure, I'd practiced with crossbows before, but those were toys compared to this one. "Is that a—"

"Deathsinger?" he finished for me. "Yeah. Used to be your mom's. It's just a little insurance policy I keep around."

This day was getting weirder and weirder by the minute. I was sure I'd wake up soon to the smell of bacon frying and find out it was all a super-intense dream.

The smash of glass brought me back to reality. A frigid wind suddenly swirled and clawed through the cabin of the car. Surprised, I swerved and skidded before regaining control of the wheel. The semi next to us blared its horn. I thought we'd been hit. But when I jerked my head to look, I saw that Dad had smashed out the back window of the car.

"What are you *doing*?" I yelled over the noise of the wind.

"Trying to get a clear shot."

"Yeah, well, maybe warn me next time! Or open a window!"

"Sorry!"

Darth's voice again: "In one mile, use the right lane to take the exit ramp to Eleventh Street."

That was going to be a slight problem. Somehow I had to get over three lanes. In a snowstorm. And through a semitruck. I couldn't go around from behind with the biker back there, so that left somehow getting past it in front.

"Hold on! I'm gonna see if I can get around this thing," I shouted to him.

"Okay, wait a minute till I get this shot off!" he yelled back. I glanced at the rearview again. Dad was crouched over the back seat with a sharp black arrow notched in the crossbow. The motorcycle was almost on us.

*Thwack!* The arrow erupted from the rear of the car. But the wind caught it, sending it arcing harmlessly away. Still, the motorcycle slowed a bit, keeping a more respectful distance.

Then the rider reached behind his back and slung what looked like a small cannon over his shoulder. I didn't need any more encouragement. My foot crushed the gas pedal to the floor, and we leapt forward, the little engine whining like a speeding lawn mower.

Finally we cleared the front of the semi. Right as I cut the wheel sharply to change lanes, I heard the boom of the gun. The cab of the big rig was vaporized where we'd been not two seconds before. The whole speeding mass pitched forward, the rear of the trailer swinging out in a wide arc right toward us.

I vaguely heard Darth's voice intone, "Take the exit on the right." But my eyes were transfixed on the approaching steel death that was about to pulverize us. I couldn't get any more speed out of the car. The giant hunk of sparking metal screeched toward us in slow motion. *We're dead. We're dead* ran through my mind. Then, following some deep instinct, I cut the wheel at the last minute and, miraculously, the semi missed us, screaming by within inches of our rear bumper.

On the GPS, Darth complained, "Recalculating." I reached out and backhanded it off the dashboard.

In my side mirror, I saw the motorcycle had somehow avoided the mess too. It was only us and him out here now, with the semi sprawled across the lanes, blocking the flow of traffic behind us.

Dad patiently worked to nock another arrow in the crossbow. I doubted the giant would miss again, so this one had to count. He took aim as the motorcycle closed the distance between us. Closer. Closer. I wasn't sure what he was waiting for.

Then the crossbow twanged again. I cringed, waiting for something to happen. I was sure he'd missed again. But the single headlight wavered slightly, then wobbled and careened off toward the shoulder and disappeared in the swirling snow.

"Got him!" Dad shouted. "Not bad for an English major, eh?"

And none too soon.

"Take the exit on the right," Darth commanded again from the darkness of the footwell.

I jerked the wheel to catch the off-ramp. We tore through the dark, snowy streets of Minneapolis. I'm pretty sure I broke about every traffic rule in the book, but I didn't let my foot off the gas until we skidded to a halt in front of a huge stone building with windows glowing welcomingly against the frozen night.

For a moment I sat there in stunned silence, "The Imperial March" playing tinnily from the GPS in celebration of our arrival. That's when I noticed I hadn't heard from Dad since the freeway.

I turned to the back seat. He looked like he was asleep amid the pile of stuff. Then I noticed a red stain seeping out against the mustard-yellow upholstery.

"DAD!" I shouted.

I threw the car door open and staggered out into the snowy night. With fingers half-frozen, I fumbled to open the back door. Finally I managed to yank it wide and stood there staring down at the unconscious form of my dad slumped in the back seat. He looked strangely gray in the dome light of the car. I knelt in the snow and took his hand in mine.

He stirred, half opening his eyes.

"Dad!" I cried, tears choking in my throat. "Stay with me. I'm right here. Just focus on my face. We'll get you some help."

He smiled groggily up at me as snowflakes swirled into the car and settled onto his face and hair. "You did it. You got us here. That's my girl. My girl . . ."

Then his eyes drifted closed.

Words formed in my brain. *Help . . . help . . .* But they fell uselessly from my lips in a hoarse whisper.

I spun around and studied the dark night, but it was an empty, pitiless void. The snow that had looked so soft and magical earlier now felt like a swarm of tiny insects stinging icily against my face. "HELP! *HELP!*" I screamed, at last finding my voice, but the storm seemed to swallow up the words almost as soon as they left my mouth.

I turned back to my dad, trying to see where he was injured. Should I move him? No, they always say not to do that, right? That moving him could hurt him more? I squeezed his hand tightly, not sure if it was more for my comfort or his. Tears of frustration started to run down my cheeks. "I don't know what to *do*, Dad," I cried. "I don't know what to do. I'm sorry. I'm so sorry . . ."

Then I felt a hand on my shoulder. With a yelp of surprise, I whirled around. It was a girl about my age. Her dark eyes studied me briefly and then looked past me into the car.

"May I?" she asked. Not waiting for an answer, she knelt beside me in the snow.

She lightly pressed two fingers against Dad's neck and looked down at her wristwatch. In the middle of the watch's white dial, a white unicorn's hooves pointed to the minute and hour. It matched her rainbow-striped unicorn backpack. I was transfixed by the stark contrast of the white snowflakes as they fell and melted against her long black hair. The strands of hair were tinted different colors at the tips like they'd been dipped in a rainbow. More snow falling. Melting.

I startled like I was waking from a daydream and glanced toward the frozen darkness, wondering where she'd come from. She'd seemingly materialized out of nowhere. When I looked back at her, she was lifting Dad's jacket to get a better look at the wound.

"Should I . . . ?" I started to ask, but she seemed to anticipate the question.

"Ambulance is on its way," she said without looking at me. "Help should be here soon."

As if on cue, the wail of a siren split the night air, and soon flashing red lights pushed back against the darkness as an ambulance and fire truck screeched to a stop behind us. Soon they had my dad on a stretcher with a thick wool blanket tucked tightly around him and an oxygen mask over his mouth and nose.

I was still holding his hand when I felt someone throw a blanket over my shoulders and try to lead me gently away. But I angrily shrugged them off and climbed into the back of the ambulance as the paramedics loaded him in. No other option was possible. I had to keep holding his hand. If I let go, I felt somehow that he'd slip away into the darkness and never return. And I'd be alone. All alone.

I studied the small crowd that had gathered through the rear windows of the ambulance as we pulled away, but the girl was gone.

# CHAPTER 5

# RED SKY AT MORNING

"Abby?"

My head jerked upward as I startled awake, sending a pile of magazines sliding from my lap to the floor. I blinked and looked around at the room. In the soft light cast by a pair of squat table lamps, a dozen unoccupied armchairs lined two walls. On another wall, a gentle cascade of water trickled into a pool while soothing piano music filtered in from overhead.

"Abby Beckett?"

I turned my head and saw a woman in a white lab coat standing in the entrance to the room wearing red-framed glasses. Her silvery, curly hair was tucked neatly behind her ears.

Oh, right. The hospital waiting room. A clock on the wall read 4:13 a.m.

"Yes, I'm Abby Beckett," I said, sitting up a little straighter in my chair and jamming a rogue wisp of hair back under my baseball cap.

"Hello, Abby, I'm Dr. Swenson. I've been taking care of your father."

I grasped the arms of my chair and half rose in anxious anticipation. "How is he? Will he be okay?"

She held up her hands reassuringly. "Yes, not to worry. He's just come out of surgery, and all his vital signs are stable."

"Oh wow, that's"—I slowly exhaled and sank back into my chair, thinking of all the worst-case scenarios that had played through my brain over the past several hours—"such a relief. Can I go see him?"

"In a little bit, yes. We're still running some tests, but those should be done soon."

I frowned. "Tests? What kinds of tests?"

She took the seat next to me and put her hand on my arm comfortingly. "Nothing to be concerned about. Your father hasn't regained consciousness since you arrived at the hospital, so we want to make certain we're covering all our bases."

My hands tightened around the armrests of my chair. Was there something she wasn't telling me? "And in the meantime?"

"We wait."

And so we waited. Tests followed more tests with no conclusive results. The morning slowly blurred into afternoon and finally dinnertime with no change in his condition. But I held on tenaciously to one thing: He was still alive. That's what mattered. He was still alive.

The hospital administration tried to put me up for the night in a separate room for family members, but I quickly nixed that. Dad liked to say my superpower was stubbornness, and I employed it fully in wearing them down until they threw up their hands and let me camp out in the chair at his bedside. Where I finally fell asleep. And dreamed of fire.

After my mom's death I'd been plagued for months by strange dreams of flames. Intense heat. Burning. Sometimes even the voice of a child crying. Those dreams had finally subsided, but now they returned as dark and terrifying as ever. When I finally gave up on sleep the next morning after a fitful night, the bed-side clock read just past six a.m. I dismissed the nightmares as fever dreams produced by my exhausted brain and opted to focus instead on helping my dad get better.

As I unfolded from the chair and stood up, I took in Dad's still form. For the first time ever, he looked human—vulnerable— amid the tangle of tubes and wires. I watched the shallow rise and fall of his chest, not completely trusting the heart monitor. The doctors had assured me he was stable and would be okay, but right now I was only trusting what I could see with my own two eyes.

His hand felt cold when I took it in mine and studied his face. "Daddy?" I said softly, resurrecting a name I hadn't used in a long time. He'd been strictly "Dad" for as long as I could remember. "Daddy, can you hear me?"

There was no stirring or change to his steady breathing. I'd never noticed the slight graying of the hair at his temples. Or the wrinkle of laugh lines at the corners of his eyes. Not that I normally sat by his bedside and studied his face while he slept. That would be, well, creepy. But this evidence of age caused my breath to hitch for a second. I'd only ever seen him as young. Vibrant. Full of life.

As I stood there quietly, I was suddenly overcome with a sense of wrongness. In the way that dreams evaporate like smoke when you wake up, I had a faint inkling of something not right, but the more I focused on the feeling, the more it slipped away.

"Bryn?" I called, thinking maybe Dad's nurse was nearby out in the hall. No reply. Then I felt it: the sensation of a presence nearby, just like on the night we'd left home. My blood turning to ice, I quickly spun and surveyed the room. But it was empty. Only the two of us.

Then why were the hairs on my arms standing up?

Suddenly there was movement at the edge of my vision. I jerked my head in that direction. There was only the wall with its large double window, the shade pulled down against the night. But something was off about the window. Its shade was outlined in the faintest red. Almost like something behind it was glowing. As I watched with morbid fascination, the red glow seemed to shift and move. Almost like flickering flames.

My heart stuttered as my nightmares threatened to merge with my waking life. Had the dreams been some sort of warning? Aesir were supposed to have a sixth sense about danger that others didn't have. This felt like that. Sort of. But sometimes I couldn't tell the difference between actually feeling something and wanting to feel it so badly that I made it up myself. Whatever this was, my alarm bells were sure going off now.

Almost in a trance, I took a single step toward the window. Then another. Now I could feel a definite heat coming from that direction. The temperature increased as I approached, but I couldn't seem to stop myself. Like I was pulled toward it. A moth drawn to a flame.

Sweat beaded on my skin as I inched nearer. My brain screamed at me to stop. I reached out to raise the shade. My fingertips touched the pull cord. All I had to do was tug and I'd come face-to-face with . . . what?

*Knock! Knock! Knock!*

My tensed muscles reacted instantaneously, jerking down on the cord so hard I ripped the blinds right off the window. Even as they crashed to the floor, I realized the noise had come from behind me. I spun and saw a figure silhouetted in the doorway of the hospital room, its features obscured in the backlight from the hallway. My hand grabbed the closest thing I could find and flung it over my shoulder like a weapon. In the same motion, I leapt across the room, sliding to a stop with my outstretched fingertips mere inches from the intruder's face.

"Wha . . . ? Ow!" the person said as he jerked backward and smacked the back of his head into the doorframe.

We stood with our eyes locked for a tense moment. My breath heaved through clenched teeth.

Then he gulped. "Uh, is that sphygmomanometer loaded?"

What? My eyes darted to the blood pressure cuff that hung limply over my shoulder.

"Sorry . . . heh . . . medical humor," said the intruder. "My, um, mom's a doctor."

I blinked. For the first time it registered that standing there rubbing the back of his head was nothing more menacing than a boy about my age. So much for my special sixth sense.

"Who are you?" I said more angrily than I meant to, frustrated and embarrassed by my overreaction. I lowered my raised hand and willed my muscles to relax. "Sorry. It's been a rough last couple of days."

He nodded. "I figured. Are you Abby? Abby Beckett?"

"Yeah. How do you know my name?"

He held out his hand tentatively. "I'm Jacob Grimsby. But everyone just calls me Grimsby. I was assigned to be your tour guide." When I looked at him blankly, he added, "For Vale? I'm supposed to show you around. You know, take you to class? That kind of thing." He let his hand fall to his side.

We were interrupted by the sound of someone humming loudly in the hallway. The smell of fresh bread made my famished stomach do flip-flops.

"I have croissants!" Dad's nurse, Bryn, sang as she appeared behind Grimsby. She was about twenty-ish, I guessed, with a long blond braid that trailed halfway down her back.

"Oh, hey, Jakey," she said. "Whatcha doing?"

*Jakey?*

Grimsby blushed and quickly stuffed his hands into his

pockets, trying to look casual. "Rolling out the welcome wagon, apparently."

"Wait," I said, "you guys know each other?"

"Oh, sure," said Bryn. She stepped past us into the room, stopping to check Dad's vitals before turning back to us. "His mom works here at the hospital too. I used to babysit him when he was just a little guy."

I turned to Grimsby. "So if Bryn was getting breakfast, how did you know where to find us?" I felt a little bad grilling the guy, but my paranoia meter was on high alert after our recent experiences.

He averted his eyes. "I just sort of followed the noise. I take it you're not a light sleeper?"

Bryn snorted. "Light sleeper? Ha! You should hear it when she starts snoring."

Grimsby grinned. "So that's what that was. I thought someone was murdering a duck with a chain saw. Slowly."

I could feel my cheeks flush a little at the turn this conversation had taken. "Okay, is everyone done discussing my sleeping habits now?"

Grimsby shook his sleeve vigorously to expose his wristwatch and then checked the time. "Yeah, we should probably be getting to class."

I stared. Class? "There's no way I'm—"

Bryn cut me off with a wave of her hand. "I think that's a fabulous idea. What were you planning to do? Sit around here growing roots until your dad wakes up?" She laid a hand on my shoulder and gently guided me toward the door of Dad's room while she kept up her lecture. "What good does that do either of you? I like you, kid, but honestly, you need to get some fresh air. Go to class. Be a kid, for Pete's sake."

I opened my mouth to protest, but she wasn't done. Her voice softening, she said, "Look, your dad knows you're here for him. He really does. But he wouldn't want you to stop living while he's getting better."

Glancing toward Grimsby, she smiled sweetly, then nudged the door closed right in his face.

"Hey!" he protested.

"Just a sec!" she called to him, then lowered her voice. "Besides, your dad is in good hands." She held up her hands and wiggled her fingers as if proving her point. Which was when I noticed for the first time the silver braided knot encircling her thumb. A Viking knot.

My eyes widened. "You're a . . ." My eyes shot toward the closed door as I whispered, "Viking too?"

The hint of a smile played across her face. My surprise probably seemed a little silly to her, but she was the first Viking I'd met in, well, at least four years.

Bryn winked at me. "Like I said. In good hands."

I stared into her eyes, my heart beating a little faster at the secret connection. Then I looked back at Dad. His heart monitor chirped out its steady rhythm. It seemed like he was okay, but what if he needed me?

Bryn pulled the door open and gently guided me into the hall.

Grimsby looked up from where he leaned against the wall next to the door.

"You, um, didn't hear any of that, did you?" I asked.

He cocked his head. "Hear what?"

"Oh, nothing. Just some girl stuff."

"She'll be ready in five," Bryn said, and pushed the door closed behind me. Then the door reopened and she poked her head out, adding, "One last thing?"

"Yeah?" I said hopefully.

She pointed her finger at my head and twirled it in exaggerated circles. "You might want to find a hairbrush." With that she shoved the bag of still-warm croissants into my hand and shut the door again.

I turned toward my reflection in the dark glass panel beside my dad's door. My hair was plastered against my head in a sort of lopsided rooster tail on one side like my pillow had exploded. I shifted my eyes back to the closed door. "Okay, I guess I'm going to school," I mumbled to myself.

"Good girl!" Bryn chimed from behind the door.

But as I stepped into the room next to Dad's, where my things waited, I suddenly remembered the feeling of the strange presence at the window. I stepped toward my own window, where the rising sun now winked through the trees, casting long, dark shadows like ghostly fingers reaching across the snowy lawn. The bare branches of a nearby maple tree nearly touched the glass as they stirred in the wind. Had the sunrise and swaying branches created the effect of dancing red flames I'd seen earlier?

I was reminded of the old rhyme: *Red sky at morning, sailors take warning.*

"Why?" I'd once asked my mom another lifetime ago. "What's so bad about a red sky in the morning?"

"That's how sailors predicted the weather back before modern technology," she'd told me. "A red sky in the morning meant a storm was coming."

As I gazed out the window, my face reflected back to me in the glass. The words echoed in my mind: *A storm. A storm is coming. A storm is coming.*

A chilly gust slipped under the slightly open window, making me shiver. I slammed it shut to block out the cold. And locked it.

# CHAPTER 6

# WELCOME TO
# MINNESOTA, EH?

All the moving boxes containing my stuff were stacked neatly in one corner of the hospital room. I found the one with "Clothes—Abby" scrawled on the side in black Sharpie. Of course everything was properly packed and labeled, because Dad was insistent that even fleeing for our lives be done in a neat, orderly fashion.

I dug out a pair of jeans and another of my mom's old red flannel shirts. The cloth's age-worn softness seemed to embrace me like a warm hug as I slid it on. I turned toward the full-length mirror that hung on the back of the door and studied my reflection. People said I had my mom's nose. Her eyes. But did I have her heart? Her courage to face our enemies no matter the cost?

I still remembered her funeral like it was yesterday. Me biting my lower lip resolutely to keep it from trembling as her coffin was slowly lowered into the ground. The fire—a cruel, random accident that had destroyed the cottage where we'd been vacationing—had stolen even the chance for me to see her face one final time. Not even the memory of the last thing she'd said to me remained. It was almost like the events of that horrific day had been burned from my mind, leaving me with only fiery nightmares. Dad said he'd been out for a late-afternoon jog on the beach and returned to find our cottage an inferno, fearing he'd lost both of us until he found me curled up in a whimpering ball in the woods behind the house.

And later, as I stood beside her grave, I silently made a vow that even though the memories of our final hours together were gone, I'd keep her memory alive by continuing the work she'd started. The words of a kid who didn't know what she was promising. To hunt and eradicate the ancient enemy of the Aesir. A line from the *Beowulf* epic sprang to my mind: *Those dark shadows of death, lurking, lying in wait, in long night keeping the misty moors.*

Grendels.

A tremor racked my body as another dark shadow loomed into my thoughts. One that had lurked fewer than ten feet away across my kitchen floor. Almost close enough to touch. Suddenly I felt chilled to the core. Even though I'd never seen a Grendel in person, I was somehow certain that's what it had been. Had it specifically sought me out? And if so, why was I still alive? Would it follow me here? I squeezed my hands into fists in frustration. Of the two people in the world I might talk with about all this, one was lying in a coma, and the other—Aunt Jess—had seemingly dropped off the face of the earth. Bryn? No, she'd probably just think it was silly—a little kid afraid of shadows.

The clatter of a cart going by in the hallway snapped me back to the present. Grimsby was waiting for me. I rubbed my hands against the chill that still lingered, then grabbed a second flannel. Then a scarf and a wool cap with a pom-pom on top and snugged everything on.

As I was about to leave, I noticed a maroon blazer draped neatly across the bed with the Vale Hall logo on the left front pocket. When I inspected it more closely, the tag on the inside collar had "Abby Beckett" stitched on it. Was I supposed to wear it? I managed to yank and tug it on over the flannels, then turned to inspect myself in the mirror. I looked like the marshmallow man stuffed into a three-sizes-too-small coat. Great.

In the mirror, my eyes fell across one of our boxes labeled "Household Items" and an idea hit me. The box's contents were a jumbled mess from the run-in with the biker, but I found what I was looking for. Dad's old cassette player.

Bryn looked up from where she sat reading a nursing textbook by the bedside when I came into Dad's room.

"This'll just take a second," I said. She smiled when she saw the player and nodded.

There was an empty plug behind Dad's bedside table, so I set up the machine and jammed a worn, old cassette into the slot, then clicked it closed. When I hit Play, the opening chords of the Beatles' "Good Day Sunshine" filled the room. A little something to keep him company while I was away.

"Be back soon, Daddy," I said quietly, and gently kissed him on the forehead.

My little mission accomplished, I headed downstairs toward the main entrance of the hospital. I paused for a second by the front doors and steeled myself against the cold, then stepped in front of the motion detector. The doors slid open, and I felt the North Carolina in me wither in the blast of the polar vortex that greeted me. If we were going to be in Minnesota for a while, I was going to have to get used to this.

I stepped out onto the sidewalk and surveyed the frozen gray wasteland beyond the doors like a visitor to some dystopian landscape. Also known as suburban Minneapolis.

If this was what the weather was like in October, then I was in trouble.

"You're not from around here, are you?" someone said.

My head was basically fixed in place beneath layers of flannel and wool, so I pivoted my whole body in the direction of the voice. Grimsby crunched across the snow-packed lawn toward me. In the light of the morning sun, he looked way less spooky than when I'd first seen him. Black backpack straps pinched the shoulders of his maroon blazer, which was a match to mine, except the "a" in Vale on his breast pocket was scratched out with black pen and an "i" was scrawled over it. Despite the cold, he was wearing khaki shorts and brown loafers with no socks. He studied my clothes curiously as he approached.

I glanced down self-consciously. "Whff?" The word came out muffled behind my scarf.

"Did you come from a lumberjack convention?" he said.

I yanked down the scarf so he could hear me. "It's like zero degrees out here."

His eyes slid toward a digital marquee on a bank across the street: 34°F. He looked back at me with one raised eyebrow.

"We, uh, use Celsius where I'm from?" I said weakly.

"Well, welcome to Minnesota. And the United States, apparently. Up here we only have two seasons: July and winter. As you may have noticed, it's not July. So you're probably gonna need a heavier coat."

"Well, I haven't had time to, you know, go shopping yet."

"Don't worry," he said, noticing the threadbare condition of my flannels. "There's a Salvation Army downtown."

He didn't know how close he was to the truth. If you ever wondered who ends up with the old clothes your parents drop off at the thrift store, it's probably yours truly. Unfortunately, one time that was literally the case, when I came to school wearing a striped polo shirt with a hole in the armpit that some girl's mom had only dropped off the previous week. She said to me, "Hey, lift up your arm for a sec." The next thing I knew, she was poking me in the armpit and calling me a dumpster diver. We didn't exactly have a lot of money on a single teacher's salary.

But all that aside, this guy was starting to annoy me. Here I was, my dad lying in a coma, me ripped from my home and deposited in this frozen wasteland, and I had to deal with him giving me a hard time about my fashion choices? I was seconds from wrapping my blood pressure cuff around his neck, but then I noticed his earnest expression. Was he actually for real?

As if sensing my confusion, he said, "No, seriously. I'll show you the Salvation Army sometime. I once got these sweet grandpa pants there. They smelled like mothballs, but they were as comfortable as silk pajamas." He nodded his head wistfully at the memory.

"So, school . . ." I said to remind him.

"Oh, right. I almost forgot. So I'm your fabulous welcoming committee of one. Jacob Grimsby, Esquire, at your service." He spread his arms and bowed comically, his black curls flopping forward. "But as I mentioned earlier, everyone just calls me Grimsby."

"Cool," I said. "I'm Abby Beckett. But I guess you knew that already." I pointed at the defaced logo on his blazer. "Vile Hall? Something I should know about?"

"Oh, it'll be more fun for you to find out for yourself. Come on, we're in the same class for first period. I'll show you around a little before that."

As we turned down the sidewalk, he asked, "So for real, where you from? Somewhere exotic?"

"Not exactly. North Carolina."

"Ah, just sick of all the sun and sea air, then?" He extracted a plastic cup from the side pouch of his backpack and sipped a bright orange liquid through a plastic straw. Whatever it was had a faintly sweet smell.

"Well, I . . ." I started.

He saw me eyeing the cup. "Oh! Sorry. I almost forgot. I brought you one too." He pulled a matching cup from the other side of his backpack and handed it to me. "Anyway, you were saying?"

I looked down skeptically at the cup, then shrugged and took a sip. As the syrupy liquid hit my tongue, my senses lit up like a pinball machine that had just gone full tilt.

I swallowed and coughed in surprise. "What is this stuff?"

Grimsby smiled proudly. "Really jolts you awake, doesn't it? I'm into that whole juicing thing." He took another long sip from his straw, then lifted his cup into the sunlight to study it.

"So, like . . . beets? Kale?"

"This one's my vitamin C booster. I start with a base of orange Tang, then add a garnish of lemon and lime Skittles, and finish off with a shot of banana Runts. Because my doctor says I need more potassium."

"You realize none of those are real fruits, right?"

Ignoring this, he said, "So why are you just starting school now? In the middle of October, I mean?"

"Oh, well . . ." I stalled as my brain struggled to put together a story on the fly. "My dad . . . he got a job here. He's an expert in Old English literature—*Beowulf*, Chaucer—that kind of stuff. So I think he's going to be teaching British literature. I'm sort of along for the ride, I guess you could say."

"Rumor is you got a scholarship to play knattleikr. That's hardly what I'd call only 'along for the ride.'"

Oh, great. It sounded like the cat was out of the bag on that one. I was really going to have to play this sport I knew literally nothing about. And probably make a major fool of myself. "It's no biggie. Really."

He stopped and stared at me like I was from Mars. Then he

shook his head as if to clear it and started walking again. "No biggie? It's only, like, the most important sport at Vale. It's practically a religion here. It's been"—he paused to count on his fingers— "well, more than three years since we won the cup. And they're only allowed to offer one scholarship each year. So, if you got one to play here, then they must be expecting big things from you." He grinned and added, "No pressure."

Suddenly I had a sick feeling in my stomach. And it wasn't just Grimsby's syrupy concoction. Why would they give me a sports scholarship when I was obviously going to be exposed as a fake as soon as I stepped onto the field? Or court. Dojo? Well, wherever they played knattleikr. I stopped at the street corner to wait for the signal to cross, but Grimsby kept walking.

When he noticed I wasn't with him anymore, he stopped in the middle of the street and turned back to me. "What are you doing?"

"Um, the light?" I said, gesturing to the glowing orange hand signaling us to wait.

Then I watched in horror as a red pickup sped toward him. Right when I was sure he was about to become the next traffic statistic, the truck braked and skidded to a stop. The driver actually smiled and waved apologetically, like it was his fault.

Grimsby turned to me with an expression like "See?"

I laughed and jogged across after him. "If you'd tried that in Charlotte, you'd be someone's new hood ornament right now."

"Welcome to Minnesota, eh?" he said.

# CHAPTER 7

# THE KEY TO EVERYTHING

On the next block sprawled a vast, grassy campus dotted with live oaks and maples. The ribbon of a stream glinted in the distance, and patches of snow melted in the early morning sun. A huge stone archway read "Vale Hall" in giant bronze letters at the base of a curving main drive flanked by matching rows of massive fir trees all the way up to an imposing black stone structure set on top of a small rise. A tall clock tower thrust up from the middle of the cluster of buildings like a finger challenging the sky.

It felt like we'd just stepped out of suburban Minneapolis and onto the grounds of a medieval castle. But not like the Disney kind, with deer and rabbits frolicking in the middle distance. This one gave off more of a Frankenstein's-castle vibe.

I froze there on the edge of campus, suddenly paralyzed by my old self-doubt and fears. Who was I fooling? I'd never be half the student my mom was.

"You okay?" Grimsby said.

I quickly recovered, pretending I'd just stopped to take in the view and hurrying to catch up with him. "Wow, it's, um . . ."

"Forbidding? Menacing? Uncomfortably off-putting?"

I laughed. "I was going to say 'huge,' but . . . No way, is that a Lamborghini?"

We were just passing by a shiny red sports car when its passenger door slowly lifted vertically like a bird's wing. A kid with perfect white-blond hair and designer sunglasses slid out smoothly like he was swaggering out of a music video. Suddenly an image popped into my head of the kid emerging from a bird's armpit. A shiny red bird's armpit. I slapped my hand over my mouth to hide the giggle that threatened to bubble out of it, hoping my eyes wouldn't give me away.

"What's so funny?" the kid said.

Too late. How do you explain to someone that you just pictured them stepping out of an armpit? "Nothing," I mumbled.

He eyed me for another few seconds, then raked his hand through his glossy locks and spun away toward the school. We followed the rest of the drop-off line, which could have been an exotic car convention.

"Don't let all the fancy-schmancy stuff fool you," Grimsby said. "Vale has the same types of doofuses and miscreants as most schools. They just drive nicer cars and wear better clothes."

We headed for a pair of towering oak doors thrown wide to a steady incoming stream of kids in maroon blazers. What looked like a Latin phrase was carved over the doors.

"Omnium rerum principia parva sunt?" I read.

"Abandon hope, all ye who enter here," Grimsby translated.

I stopped and looked up at the words. "Really?" But Grimsby was already several steps ahead of me. I rushed after him. "You're kidding . . . right?"

"Ms. Beckett. Welcome."

I spun toward the voice, surprised to hear my name. At the top of the entrance stairs stood a thin, grim-looking woman with graying hair pulled back into a tight bun, wearing a dark skirt and matching jacket. She extended her hands toward me, so I awkwardly stuck mine out and she clasped them firmly in both of hers.

"Um, thank you," I said.

Her smile was the barest tightening of her lips. "I'm Professor Roth, the headmaster here at Vale Hall. I wanted to be the first to welcome you and wish you well in your pursuits at our school. Your mother was very well-regarded during her time here." She paused and studied me with a penetrating gaze. "We expect great things from you as well."

Maybe it was the crushing weight of those expectations. Or the way she still held my hands trapped in hers. But abruptly I felt on the verge of hyperventilating. I shot a look over my shoulder, trying to locate Grimsby, but he seemed to have disappeared.

"Perhaps we can find a time to speak at greater length soon," Professor Roth continued, and I felt the lessening of pressure as she released my hands.

"Uh-huh," I managed. "Yeah, catch you later." I groaned inwardly even as the words came out of my mouth. *Catch you later?* I backed away, wishing I could simply melt into the crowd of kids, then felt a hand on my shoulder.

I spun and saw Grimsby regarding me with his eyebrows halfway up his forehead. "What was that about?"

"Oh, nothing." I felt my pulse slowly returning to normal. "She just wanted to, you know, welcome me to Vale."

"Well, sorry I sort of disappeared there. I'm not exactly numero uno on her favorite students list." He studied me appraisingly. "But maybe you have a shot at it."

"Why? What do you mean?"

"It's not like she makes the time to personally welcome every student. You're obviously special."

The medieval castle theme continued on the inside of the school. Huge dark stones fitted tightly along the walls were interspersed with heavy timber beams supporting the arched ceiling. High on the walls, sconces held what looked like real torches, which cast a flickering light through the maze of classrooms and corridors.

"Hold on a sec. I'll be right back," Grimsby said.

I turned toward him in time to see him disappear through a nearby doorway. A sign next to the door read "KNUT" above the glowing red words "On Air." I took the opportunity to quietly slip the smoothie he'd given me into a nearby trash can, my head still buzzing from my earlier sip. Watching the sea of unfamiliar faces as they passed, I felt very alone. Wishing I hadn't left my dad's side. Would he somehow sense I was gone? Was he feeling scared and alone too? Maybe this had been a mistake. I should have been spending my time with him, not going to class and—

"Sorry about that. All set." Grimsby's voice broke into my thoughts as he reappeared at my side.

I took a long, slow breath, fighting down the panicky feeling. Dad was going to be fine. The doctor had promised.

Grimsby frowned at me. "Are you sick? You look a little pale."

"I'm fine," I said, and nodded toward the door he'd just come from. "What was that about?"

"Oh, that's the school radio station. So great you *K-NUT* believe your ears." He paused expectantly.

I groaned.

"Hmm, I guess I still need to workshop that one a little more." He shrugged. "Anyway, I normally help out with morning announcements, so I just wanted to remind them I'm out today on account of showing you around."

"They let sixth graders on the air?"

"Well, technically I'm the backup to the backup's backup. So I haven't actually been on the air yet. But I'm just one good laryngitis outbreak away from my moment in the sun."

He pointed to another door up ahead. "So our first class is world history with Dr. Ruel. Everyone just calls him Doc for short. Supposedly he has like a dozen PhDs, so what he's doing teaching here instead of some Ivy League school is a mystery. Anyway, he's the most popular teacher at Vale. Just remember the key words: 'I'm having trouble picturing that.'"

"Why? What does that mean?" I asked.

"Just wait. You'll see."

"Mr. Grimsby, I hope you're not planning to take that food into the classroom," said a voice behind us. I turned to see a tall, thin man with graying hair, his arms crossed and eyebrows raised.

"Uh, no, sir," said Grimsby.

"I didn't think so." The man was still talking to Grimsby, but his gaze had fixed on me, pinning me with an uncomfortable stare for what seemed like an eternity. Finally, without another word he turned and continued down the hall.

I blinked and shuddered as I watched him go. "Who was that?"

"That's Mr. Wendel," Grimsby said. "Science teacher. Prefers using students instead of rats in his experiments. Let's just say you don't want to get on his bad side."

Grimsby looked at my empty hands, then tilted his head to study my backpack. "You must have been hungry, eh?" He slurped at the last of his breakfast.

I'd been hoping he wouldn't notice. "Uh, yeah. Starving."

Which was the truth. I was kicking myself for forgetting Bryn's croissants at the hospital. The couple of sips I'd had of the orange concoction still rolled sourly in the pit of my stomach.

He shrugged. "Go ahead and grab a seat. I'll join you in a sec. Doc lets us sit anywhere we want."

The classroom was half-full already when I entered, but I spotted a couple of seats in the back and wedged my flannel-wrapped bulk into a desk. It was uncomfortably warm inside with my extra layers. I looked down, thinking I was going to have to find somewhere to ditch some of the clothes, when someone stopped in front of me.

"Hey, chica, that's my seat."

*Chica?* I looked up into the face of a boy with blond hair, smoky-gray eyes, and perfect white teeth. I disliked him immediately. "Excuse me?"

"That seat." He gestured to where I was sitting. "It's mine. Move it."

Normally I consider myself a reasonable person. But being chased by a gun-toting giant, witnessing my dad's near death, and barely having had any decent sleep or food for the last few days had left me in no mood to conduct a peaceful negotiation.

"So? There's lots of others," I said, waving my hand to indicate the dozen or so empty desks. "I was told we could sit anywhere we want."

As he frowned down at me, he ran his fingers through his hair. Wait. This was the same kid from earlier. Armpit boy. I hadn't recognized him immediately without the sunglasses.

A slight narrowing of his eyes indicated he'd registered who I was in the same instant. "Hey, you're that girl from outside. Lady Ha-ha." He gestured to my threadbare clothes. "Or no, wait, wait, I've got it . . . Taylor *Thrift*?"

I squashed down an urge to drop-kick him into the hallway. Already I'd nearly resorted to violence twice in one morning. The day wasn't off to a great start.

He was smirking at me now. "So, Ms. Thrift, why haven't I seen you around here before? Are you new? What's your name?"

"My. Name. Is. Abby. Beckett," I said, biting the end off every syllable. "And yeah, I'm new. Why? Who are you?"

He spread his hands out, palms turned up. "Everyone knows who I am. I'm Chase Lodbrok." He leaned closer and finished in a mocking tone. "Now. Get. Out. Of. My. Seat."

Other kids were starting to turn around in their seats to witness our standoff. But I wasn't backing down. *Everyone knows who I am.* Spare me. "Lodbrok?" I shot back. "Did you know in Norse that means 'fuzzy pants'? So why don't you . . . and your fuzzy pants . . . find another seat?"

Chase's grin stayed frozen on his face, but his eyes went cold. "I don't think you get it," he said. "So let me explain it more slowly. I sat here yesterday. And the day before that. And the day before that. So it's my seat."

I held his gaze. "This is today. What does yesterday have to do with me?"

"An excellent question, Ms. Beckett," a voice boomed from the front of the room.

I looked past Chase to a short man standing by the whiteboard with a perfect horseshoe of hair around a shiny bald head, giant Coke-bottle glasses, and a handlebar mustache. Dr. Ruel, or Doc, I guessed. The whole package didn't exactly say "most popular teacher in school" to me.

He gestured to my new friend to take another seat. Chase glared at me and then slammed angrily into a seat in the next row.

Doc watched him for a minute, then looked up at the class and continued, "Indeed, what does the past have to do with any of us, really?"

"Sorry, no, I didn't mean—" I started.

"No, it's quite all right," he said, holding up a hand. "It's a valid question." He turned to the whiteboard and wrote in large letters "WHY DOES THIS MATTER?"

Turning back to the class, he said, "An important question to answer if we're to be certain we're not spending all this time in idle study."

He scrawled "1492" on the board. "All week we've been studying the age of exploration. Now, at some point you all likely learned the rhyme 'In fourteen hundred ninety-two, Columbus sailed the ocean blue.' There they are: the *Niña*, the *Pinta*, and the *Santa María*, appearing on the coastline of a new land. But were they the first non-native peoples to arrive in North America?"

Grimsby caught my eye as he slid into a desk a few rows over and winked. Then his hand shot up.

"Yes, Mr. Grimsby?"

"Um, sir, I'm having trouble picturing that."

Doc stared at him for a beat, then nodded and, without another word, turned back to the board, his hand launching into action as he started to sketch a ship, then two more ships. Soon a rippling ocean, waves crashing on a beach, and even a little house with a thin line of smoke trailing from the chimney filled the board. As I witnessed this for the first time, it reminded me of this painter, Bob Ross, that my mom always used to watch on TV. He could somehow make a simple stroke of his paintbrush look like a bird, or a tree, or a mountain range. Similarly now, the class watched in fascination as Doc transformed the whiteboard into a masterpiece of historical edification.

As the lecture went on, I could start to see why everyone liked this teacher. His teaching style was like a stage performance—a mash-up of fascinating historical tidbits, artwork, and deadpan humor. I tried my best to follow along, but half an hour later, the notebook Grimsby had let me borrow was filled with a confusing jumble of words and arrows interspersed with pathetic stick-figure attempts to reproduce Doc's art. By tomorrow, I was sure I wouldn't be able to make any sense of it all.

A quick movement caught the corner of my eye. I looked up from my notebook in time to see Chase blow into a straw, sending a tiny white projectile into the hair of the girl in front of him. The back of her head and the floor beneath were covered with little white flecks of paper. He shook with silent laughter and fist-bumped the guy next to him. Doc kept lecturing, oblivious in the front of the room. I waited for Chase to reload, then loudly cleared my throat.

Doc turned just in time to see another spit wad take flight. Chase jerked his hand under his desk, but it was too late.

"Mr. Lodbrok," Doc said, frowning. "Please see me after school today for detention. Maybe some time cleaning my class-room floor will help you remember to refrain from disrupting my class."

The girl in front of Chase realized what had been happening and shook her head, sending a shower of paper bits to the floor as she shot Chase a dirty look.

Doc surveyed the room and stopped on me. "Now, Ms. Beckett, something tells me you might know the answer to my question."

"Um . . . sorry?" I stalled, looking down like somehow the answer was going to magically appear on my page. But my notes looked like a traffic accident.

"The first Europeans to set foot in the New World were . . ." he prompted.

I paused. "Uh, the Vikings?"

"Are you asking me or telling me?"

"I'm pretty sure it was the Vikings."

"Very good," Doc said. He drew a line through 1492 and wrote "999" below it.

"The discovery of the New World is commonly credited to Columbus because he established the first permanent European settlements here. But the Vikings actually landed in North America almost five hundred years earlier. Some say our own Bjarni Herjólfsson, or as I believe some of you refer to him, Bellyflop Bjarni"—he paused as chuckles filled the room— "was the first European to sight the New World even before that."

In my notes I drew a stick figure of a chubby guy diving into a swimming pool and scrawled "Bellyflop Barney?" above it. I'd have to ask Grimsby about that later.

"The Vikings have a reputation as raiding barbarians," Doc continued, "but they made significant contributions in technology, government, and the arts. Indeed, we might even go so far as to ask where we'd all be without the Vikings. Don't you agree?"

He looked at me mysteriously. I wasn't entirely sure if he really wanted me to answer or if it was just a rhetorical question. A chime signaled the end of the period.

Doc shifted his gaze and said, "Okay, class dismissed. See you all tomorrow. And don't forget to study. There's always a chance for a pop quiz."

A chorus of groans joined the sound of chairs scraping the floor. I rose to go.

"A minute, Ms. Beckett," he said with his back still to me.

Grimsby pointed toward the hall. "Meet you outside?"

I nodded.

"That was a mistake," Chase said as he shouldered past me on his way out the door.

"Have fun in detention," I replied.

"Ms. Beckett?"

I turned to see Doc glance from Chase back to me before he spoke again. "I apologize that I haven't been able to formally welcome you to Vale yet. I'm sure you don't remember me from your mother's funeral?"

I tilted my head, struggling to recall any of the blur of faces that had paraded before me that day as I'd stood in a state of mute shock.

He adjusted his glasses and nodded. "No . . . no, I didn't think so. Well, your mother and I actually attended Vale together many years ago. I knew her quite well. I was particularly saddened by her passing, and indeed to hear the further news recently of your father's condition." He paused and looked at me with that intense gaze of his. "I expect that you're feeling a bit lost at the moment?"

I looked down at my notebook. Lost. Scared. Angry. So many different emotions. "I guess you could say that."

Doc chuckled. "I assumed as much." He slipped his hand into the front pocket of his shirt and extracted something, which he held out to me. "Which is why I thought having this might be particularly useful in starting to get yourself, let's just say . . . unlost."

I took the item in my hand and studied it. It was a shiny black plastic card about the size of a credit card with "G39" stenciled on it in gold letters. I looked up at him. "What is it?"

He glanced toward the classroom door before replying cryptically, "Simply the key to everything."

The key to everything? That didn't seem simple at all.

Noticing my skeptical look, he winked. "But you might find that the gold frame is an excellent place to start seeking the answer to that question." He tilted his head toward the door. "And, if I may make the suggestion, your friend Mr. Grimsby may serve as an excellent fellow seeker."

So many questions sprang to mind. But just as I was about to reply, a pair of students entered the class. Doc's gaze shifted to the clock on the wall. "Let me not keep you from your next class. We'll talk more later. Welcome to Vale."

# CHAPTER 8

# FISH JELL-O

Two periods later we emerged from our British literature class with an assignment to write the first draft of our own sonnet by the next class.

"Brit lit, how do I despise thee?" Grimsby groaned. "Let me count the . . ." He glanced over at me. "Oh. Sorry, I think you said your dad teaches that."

I shook my head. "It's okay. I know he'll be back to terrorizing students with twenty-page essays on Old English etymology soon." I wasn't sure I really believed that, but saying it out loud made me feel like it was somehow more likely to happen.

"Um, yeah, I can hardly wait." Grimsby laughed. "Anyway, on to the best period of the day: lunch."

I put my hand on my stomach. "Finally. I forgot Bryn's croissants, so I could probably eat a horse."

"Sorry, that was on yesterday's menu," he deadpanned. "But maybe horse soup today if you're lucky."

When we entered the school cafeteria, I was immediately reminded of the great feasting halls of Norse legend. The room's wooden rafters swept gracefully upward to a vaulted point supported by pillars as thick as trees. At either end of the hall, fires roared in enormous hearths, and more of those strange sconces ringed the room, filling it with flickering orange-and-yellow light. Great rectangular wooden tables arranged in three rows each at least a hundred feet long were filled with students chatting and laughing or scrambling to finish their homework before their next class.

"I almost forgot," Grimsby said. "What did Doc want earlier? When he talked to you after class?"

I shrugged. "I guess he just wanted to welcome me to Vale." Then, remembering the black card, I slid it out of my pocket and held it out toward him. "Also, he gave me this."

Grimsby studied the card. "What is it? Some sort of high-end credit card?"

"I was hoping you'd know. At least, Doc seemed to think you could help. He called it 'the key to everything.'"

"Sounds mysterious," he said, frowning.

"Yeah, no kidding. Oh, and he said something about a gold frame. Does that mean anything to you?"

"A gold frame?" Grimsby rubbed his chin and then shook his head. "Sorry, not a clue."

I slid the card back into the pocket of my blazer. "Okay, well, if any inspiration hits you, let me know."

As we scanned the crowd for empty seats, I spotted the infamous Chase Lodbrok. "What's the deal with that guy anyway?"

Grimsby sighed. "You've got your three main social classes at Vale." He pointed as we passed by the tables. "Sports types, spoiled rich kids, and the basic criminal element. Or as I like to call them—jocks, jerks, and juvies."

I studied the kids at the tables. Even most of the juvies had three-hundred-dollar designer jeans.

"Chase Lodbrok," he continued, gesturing with his chin at the blond kid surrounded by a group of adoring fans, "has the unique distinction of belonging to all three. Which, I guess, is why he's the most popular kid in school."

"Oh great, so I just hosed my social status in one morning?"

He shrugged. "Basically." He flopped his backpack into a chair at an empty section of one table near the trash cans. The air was ripe with the scent of old banana peels and discarded tuna fish sandwiches. I could see why this corner was empty.

We joined a line of kids waiting to get lunch, and Grimsby handed me a tray. "Stick with the pizza. It's your best bet."

But when we got to the front of the line, another familiar scent transported me to a vivid memory of my five-year-old self, a yellow plastic tablecloth spread over a kitchen table, eating dinner with my mom and dad. We were all smiling and laughing.

"Wait, is that . . . ?" I slid my tray down the stainless-steel rails and stopped in front of a steaming pan of food. My eyes teared up. Partly because of the toe-curling odor. But mostly from the memories.

"You know lutefisk, dear?" a voice asked in a thick, vaguely Scandinavian accent. I looked up at an elderly woman dressed in a standard-issue white apron and hairnet over purple hair. Her face was beaming like I'd just made her day. She poised her ladle over the steaming dish. "You like?"

"Yes, please!" I nodded enthusiastically and held out a plate for her to scoop a large serving onto it.

Grimsby reappeared at my side shaking a bottle of strawberry milk as I headed back toward our table. His face screwed up in a look of revulsion, and he pinched his nose with his free hand. "Pizza, dude. I said stick with the pizza."

"No, this is good stuff," I said. "Really. My mom used to make it for my dad and me all the time. It's sort of like fish Jell-O. You want to try some?"

"Fish. Jell-O." Grimsby's face turned a distinct shade of green as he stared at the gelatinous lump on my plate. "No thanks. I'm, uh, trying to cut back."

I shrugged. "Suit yourself."

When we arrived back at our table, I did a little stutter step and nearly dropped my tray. An Asian American girl with a rainbow unicorn backpack and dark hair with multicolored tips was sitting across from where I'd left my bag. Her head was bent over a textbook that lay open in front of her, and the fork in her hand slowly moved across the page, tracking her reading. It had to be the same girl who had rescued my dad and me when we'd arrived at Vale. She'd changed clothes, but her backpack and hair were unmistakable.

Grimsby dropped into the seat next to her, then fished around in his backpack and pulled out several items. Ignoring a neat little Tupperware with something that looked like a salad inside, he lined up the bottle of strawberry milk, a bag of neon-orange cheese puffs, and a giant blue-frosted cupcake on the table in front of him.

"You know you have the worst eating habits, right?" said the girl, looking up for the first time from her book at Grimsby's food selections. She pulled a small salad closer to herself and stabbed her fork into it.

"It's all about colors," Grimsby said to her. "The more colors on your plate, the healthier you're eating. It's in all the nutrition books."

She sighed and adjusted her position to accommodate her backpack.

"Why don't you ever take that thing off?" asked Grimsby, pointing a neon-orange-dusted finger at the unicorn-themed bag on her back.

"Why don't you mind your own business?" she shot back before forking a piece of avocado into her mouth.

I stood there stunned as I witnessed this exchange. Surprised that this girl I'd only briefly glimpsed during one of the darkest moments of my life, who I'd started to believe was either an angel or a figment of my imagination, was suddenly sitting there across from me. Eating a Cobb salad.

"You two, uh, know each other?" I finally said.

Grimsby glanced up at me across the top of his cupcake. "Are you planning to eat standing up?"

"Oh," I said. "Right." I hooked a chair leg with my foot and pulled it out, then sat down.

Grimsby swallowed a large bite of cupcake, then tilted his head toward the girl. "Sorry, yeah, this is my mother. Or at least she acts like she is."

The girl stuck out her tongue at him. "Also his best friend, Gwynndolyn R—"

"Gwynndolyn R. . . ." Grimsby singsonged. He rolled his eyes. "It's just Gwynn."

My eyes bounced from Grimsby back to Gwynn. "Well, I'm, um, just Abby."

"Nice to meet you, Just Abby," said Gwynn, shooting a look at Grimsby. "Are you new here? I don't think I've seen you around."

Surely she recognized me. Unless there was some other rainbow-haired girl at the school who wore a unicorn backpack.

"Yeah, well, I think we . . . actually sort of met when . . ." I started, but her eyes darted toward Grimsby, and she gave a little shake of her head. "Oh, oh, right," I said quickly. "Yeah, this is my first day."

She smiled. "Well, welcome to Vale. Is that lutefisk you have there? Looks good."

"See?" I said to Grimsby. "I'm not the only one."

But he was already distracted, watching as Mr. Wendel, the science teacher I'd met earlier, yelled at some kids nearby to quiet down already.

Gwynn flipped her book closed, pushed back her chair, and stood up. "Well, it's useless trying to study with all this racket. I'm gonna find someplace quiet before next period. See you around?"

I stared up at her, wanting to ask so many questions. "Definitely. And thanks for . . . you know."

"Don't mention it." She smiled, then turned and strode across the cafeteria.

I watched her disappear out of sight, then swung my head around to see what had Grimsby so transfixed. Mr. Wendel was now leaning menacingly over a pair of boys. A big vein throbbed in his forehead like he was about to blow. I mean, it was pretty loud in there with everyone talking over each other. I've noticed that old people—like maybe thirty and over—seem to have a thing about loud noises.

Noticing me watching, Grimsby said, "Mr. Wendel is probably the last guy who should be doing cafeteria duty. I heard one time he went so nuts he actually duct-taped a kid who fell asleep in class to her desk and left her there. All weekend."

I narrowed my eyes. "No way. You're just yanking my chain, right?"

He shook his head. "No, true story. Like I told you earlier. You don't want to get on his bad side."

I blinked and shook my head. As I looked down for my fork, a muscle spasmed in my shoulder, probably from sleeping in a chair all night. I rolled my shoulders, then raised my hands over my head and stretched, trying to work out the kink.

That's when it happened.

Out of nowhere, a projectile hurtled through the air. With a loud slap, it splattered wetly across the front of Mr. Wendel's shirt. As the pieces slid slowly down his tie, I could smell it even from where I was, like a putrid scent grenade loosed in the cafeteria. Lutefisk. I couldn't believe some kid would nail a teacher with a lump of that stuff. Poor Mr. Wendel. Actually, poor kid as soon as he figured out who did it.

Mr. Wendel stared while the fish chunks left greasy gray skid marks down his navy-blue tie, then raised his head, slowly scanning the deathly silent cafeteria.

I realized then that my arms were still in the air, frozen in mid-stretch. I *also* realized that this could possibly, just maybe, look incriminating. So I jerked them down to my sides.

But it was too late.

The quick motion attracted Mr. Wendel's attention. He turned his red-faced, furious gaze directly on me.

A sick feeling hit my stomach as Mr. Wendel's stare dropped to my tray and the bowl of smelly fish in the middle of it. My eyes darted frantically around the cafeteria. Surely there had to be someone else with this stuff on their plate. That's when I noticed Grimsby's seat was empty. Had he really ditched me again? Some friend he was turning out to be.

Then I saw Chase and his friends a few tables over, purple-faced and doing their best not to explode with laughter. He was holding something under the table. Even without seeing it, I knew immediately what it was.

And I knew I was dead meat.

Mr. Wendel stalked wordlessly toward me. I stared transfixed at the throbbing vein on his forehead, feeling my own pulse racing faster and faster. Soon he stood right in front of me. Looming over me with a maniacal glint in his eyes. He opened his mouth to speak. I cringed.

Then just at that moment, a screech of static filled the air, and from the overhead speakers came a loud voice. "ABBY BECKETT. WILL YOU PLEASE REPORT TO THE HEADMASTER'S OFFICE. REPEAT. ABBY BECKETT. TO PROFESSOR ROTH'S OFFICE. IMMEDIATELY."

Looking like a cat that had just been cheated out of a particularly delicious mouse, Mr. Wendel stared at me, then wordlessly lifted his arm and pointed in the direction of the headmaster's office.

# CHAPTER 9

# THE GOLD FRAME

Maybe I imagined it, but as I rose to go, it seemed like every-one's expressions were the same as you'd see on people watching a funeral procession. Then the deathly quiet was suddenly broken by a high-pitched, repetitive squeaking noise like a shopping cart wheel that needed oil.

*Eee. Eee. Eee.*

I looked around and saw an aging janitor in a gray jump-suit pushing a trash can–and–bucket combo with a mop handle protruding from it. He smiled at me kindly across the sea of heads, then pulled the mop out of the water and started swabbing circles on the floor where the fish juice had splattered in a puddle at Mr. Wendel's feet. Mr. Wendel was still staring daggers at me, but I shifted my gaze to the floor and wordlessly continued out of the cafeteria and into the hall he'd indicated.

Eventually I came to a sign reading "Office of the Headmaster" at the foot of a flight of stairs leading upward. At the top was a long hall with both the walls and ceiling covered in polished oak paneling and lined with oil paintings of what I guessed were past headmasters. Each pair of stern eyes seemed to regard me disapprovingly as I passed. I could almost feel the walls closing in around me. I didn't know why I'd been summoned to Professor Roth's office, but I had the distinct impression of escaping the frying pan only to land right in the fire.

At the end of the hall, a bronze placard beside a closed, solid oak door read "Professor Roth—Headmaster." Just as I was building up the nerve to knock, I heard a scuff of shoes behind me. I whirled around to see Grimsby taking a great interest in one of the oil paintings of a past headmaster.

"You'd think the artist could have left out that giant, hairy mole on this guy's forehead," he said.

"There you are," I said. "Thanks for bailing on me back there."

He turned to look at me and put his hands up in mock surrender. In his left hand was a drinking glass from the cafeteria. "Whoa, what do you mean? I probably just saved your life. You should be thanking me."

I crossed my arms. "*Thanking* you? For what? I—"

He held the cup over his mouth and said, "Abby Beckett, will you please report to the headmaster's office?"

My eyes widened in surprise. "Wait . . . that was you? But how?"

Grimsby grinned. "Let's just say my first airtime on KNUT came a little earlier than expected."

I continued to stare at him as the pieces fit together, remembering him stopping off at the school radio station earlier in the day. He'd probably risked getting in big trouble to help me out. "Wow, that was . . . huge. Thanks. Really."

"Hey, what are friends for?" he said.

I laughed, then swiveled my head to look up and down the hall. Empty, if you didn't count the gallery of glaring headmaster paintings. "We should probably get out of here before . . ." I trailed off as something clicked in my brain.

"Something wrong?" Grimsby said.

I studied the portraits all around us. "No, I . . . just remembered how Doc said something about a gold frame being an excellent place to start looking for answers, or something like that."

"Oh, interesting. You think he meant one of these? There are plenty of gold frames here." He stared around the hallway. "But which one?"

I suddenly had a sinking feeling. There were probably fifty paintings of former headmasters lining the walls. And they all had gold frames. "I don't know." I turned to the one closest to me. "Maybe there's something peculiar about one of them?"

"Like what?"

"Not a clue. I guess look for anything unusual."

We did a quick search down the hallway, studying each frame as we passed. Grimsby leaned so close to inspect one of the frames, his nose nearly touched it.

"Speaking of unusual," he said casually, "what did you mean earlier when you said to Bryn, and I quote, 'You're a Viking too'?"

I stared at him blankly for a few seconds. "I thought you said you couldn't hear anything."

"I lied."

Fantastic. I lowered my head and pinched my nose to ward off the headache that suddenly throbbed at the front of my skull.

"Look," he said. "You seem like you kind of need a friend. And even Doc suggested I might be able to help somehow. You can trust me. Really."

I opened one eye and looked at him skeptically. "Oh, really? After you just told me you lied to me?"

He looked away. "Well, usually."

I studied him standing there, with his floppy hair, too-big blazer, and pale, skinny legs. And I laughed. I couldn't help it. It just came out. "Usually? Well, forgive me if I don't find that *super* encouraging."

He grinned. "No, for real, I'm a highly trustworthy individual. So why don't we start here: The Vikings don't only exist in history books, do they?"

I'd kept this part of me secret for so long that it was hard for my brain to even form the words to tell another person about it. "Okay, you're right. They—"

Grimsby raised an eyebrow.

"Fine, *we* never actually disappeared. We figured out that instead of raiding and pillaging, we could be more effective by assimilating into different cultures and working behind the scenes."

"Wow, you just made Vikings sound super boring. But you still get to whack people when you have to, right?"

I laughed. "Sometimes I guess that still happens." I opened my eyes wide and held up my hands. "But *I've* never done that, of course. Killed someone, I mean."

"Wow, so let me get this straight. You're a Viking warrior. No kidding. Like a stone-cold member of an ancient civilization of bone-crushing giants."

"Well, technically, I'm not a warrior yet. You have to be at least fourteen for that. And only then if you've also got some wicked good skills. Until then I'm a thrall, which doesn't sound even half as cool."

"Thrall . . . *thrall*," Grimsby mouthed, letting it roll around on his tongue, then shaking his head. "Yeah, I'd stick with the warrior thing. That's our ticket to the upper echelons of middle school society right there."

"*Our* ticket? I'm telling you this in confidence, remember? You have to promise not to tell anyone."

His face fell. "What? But think of all the—"

"I'm serious."

"*Fiiiine*," he moped. "I won't tell anyone."

"So now that you know," I said, "can we please get back to checking these frames?"

I bent down to run my fingers along the edge of one of the frames, hoping to indicate that I was done talking about the subject for now. While I'd initially felt a little sick to my stomach at divulging my secret to another person, now more than anything I felt . . . well, relieved. It was actually kind of nice to feel like I had someone to share it with for once. Like I was suddenly a little bit lighter somehow.

Just then I felt my back pocket vibrate. When I extracted my phone, the name on the display was Bryn, my dad's nurse.

"Bryn?" I said, suddenly feeling out of breath. "Is everything okay with my dad?"

"Sorry to call you at school," came Bryn's voice. "I just thought you'd want to know right away. The doctors think they've figured out what's wrong with your dad. Hold on. I'm texting you a photo."

My heart knocked against my ribs as I waited, not missing the fact that she hadn't answered the question: *Is everything okay with my dad?* After a few seconds, a text came through. When I thumbed it open, I saw a photo of a clear disk made of two halves of glass fitted together. Inside was what looked like some sort of thorn or claw.

Nervous butterflies stirred in my stomach. "Wh-what's that?"

"Hold on. I have Dr. Swenson right here too. She can explain it better."

"Hi, Abby." Dr. Swenson's voice came over the line a few seconds later. "I hope you'll forgive me for not sharing this news in person, but I have to be away for most of the afternoon and wanted to make sure you knew what we knew. Are you familiar with the legend of the svefnthorn?"

I stared down at the screen of my phone. Whatever it was, it was sharp and dangerous-looking. "No, what is it?"

"Svefnthorn translates roughly to 'sleep thorn' in English. It's an artifact described in some ancient medical texts. Its sting was said to put one's foes into a deep sleep. I've never seen a real one. Indeed, until now I wasn't even sure they were more than a legend."

My exhausted brain was having trouble making the connection. "Okaayyy . . . so what does this have to do with my dad?"

"When we examined your father's wound, instead of the usual pellets that we'd expect from a shotgun blast, this is what we found. In fact, we removed several of these from his upper chest and shoulder. We think this is the reason for his current condition."

I felt my breath start to come faster and struggled to shove down the grim scenarios that came flooding in. "Condition? What do you mean? You called this a sleep thorn, right? So he's . . . asleep?"

"Essentially, yes. It's more like a sort of coma. According to the texts I could find, usually a person stung by the thorn would drop into a deep sleep and regain consciousness after a few hours."

"It's been way longer than that," I said, feeling like I was stating the obvious. "So why hasn't he woken up yet?"

There was a pause on the other end of the line that may have been less than a second but felt like hours. "To be perfectly honest with you, we don't know yet," came Dr. Swenson's voice at last.

I pressed the phone tighter to my ear. "Should I come to the hospital? If there's anything I can do . . ."

"All his vital signs remain stable. And now that we have a better understanding of what we're up against, my team will be able to analyze the toxin released by the thorn and attempt to engineer a countertoxin. Best-case scenario: It may wear off and he'll wake up on his own. So finish off the school day. We'll take good care of your father."

I nodded mutely like she could see me. Why had the giant on

the motorcycle been firing these strange thorns? And why hadn't my dad woken up yet? It didn't make any sense.

"Okay, Dr. Swenson, thanks so much for letting me know."

After hanging up, I stood staring blankly at the photo of the svefnthorn. Despite Dr. Swenson's reassurances, I was struggling to feel relieved by the news. Probably because there was something in her tone just like when my dad tries to withhold information, thinking he's protecting me.

"Abby?" Grimsby said. "Everything okay?"

Not sure how to respond, I blinked and slid my phone back into my pocket. "Yeah. Fine, I guess." I gestured toward the wall nearby. "Find anything?"

He pointed to a nameplate beneath one of the portraits. "Maybe. Take a look at this."

The nameplate read "Jason 'Jay' Gould, 1881–1885." I turned to him, nodding excitedly. "Maybe Doc didn't mean 'gold' as in the *color* gold, but 'Gould' as in his last name."

"Exactly what I was thinking."

"Hey, can I borrow that glass you're holding?"

"Sure," he said, handing it to me. "What's up?"

I leaned closer, holding the cup like a magnifying glass over the tiny words I'd spotted below the nameplate. "'Press here,'" I read aloud.

I reached out with my pointer finger and tentatively pressed the nameplate. With a soft beep, the plate depressed like a button, and a panel in the wall slid away, revealing a small slot behind it.

Grimsby turned to me with a surprised expression that mirrored my own. "Now what?"

"It's got to be . . ." I removed Doc's G39 card from my pocket, then slid it into the slot and waited. Nothing happened for a few seconds, then suddenly an entire section of the wall slid away to one side, leaving us staring into an empty elevator car.

Grimsby took a step back in surprise. "Whoa! Secret Vikings. Hidden elevators. And I thought this was gonna be a normal Tuesday." He bowed slightly and gestured toward the elevator. "After you."

Inside we stood staring at the button panel.

"Which floor?" he asked.

"Good question." I stared down at the card I'd retrieved from its slot, then studied the walls of the elevator car. "I don't see another slot. And there's no thirty-ninth floor. There are only buttons for nine floors here. And G. For 'ground,' I guess."

"Or 'garage.' I bet Vikings have some pretty sweet rides."

I pushed the "1" button to see where it went, but after a few seconds, the whole panel flashed and the door dinged open again. Next I tried the "2" and "3" buttons with the same results.

Grimsby held up a finger like he had an idea. "Let me try . . ." He punched in the sequence G-3-9. This time the entire panel lit up. The door closed and the elevator started moving downward.

"Nice," I said.

He shrugged. "Glad to— *Ahhhhhhh!*" He finished with a cry of terror as suddenly the elevator plunged downward like its cable had snapped.

"What did you do?!" I screamed. I clutched a metal handrail on the wall and held on for my life.

"I don't know! I was trying to get to another floor. Not plummet us to our deaths!"

I frantically started mashing all the buttons at once with the palm of my free hand, trying to stop our free fall. But the lit panel simply blinked frustratingly back at me. The elevator kept speeding faster and faster. I would have screamed, but it felt like my stomach was jammed in my throat.

Finally the elevator jerked to a halt, sending us crashing to the floor. That's where we lay sprawled in a tangle of arms and legs when the doors dinged open.

"Would you two stop messing around already?" said a familiar voice. I looked up from the floor. Gwynn, aka rainbow unicorn girl, smiled down at us with one eyebrow raised. Except she wasn't wearing her backpack anymore. And on her back were what looked very convincingly like feathery white wings.

# CHAPTER 10

# ASGARD

"Is this heaven?" Grimsby asked a little dazedly, apparently spotting the wings too. Then he gasped, evidently remembering the direction we'd just traveled, and his eyes grew wide. "Or the *other* place?"

"We're not dead," I said, handing him one of his loafers, which had somehow ended up lying on my ear, and pushing myself off the floor. "I think."

"Not yet," added Gwynn helpfully as she eyed Grimsby.

I squinted past her at a short tunnel leading to an enormous room. "Where are we?"

She spread her hands and said, "Welcome to Asgard. Also known as Viking central command for North America."

I sat up quickly. "Whoa, what?! You're telling us the Vikings . . . have a secret headquarters . . . right here under Vale Hall?"

She smiled wryly. "Well, it *was* a secret, anyway." And she shot a glance toward Grimsby before turning a withering gaze on me.

She had a point. But I'd only caved with permission. Sort of. Which meant that Doc was . . . who, exactly? To change the subject, I said, "You have, uh . . ." I pointed to my back and made a vague flapping motion like wings. "So you're a . . . Valkyrie?"

I was familiar with Valkyries, of course, from stories my parents had told me when I was little. They were winged women who carried fallen warriors to Viking heaven. But I'd always thought they were just characters from fairy tales.

She shrugged casually and nodded, then slid a finger over one feathery wing. The wings had multicolored tips just like her hair. For a brief second, a sad look crossed her eyes as she caressed her wing, but then she blinked and turned to us, all business. "There's a lot you need to know. Doc said you might be, um, dropping in."

My eyes lit up as I suddenly made the connection. "The Valkyrie thing! That's how you—"

"Found you and your dad?" she finished for me. "Yeah. Valkyries have a sort of radar for people in peril. You know, the whole taking-dead-souls-to-Valhalla thing."

"Wow, well . . . thanks," I said. "Really. I don't know what my dad and I would have done if you hadn't found us. Oh, and thanks for not taking him to Valhalla."

She laughed. "No problem. Now, why don't you two follow me? I'll give you the grand tour."

"It's okay if Grimsby comes along?"

She glanced in his direction, then shrugged. "I guess we can't just leave him here unchaperoned." She narrowed her eyes mischievously. "We can always wipe his memory later."

Grimsby let out a little strangled noise and threw his hands protectively over his head. "Hands off the merchandise!"

On the threshold of the next room, I froze and breathlessly took it all in. The cavernous space looked like what I guess you'd get if the NASA command center and a medieval castle had a baby. Giant television screens played news feeds from around the world. And everywhere was a flurry of activity. People in heated debates in front of whiteboard-sized maps. People moving among sleek, glass-topped desks and typing at computers. No, not just people. *My* people.

"These are all . . ." I started.

Gwynn nodded. "Vikings."

My heart swelled with a sense of pride. A feeling of . . . not being alone for the first time in such a long time.

"This way," Gwynn said, and led us farther into the room.

The walls were lined with more of the torches that filled the halls of Vale above us. But as with those other torches, I couldn't get over the feeling that there was something off about them. When I stepped closer to a sconce on a nearby wall, it didn't take me long to figure out what the problem was: It wasn't giving off any heat.

"It's a hologram," said Gwynn. She waved for us to follow her.

"But it looks so real!" I poked my finger and then my entire hand right through the flame. I was relieved when my hand didn't come out burned black like an overcooked hot dog. Kids, don't try this at home.

When I turned, Gwynn was already halfway across the room. As I hustled to catch up, I noticed what looked like massive tapestries along the walls depicting battle scenes, feasts, and epic adventures. But these weren't ordinary tapestries. The figures in

89

them moved as if they were alive, two battling Vikings even leaping from one tapestry to the next as their swords clanged together.

"Millions of electronic pixels are embedded in the cloth," said Gwynn, following my gaze. "Basically, live-action tapestries. Sort of a modern upgrade from the old days."

I watched a dragon ship slice through a wave with a spray of water that doused the revelers in a neighboring tapestry, causing them to roar and shake their fists in complaint. I spun in a slow circle, wanting to take in everything. I had to admit, I was impressed. I'd had no idea there were so many of us. Or that we were so high-tech. This whole space. Her wings. The Vikings . . . I had so many important questions to ask.

"Can you get ESPN on those?" Grimsby said excitedly. That was not one of those questions.

"Actually, yeah," Gwynn said. "You should see it in here on Sundays when the Minnesota Vikings are playing."

"Coooool," he said. He couldn't seem to get over her wings. He reached out to touch one like he couldn't believe they were real, but she smacked his hand away. "What gives? I've known you since I was, like, two years old, and you never told me you have wings?"

"You never asked," she said with a shrug.

Gwynn led the way through a set of large steel doors inlaid with intricate carvings. "The complex here is built in a wheel-and-spoke model patterned after the ancient Viking fortress at Trelleborg in Denmark. We have living quarters, medical offices, stores—everything we need to be completely self-sufficient if necessary."

I glanced up at the ceiling, picturing the world above continuing oblivious to the presence of a city of Viking warriors living under its feet.

Gwynn stepped up to what looked like a dragon-head prow fixed on the wall. A thin beam of light scanned her face, and after a second the dragon's eyes glowed green. A door slid open, and we were blasted by a twin assault of heat and the noise of metal ringing against metal.

"The forge," she shouted over the noise. "This is where they make all the good stuff!"

The huge, cave-like space was dim, like stepping into a twilit world. It was illuminated only by the pulsing orange glows of numerous fires that reflected in the steam that billowed out of sight into the looming blackness above. The smells of molten metal and a humid dampness permeated the air. Nearby, a leather-aproned blacksmith whose height would have easily qualified him for the NBA hammered at a glowing sword blade. His face was hidden behind a welder's mask, but by the journeyman's braid at one end of his flowing golden hair, I guessed he was probably only a few years older than me. His muscular arms flexed with each blow, sending sparks raining around him with each stroke. He looked up as we approached and nodded at Gwynn before plunging the sword into a nearby water trough. Steam hissed and rose from the cooling metal.

Gwynn's face flushed as she watched him work. "Did you hurt your arm?" she said, pointing to a bandage wrapped around one bicep.

The giant glanced down at his arm. "Work injury," he grunted before returning to hammering the glowing metal.

"Friendly guy," Grimsby joked under his breath as we continued our tour.

"I, um, think your backpack is on fire," I said, pointing to his back.

"Huh? What?" He frantically spun around in a circle, then finally shrugged off his backpack and threw it on the ground, stamping on it until the small flame went out.

"Sorry," said Gwynn. "Should have warned you both to watch for stray sparks."

"Thanks for telling me *now*," Grimsby said. He lifted his backpack off the ground and frowned at the charred front pocket.

I picked up a short throwing knife from a nearby table as we passed by. "Isn't the forge kind of . . . old-school by comparison with the rest of Asgard?"

Gwynn plucked the knife from my hand and expertly twirled it in her fingers. "Sometimes the old ways are the best. We're still trying to reproduce the methods of the original Viking masters. Their blades were said to defeat even magical charms. Unfortunately, those skills remain lost to history."

I watched another Viking worker grind a razor-sharp edge on a wicked-looking battle-ax. I was thinking maybe I could use a new ax when Gwynn said, "Oh!"

I turned to her. "What's up?"

"While we're here, let me show you something." She led the way across the space to a heavily scarred table. It was covered with neatly arranged tools. Something about it looked oddly familiar. Gwynn snapped on a desk lamp and blew across the table, sending millions of dust motes swirling in the arc of amber light.

Grimsby sneezed and waved the dust away from his face. "So it's an old"—he coughed—"table. What's the big deal?"

Gwynn turned to me. "This was your mom's. The table. The tools. All of it."

This took a few seconds to register. I realized then why it looked so familiar. It was an exact replica of the one from our basement back in North Carolina. Same tools. Same books.

A sudden sharp pang stabbed at my heart. My mom? Worked here? Why hadn't she ever told me? It was like I'd just discovered an entire part of her life she'd kept hidden from me. Hot tears blurred my view of the workbench. Probably I was overreacting, but it made me wonder what else I didn't know about her.

Then I noticed a gap on the bookshelf. I ran my sleeve roughly across my eyes and stepped forward. What had been there? I thought back to the shelf at home, and then I remembered. Her journal, where she'd recorded all her work. It was missing.

"Is something wrong, Abby?" Gwynn said, looking at me with concern.

"It's nothing." I quickly surveyed the rest of the workbench, but the journal was nowhere in sight. I cleared my throat, embarrassed. "So my mom actually worked here? I had no idea she ever came to Vale. I mean, after her days here as a student."

"Yeah, I guess she was actually sort of a local legend. The Aesir would gather here at Asgard at least a couple times every year. And she was always consulting on some project or another with the Vikings. But I overheard once that she was working on something even bigger."

I frowned. "Something bigger? Like what?"

She shrugged. "Your guess is as good as mine. I never heard what it was."

Grimsby frowned. "So your mom was some sort of blacksmith?"

I shook my head. "Not exactly. She used to call herself a seeker of knowledge—science mostly, but also history, art—all sorts of fields. I remember when I was little how she'd be up at all hours of the night poring over books with titles I couldn't pronounce or tinkering on a project in our basement."

As we moved on to continue the tour, I couldn't help staring back over my shoulder one last time, imagining my mom bent over the table working. When we reached the other side of the room, another door slid open, welcoming us back to the cool quiet of the hall.

"Okay," said Grimsby, tilting his head to the side and squinting one eye like his ears were still ringing. "Let's see if I've got this right. The Vikings still exist. In a secret underground bunker. Here in Minneapolis. Couldn't they have picked someplace nicer? Like Miami maybe?"

Gwynn considered before replying. "Yes, yes, yes, and no. At over six feet tall and more than two hundred pounds on average, can you imagine Vikings in a tropical climate? You'd need a lot of deodorant. It wouldn't be pretty."

"But why underground? Are they hiding or something?"

"Not exactly. Hiding, I mean. Think about it. It's no accident that the largest Scandinavian population outside northern Europe happens to be here in Minnesota. Plus there's the football team. The Minnesota Vikings. Not exactly subtle. The rest of the world believes that the real Vikings faded into legend. We have a strict vow of secrecy." She shot a glance in my direction. "Because, let's just say, there are plenty of people who would love to destroy the Vikings if they knew what we were doing."

"But this entire place," Grimsby said, taking in the whole of Asgard with a sweep of his arms. "Doesn't it bug them being underground all the time?"

"Ha!" I laughed. "You're talking about a civilization that's basically used to not seeing the sun for half the year. In Iceland in the wintertime, the sun rises around noon and sets at three thirty. Trust me, this is nothing."

Gwynn nodded her agreement. "And anyway, this next room may change your mind about that."

We stepped out of the hallway onto a circular cobblestoned plaza about the size of a football field. It was lined with multi-colored buildings constructed of stout timbers, just like in a northern European village. Overhead a huge dome-shaped atrium stretched upward at least three stories high. It was composed entirely of massive triangular glass panels through which sunlight streamed, filling the room with the welcoming glow of a summer afternoon. Looking upward, we could see wispy clouds drift lazily by in the azure-blue sky. In the center of the room was a pond with grass around it and even a gnarled old weeping willow growing over it as if the pond were a basin for its tears. Rough-hewn wooden tables sat scattered around the room, with people seated at them talking, eating, or reading.

"Wait," said Grimsby, turning back and then forward again, clearly disoriented. "Did we somehow walk all the way back to the surface?"

Far above, I saw what looked like a red-winged creature with a long pointed tail soar through the sky. Then something clicked. "Oh, I get it. This is another simulation, right?"

Gwynn smiled. "Yes and no. The sunlight itself is real, captured on the surface and magnified through a complex set of mirrors and prisms until it reaches here. But we can change the scenery to a variety of things. Thunderstorms. Snow showers."

"Dragons?" I added.

She nodded. "That was Doc's idea, actually. He wanted to add some playful elements to keep things interesting."

"Oooh, I want to try!" said Grimsby, looking around. "Where's the remote?"

"Um, it's not exactly something they let anyone control," said Gwynn. "Anyway, I think you're going to want to see what I have to show you next." She led the way across the plaza, indicating the buildings around its edges. "This is what we call the village square."

"But it's a . . . circle?" Grimsby said.

She rolled her eyes. "Yeah, well, it's more the idea than the actual shape. The goal was to create a community gathering place and central hub much like town centers back in the old country. We have everything from bakeries to tailors and—"

"Starbucks?" I cut in, staring across the room at a familiar green-and-white logo over a storefront.

"Even Starbucks," Gwynn confirmed.

"That settles it," Grimsby said. "They *are* everywhere."

"As well as lots of other food options," Gwynn said, leading the way across the room to a row of restaurants. "We've got your standard fare over here like pizza and burgers. And over there"—she pointed—"are the more traditional Viking foods."

One restaurant advertised stuffed boars' heads on spears next to another called Bucket o' Haggis.

Grimsby shuddered. "Haggis? That's, like, sheep intestines, right? But isn't that a Scottish food?"

"That's a common misconception," I said, then shrugged apologetically when Grimsby turned a raised eyebrow in my direction. "Hey, my dad hardly ever has time to cook, so I pick up what I can from the Food Network. Anyway, it was actually the Vikings who introduced haggis to the people of Scotland. The Vikings eventually moved on, but they left their food behind."

"I don't think that was entirely accidental," Grimsby said with a grimace.

Gwynn opened her mouth to continue when Grimsby cut in. "What. Is. *That?*" His eyes were fixed on a stainless-steel box that looked like an oversized refrigerator set against a green building with a giant 7-Eleven logo on it. On the front of the machine, a touch screen was filled with dozens of colorful icons.

"Oh, that's the Slurpee machine," said Gwynn. "Its nickname

is Slurpus Maximus. It has about every flavor combination you can imagine, and probably a lot you've never heard of."

"I didn't figure Vikings for Slurpee fans," I said.

"Sure, Vikings invented Slurpees, of course." She gave me a look like I should have somehow known this. "They didn't cover that in your cooking shows?"

"Sorry," I said. "I guess I missed that episode."

"Yeah, well, when you're surrounded by ice for ten months of the year, you find creative ways to use it. Go ahead and try it if you want."

Grimsby was already way ahead of her. He stood in front of the machine wide-eyed. After assessing his options, he started moving his finger over the buttons like a little kid with a new toy as he read the labels. "Let's see . . . Wild Cherry—of course. Spam? That's just wrong. Banana Split—definitely have to try that one later." His finger stopped over a button with an icon of a movie camera on it, and he turned to Gwynn. "Movie Theater Combo?"

She nodded. "That's one of the more popular ones. See if you can guess what's in it."

He jabbed eagerly at the button, and a cup fell into the dispenser. The machine whirred and a thick icy stream like liquid chocolate sprayed into the cup until it had formed a perfect peak just above the cup's rim. Finally, a thin straw shot out of the machine with a *fwip* of air and tucked neatly into the center of the concoction.

Grimsby's hand trembled as he reached for the icy cup and took a sip. A big smile spread across his face. "Let's see . . . I'm detecting buttered popcorn." He licked his lips as he considered. "Coke and . . ." He took another sip. "Yeah, Junior Mints! It's like going to the movies in a cup!" He eagerly looked around at the other shops. "Be right back. I want to see what else they have around here."

"I guess I should make sure he doesn't break anything," Gwynn said. "You want to join us?"

"You guys go ahead," I said, taking a seat at a nearby table. "I have something I want to check on anyway."

I opened the browser in my phone and typed "svefnthorn" into the search bar. Immediately thousands of results came back. That seemed promising. But after clicking on several of them, my initial excitement quickly deflated. The legends were maddeningly vague and even contradictory about how the svefnthorn worked. In one story, a king was pricked with the thorn and woke up on his own a few hours later. In another, the thorn's hold had only been broken when the hero crossed a magical circle of fire.

I was startled out of my thoughts by a loud gurgling noise nearby. When I looked up, Grimsby stood a few feet away slurping the last dregs of Slurpee out of his cup, his blazer pockets bulging with more Viking treats he'd discovered.

Gwynn slid into the seat across from me, shaking her head. "We may never get him out of here." She pointed toward the phone. "News about your dad?"

I filled her in on the svefnthorn and what I'd found out so far. "I don't know what to think. My training books didn't exactly include any chapters on magical fire circles."

She reached across and squeezed my hand. "If there's anything we can do to help, just say the word."

Grimsby sank into a seat beside me, pinching the bridge of his nose. "Oww, brain freeze!"

One corner of Gwynn's mouth tilted up as she turned back to me. "Or . . . at least, you can count on *me*—"

"Abby Beckett?" came a voice from behind me.

I twisted my head around. A short woman with a harassed look about her stood looking down at me. Her hands seemed to flit in continuous motion like birds looking for a place to land, adjusting her glasses, smoothing the front of her skirt, and finally clasping and unclasping.

"I'm Abby," I said.

"Oh, good," said the woman. "I'm the assistant to the headmaster, Professor Roth. She requested that I escort you to her office."

Oh no! What time was it? I checked the screen of my phone and felt my stomach drop into my shoes, realizing that I'd completely missed all my afternoon classes. On my first day. I shot a quick look at Gwynn, who only grimaced and shrugged. "Can I ask what it's about?"

She shook her head. "She didn't say. Only that I should bring you as soon as possible."

I stood and took a quick breath to settle my racing heart. "Okay, I'm ready." *I think.*

# CHAPTER 11

# THE GREY COUNCIL

The assistant led the way wordlessly toward Professor Roth's office, the only sound the click of her shoes on the cold stone floor. When we entered the hall of headmaster paintings, I again felt their disapproving gazes, and my mind naturally turned to all the worst-case scenarios of what I was walking into. A month of detention for plastering lutefisk all over the front of a teacher's shirt? A week's solitary confinement for spilling my secret to a non-Viking? The traditional Viking punishments had been legendary for their gruesomeness. But we were more evolved now. Right?

The headmaster's office door stood open. The assistant stopped at the doorway and gestured me inside. I gulped and stepped into the room. Upon entering, I was immediately struck by the room's size, less an office than a royal suite. The focal point was a massive stone fireplace centered directly in the wall ahead. A roaring fire threw flames nearly half the height of the eight-foot black maw. To one side of the fireplace stood a large wooden desk, with a high-backed chair like a throne behind it. The room was lit only by the firelight, heavy curtains drawn against the pale

October daylight. The flames cast flickering shadows across the other walls, which were covered with shelves filled with books, vases, and other miscellaneous artifacts. A glass display case held a giant bladeless sword hilt, ornately carved and looking like a relic from an ancient time.

I stopped and looked up at a display on one wall illustrating the growth of Vale's campus over the years. An old sepia photo showed a small cluster of buildings surrounded by trees. Next to it a similarly old-looking aerial photo showed the campus from above in the early twentieth century. More photos and maps followed Vale's growth into the future, including artists' sketches of new buildings yet to be constructed. Scenes of sleek glass edifices glinting in the sun depicted a bright future for Vale.

The door behind me closed with a soft boom that echoed through the large room. Professor Roth's heels clicked on the stone floor as she approached and stood beside me, looking up at the display.

Her voice was quiet when she spoke. "What we have started here is just the beginning of Vale Hall's shining future. A rebirth as well as a reinvention. We find ourselves at a critical juncture when every Viking must ask: Will I be a part of that future, or will I cling to our past?"

Was she actually asking me? Or was it a rhetorical question? Confused, I opened my mouth and closed it again, not sure how to respond.

Finally she turned and walked toward the large desk. "Ms. Beckett, we have much to discuss. If you would please join us."

Us? I looked around the room and noticed for the first time a pair of figures seated toward the head of a long table set apart from the fire. They broke off their conversation and turned toward us as they heard us approach. In the dim light, I couldn't make out their faces.

Professor Roth stopped at the desk, opened a drawer, and lifted a bundle of gray cloth from its depths. She threw the cloth around her shoulders and pinned it like a cloak at one shoulder. The other two figures stood. They were wearing similar gray cloaks. What had I just walked into? Surely this wasn't about throwing food in the cafeteria or cutting class. Something tickled my memory, but I couldn't quite put my finger on it.

Professor Roth gestured me toward a chair at the table and then chose one herself. Four seats with high carved wooden backs and crushed-velvet cushions were arranged around the head of the table. Only one was unoccupied.

"Ms. Beckett," said Professor Roth as she sat, "you have been afforded a unique opportunity today." She paused, looking at the other two figures. "The chance to have an audience with the Grey Council."

I gripped the armrests of my chair to keep from completely embarrassing myself by sliding in a dead faint to the floor.

The Grey Council. The cold, faceless "they" who had seemed to run my entire life from a distance. The leadership body of the Vikings were right here? At Vale Hall? After discovering a hidden city of Vikings beneath my feet, I guess it shouldn't have come as such a surprise. But the Grey Council was almost mythical, so to see them here in flesh and blood was hard to get my head around.

"I'm sure the past few days have been very trying for you," Professor Roth said. "And we realize that your father may not have filled you in on the full reasons behind your move here to Vale. Indeed, he himself was largely unaware of the extent of the Viking presence here." Her hands came together in what looked vaguely like a conciliatory gesture. "But we hope to provide you some answers now."

I paused my mental review of punishments they might be about to inflict on me. Full reasons behind our move? What did she mean by that? The other two heads nodded, but the roaring fire behind them kept their features obscured in shadow.

"Ms. Beckett," continued Professor Roth. "May I call you Abby?"

"O-okay," I managed weakly. *Come on, Abby, where's that fiery spirit Dad always talks about?*

She gave me a thin smile and nodded. "Very well. Abby, as you know, the Vikings of the Aesir order—an extremely select group that has included many members of your own family—hold a very singular commission: to hunt the creatures known as Grendels."

I nodded. I'd also gotten the impression from my mom that this commission had been a growing source of contention between her and the Viking leadership.

"Further, the need for this constant vigilance has grown weaker down the ages. Supposed Grendel sightings have become fewer and further between. In fact, we have come to believe that some Aesir have even fabricated such sightings as a way to justify the continued existence of the Aesir order."

I sat up straighter at this, suddenly finding some of my fire. "My mom would never—"

Professor Roth held up one hand. "I'm afraid that your mother's activities in devoting much of her life to researching the Grendel problem were more archaeology and historical inquiry than modern forensic work."

"But . . . but my mom's journal," I said, struggling to keep my voice even. "She meticulously recorded Grendel sightings from the past several centuries. From all over the world. Are you suggesting those were all hoaxes?"

Professor Roth's gaze was unwavering. "Did your mother in fact ever see a Grendel with her own eyes?"

I thought back to my dim recollections of conversations I'd had about Grendels with my mom. I'd never actually read her journal, only occasionally heard her talk about what she recorded in it, saying there would come a time when I was older when she'd share it with me. But that time had never come. And now she was gone.

"I don't know," I conceded, letting my gaze fall to the floor. But my blood instantly chilled at the memory of the dark shadow that had invaded my home. Its terrible voice. *Hello, Abby.* I jerked my head up again. "But I have."

Professor Roth's eyes flicked toward her companions before meeting mine again. "You . . . have what, exactly?"

"I've seen a Grendel."

I told them about my encounter in our home in Charlotte. The feeling of dread that had gripped me. How it had known my name.

And how I had since come to think—no, to *know*—that it had been a Grendel.

As I finished, the room was completely still for a few seconds. Then Professor Roth turned away to stare at the fire for a long time. I fidgeted in my seat as the other two figures rose and joined her in a whispered discussion. I strained my ears trying to over-hear some of what was being said, but it was no use.

Finally, they seemed to arrive at some consensus. Professor Roth swiveled on one heel back toward me. I leaned forward, waiting to hear what she would say.

"Impossible," she said with finality.

I shook my head in surprise. "What?!"

She steepled her hands thoughtfully in front of herself. "What you saw could have been any number of things. Or even nothing at all. A product of an overactive imagination, perhaps."

I jerked up out of my chair in agitation, then sat down again. "But I saw . . . I even *heard* it say my name. How could that have been nothing?"

One of the figures who had so far been silent spoke then. "What were you doing immediately before this incident? What were you thinking about?" A man's voice.

I turned my head toward him as I thought back to that night. "Training. Or actually, I had just finished training and was look-ing at a picture I'd drawn years ago . . ." I trailed off as it came back to me, and I realized where he might be going with this. "Of my mom and me fighting a Grendel."

He nodded. "And you said that you heard your father calling

your name when he returned home. Could your agitated state merely have caused you to conflate his voice into this illusion? You were already in a highly suggestible mental state and mistook the intruder for a Grendel. But the bottom line is, had it been a Grendel—"

Professor Roth finished for him. "It's unlikely you would be here to tell of it."

The room went silent again as they let their words sink in. My eyes went out of focus as I studied the crackling flames, not sure what was real anymore. Before I even realized I was speaking, I heard my voice airing my thoughts to the room: "If it really was a Grendel, why am I alive? But if it wasn't a Grendel, who broke into our house? Who attacked us on the road? And why am I here at Vale Hall at all?"

Professor Roth came around the table and rested her hands on the back of my chair. "Those are all excellent questions. And your last question is exactly the reason that I called you to my office today."

I twisted my head to look up at her, trying to read anything in the flickering light playing on her face.

"You see, Abby, we have been recalling all the Aesir to Vale recently. It has been ages since a confirmed Grendel sighting. The Aesir have spent that time seeking out any proof of their continued existence. Combing the globe for any signs that that fearful race of creatures still lives. But now we feel that the time has finally come to close that chapter of our history. That in fact there is only one logical conclusion at this point: The race of Grendels is, indeed, extinct." She paused. "And therefore the Aesir are . . . no longer necessary."

I sucked in a sharp breath, feeling like my whole reason for existence had just been washed away like a sandcastle under a wave. My parents had trained me practically from birth for this one purpose. I was a Grendel hunter. Now what was I? Just an average kid struggling to pull a C in pre-algebra? Why had my mom believed so strongly that Grendels still existed? She had been a scientist—a brilliant one. And scientists rely on facts and provable theories. She more than anyone had been convinced that we weren't wasting our time hunting shadows.

"No," I blurted out, surprising everyone, including myself. I had said it in almost a whisper, but the word echoed in the room.

The man who had spoken earlier leaned toward me, the firelight catching his pale gray eyes. "I'm sorry, did you just say . . . no?"

I hurried to add, "My mom didn't believe that. And I . . . I don't either."

My words hung in the air for a few seconds. There was silence in the room as three pairs of eyes stared at me with a combination of shock and disbelief.

Professor Roth cleared her throat and shot a look at her fellow council members before turning back to me. "No, you're correct," she said gently. "It's true your mother didn't agree with this conclusion. But I'm afraid she was alone in her opinion."

The man with the gray eyes pushed back from the table with a rumble of chair legs on stone, then rose and crossed to a nearby bookshelf. He studied the spines, then extracted a thin leather-bound volume. "If I may," came his deep voice.

Professor Roth motioned for him to continue.

As his face turned toward the light, I made out the features of a man maybe in his forties, with a powerful, chiseled jaw and piercing eyes. An expensive-looking suit and tie were visible beneath his gray cloak. He thumbed through the book and, finding what he was looking for, traced the words on the page briefly with his finger, then looked up at me.

"You're familiar with the Beowulf legend, I assume?" he said.

"Sure," I said, studying the book in his hands with interest. "It's, like, the Aesir's bible. My dad says it's probably the oldest and most important work in English literature."

"Indeed," he said flatly. "It is also a record of the last confirmed Grendel sighting."

My eyes jerked upward to his face. Wait. What?

The man inclined his head toward the text and read aloud: "'Grendel in death endured a stroke of hard sword fiercely swung; his head was cloven from him.'" Flipping forward a few pages, he continued, "And now Beowulf speaking: 'This do I promise thee henceforth, that thou wilt not from that quarter have need to fear.'"

He looked up. "As you likely know, Beowulf was not just a legend. He was, in fact, an Aesir himself. After this death blow, he commissioned the Aesir to be guardians. A secret society to stand vigilant down through the ages against the re-emergence of the Grendel race. From his very mouth, we have here a promise that we need no longer fear these foul beasts. Still, he felt it prudent to keep watch in the event that any of that evil breed had somehow escaped his sword. Now the passage of so many years has shown that this is no longer necessary."

"Then why did my mom think there was still a danger?" I said. It came out harsher than I'd meant it to.

The man's nostrils flared angrily, and I suspected I'd touched a sore point. "Because your mother was a fool," he said icily. "She spent her life in the pursuit of shadows. And died in disgrace."

I leapt to my feet with my hands balled into fists. "She wasn't a fool! She was smarter than you could ever hope to be!" My words sounded like a flimsy playground response even as they left my mouth. I willed hot tears not to spring to my eyes and make me look even more like a child but felt a tiny drop run down one cheek.

"Unferth," said the third figure, speaking for the first time as he stood and placed a hand on the other man's arm. I finally caught a glimpse of this third person's face as he turned. Large glasses framed familiar features. It was my world history teacher, Dr. Ruel. What? He was one of the Grey Council? I was so disoriented now that the room seemed to tilt under my feet.

But Unferth wasn't done. "It's true your mother was brilliant at the start," he conceded. "We could never have made the advances we have without her. But her passion evolved into a mania that further and further separated her from reality. It was only her death that saved her from shaming your entire family."

"Enough!" said Professor Roth, speaking with a firmness that left no doubt that the discussion was over. Unferth spun angrily away toward the fire.

I was trembling, wavering between rage and tears. I couldn't remember ever being so furious.

Doc stepped around the table and placed a calming hand on my shoulder.

Professor Roth shifted her glare from Unferth's back and turned to me. "I'm very sorry you had to hear it like this and under such circumstances, given your father's current condition. But the fact remains that we already voted on this. Neither your mother's beliefs—nor indeed what happened to you and your father—change the fact that we have decided to"—she paused as if searching for the right words—"disband the entire Aesir order. Effective immediately."

# CHAPTER 12

# THE OVEN MITTS OF DOOM

Later I found myself outside sprawled on my back in a snowdrift, staring up at the stars as the sky darkened from purple to black and thinking deep thoughts about the pointlessness of my existence. Feeling the ache of missing my dad's solid presence in whatever life threw my way. He always had a sort of radar for when I was in a deep funk, and with that an accompanying knack for helping me over, around, or through it, whether it was by telling a funny story or just hugging me quietly while I sobbed on his shoulder.

I heard footsteps crunching toward me through the hard-packed snow. Dad? My heart knocked a solitary hopeful beat against my ribs, but then Grimsby's face obscured my view of the Big Dipper.

He flopped down next to me. "What are we doing? Making snow angels?"

"I'm done," I said. "I want out. I can't do this."

"Don't beat yourself up about it. It's only your first time. You just move your arms and legs back and forth like this." When I didn't reply, he continued, "Hey, I'm not very good at this, but I'm picking up a vibe that something's wrong."

"Only everything." I swung my arm wide to take in the whole of the Vale campus and, while I was at it, the entire state of Minnesota. "A week ago, I was living happily in North Carolina. And now my dad's in some sort of coma. And apparently my whole life has been pointless. And I can't . . . stop . . . shivering," I finished with a last, violent tremor.

"Yeah, Doc spotted me and pointed me in the last direction he'd seen you running. He said he thought you could use a friend."

I winced, remembering my embarrassing flight from Professor Roth's office. "Thanks, yeah, it's nice to talk to someone who doesn't think I'm completely nuts."

"Well, I wouldn't go that far . . ."

I punched him in the arm. "Hey . . ."

"Sorry, couldn't help myself." He stuffed his hand into one of his blazer pockets. "Peace offering?" His hand emerged clutching meatball-sized spheres of what look like dough covered with powdered sugar. "You've *got* to try these! *Soooo* good! I found them at a bakery back in Asgard."

I turned my head and studied the greasy dough balls. Some maroon lint from his blazer pocket was mixed with the sugar coating. "I . . . think I'll pass. What are they anyway?"

He shrugged. "Suit yourself." He popped one into his mouth and mumbled, "They're called ableshivers . . ." He considered, then tried again. "Ableskiffers?" He shook his head and shrugged.

"Well, something like that. They're basically doughnuts filled with raspberry jam. But they're like little bites of heaven."

I looked back toward Vale. "So where's Gwynn?"

"Off looking for her Latin book. Said she thinks she left it in the library."

"Vale has Latin classes?"

"No, it's some sort of independent study. She has this idea she wants to be a doctor. Only sixth grader I've ever heard of who's already premed. I told her the only Latin she needs to know is 'Semper ubi sub ubi.'"

"Huh?"

"Always wear underwear." He turned to me and grinned.

His words caught me so unexpectedly that a laugh burst out of my nose. "Ow, I just snorted!"

Then we were both laughing, lying there in a snowbank in the dark. And somehow the stars didn't look quite so bleak anymore.

Finally Grimsby sat up and started brushing himself off. "We should probably get going. I told Gwynn I'd meet her back in the entrance hall."

"Yeah, okay." I sat up. "Hey. Thanks. I needed a good laugh right then."

He held out his hand and helped me to my feet. "Anytime."

As we approached the main building, we slowly merged with a sea of gray-and-white-permed heads. It was like some weird flash mob composed entirely of senior citizens had materialized out of the night.

"Where are all these people going?" I said. "Is there a Beatles concert here tonight or something?"

"Bingo," said Grimsby.

"Wow, that was like a totally random guess. You mean the Fab Four are really going to be here? Actually, no, I think only two of them are still alive. So Fab Two?"

"No, you yutz, I mean B-I-N-G-O. As in the game? They have it every Tuesday night at Vale. How else do you think they pay for— *Whooooaa!*" Grimsby suddenly tripped and did a face-plant in the snow.

There was a loud *yip!* followed by a scrabbling noise in the dark.

"Oh! I'm so sorry!" said a voice behind us.

I turned to see a grandmotherly type scooping up a tiny Pekingese dog that looked like a mop with a face.

"Did my little Skol hurt you?" she asked. "He's always getting into trouble, isn't he? Yes he is. *Yes* he is." She said this last part to the dog as she nuzzled his nose with hers and made little cooing noises at him.

"Don't worry about me. I'm fine," said Grimsby sarcastically as he pushed himself to his feet and brushed snow off his blazer.

Skol growled in the woman's arms. Grimsby raised his hands and backed up a step.

The woman turned to us and blinked as if just remembering we were there. She wore a knitted sweater colored like a neon rainbow. Her tangerine-colored cat-eye glasses were framed by a large permed coif tinted a light shade of blue. Tar Heels blue. A sudden wave of homesickness came over me. Sure, North Carolina hadn't been all cheeseburgers in paradise—not by a long shot—but it was home. Here, with the snow, all the unfamiliar faces, and of course my dad lying in a coma . . . wasn't exactly feeling very homey.

As the woman leaned down to set her ball of fluff on the ground again, her sweater fell open, revealing a black T-shirt underneath with the classic photo of the Beatles crossing Abbey Road on the front.

Grimsby leaned toward me and whispered, "Isn't it weird how we were just talking . . ."

"Oh, are you Beatles fans too?" said the woman, noticing our stares as she straightened up and glanced down at her T-shirt. "Not too many young people these days know the classics anymore. Now, Pauly Mac, he's such a nice boy."

Pauly Mac? I assumed she meant Paul McCartney. But the way she called the geriatric lead singer of the Beatles a boy struck me as a little odd. If he was a boy, how old did that make her, exactly? She gave me a toothy smile. "And you look like a nice girl, dearie." She reached out and pinched my cheek between her thumb and forefinger.

I winced and smiled weakly. "Um, thank you, ma'am. I—"

"And so sad," she continued as if I hadn't spoken. "So lost." As she peered into my eyes, I had a weird sensation like she was staring right into my soul. At last she released her grip on my cheek and looked around with her hands on her hips. "Now, where did I put my . . . ?"

I noticed a huge Day-Glo-orange beach bag at her feet. "Bag?" I asked, reaching down to lift it for her. On its side, printed in big pink letters, were the words "Sun's Out, Fun's Out!"

"Oh, yes! Thank you! I'm always losing things. I guess the old gray matter's not what it used to be, you know?" She laughed and flapped her hands in what I guessed was supposed to be her thoughts flitting away on the wind. Or possibly jazz hands. I couldn't tell. Since she didn't immediately break into a musical number, I assumed it was the first one.

As I attempted to lift her beach bag, I stumbled forward, surprised at its weight. My brain was expecting two, maybe three pounds max. But instead I could barely lift it.

Grimsby raised an eyebrow. "Need some, uh, help there, Hercules?"

"Got it," I grunted after finally managing to sling the bag awkwardly over my shoulder.

The woman leaned down to rescue Skol from a snowbank. I snuck a covert glance into the bag while she was distracted, but whatever was so heavy was hidden under a pink-and-lime-green-chevron-patterned afghan blanket folded on top.

"What's under there?" Grimsby asked, quietly echoing my thoughts as he leaned in to eye the bag. "The stuffed bodies of all her previous dogs?"

I shrugged and turned back to the woman, who had scooped up Skol and was nuzzling him again. "I guess you won't be able to carry both this and your dog. Maybe I can, uh, carry your bag for you?"

Her gratified look was like I'd just offered to file the bunions off her feet for the rest of her life. "Oh! I couldn't . . . You must be busy! Homework to do and all that."

But I couldn't leave an old lady there with a super-heavy bag in the cold. Plus, she sort of reminded me of my own grandmother. Or what I figured my grandmother would have been like if I'd ever known her. All my grandparents had already been gone by the time I was born.

"It's no problem," I said. "It's the least I can do after my friend tackled your dog." I grinned at Grimsby, earning a frown in reply.

"Oh, you're a dear, Abby! I'm just headed up to the bingo game. Tonight's the night that I'm gonna win. I can just feel it!" She crossed her fingers on both hands, and a big grin spread across her face.

"Okay, I . . ." I started to take a step forward, then froze as her words registered. "Wait, how do you know my name?" I asked warily. "Do I . . . know you?"

A strange look flitted across her face, then was gone. Or maybe it had only been a trick of the shadows in the lamplight. "Oh! Well, I must have heard your friend say it earlier."

I frowned and turned a questioning look at Grimsby. He shrugged and shook his head like he couldn't remember. "Well, I'm Abby," I said. "But I guess you knew that already. And this is my friend Grimsby."

"Pleased to meet you." She beamed. "Most people call me Granny V. But you can call me what you like. Just don't call me late for supper, I always say!" She laughed at her own joke. "And speaking of being late, we'd better hurry! If I don't get there soon, old Jack Manworth'll steal my seat."

I shook off the strange feeling Granny V had given me, chalking it up to paranoia after the events of the past few days.

We followed the scent of Bengay joint cream to a room filled with a gray haze. In the front, a guy chewing on a cigar and wearing a battered Twins cap looked up as she arrived. Jack Manworth, I assumed. I half expected an altercation, but instead his eyes grew wide, and he quickly cleared space for her without a word.

Granny V turned her smile on us again. "I like to sit right up front. The old eardrums, they ain't what they used to be." She jammed her forefinger into one ear and wiggled it around before extracting it and using the same finger to point to a seat.

I gratefully plopped the heavy bag down onto the table. "There you go. Guess we'll be going now."

"So soon?" Her mouth fell into a frown so sad you'd think Grimsby had just strangled her dog. "I was hoping you might want to play a round of bingo with me. You know, as a thank-you for carrying my bag."

I glanced at Grimsby, then back at Granny V, feeling anxious to see if there were any updates on my dad's condition. "Sorry, no, we can't stay. I have somewhere I need to be."

"Oh?" said Granny V casually, looking down as she arranged her things on the table. "You never know. I may be able to help you with that. In fact, I sense that you are looking for something."

Grimsby frowned. "Looking for something? Yeah." He checked

his watch. "I'm looking for some dinner. Maybe a burrito and a Yoo-hoo?"

Granny V shook her head. "Bigger than that." She lifted her gaze and stared directly at me. "Something to do with your father, perhaps?"

I stared at her for a second, sure I'd misheard her. "Sorry, what did you say?"

She held my gaze, unblinking. "Your father. You don't know how you can help him. But I do."

A tight panicky feeling gripped my chest, like the time I'd been swimming in the ocean in the Outer Banks and suddenly spotted a fin poking out of the water. I turned to Grimsby, but he looked as baffled as me. How did this woman know anything about me? Or my dad?

"Okayyyyy . . ." I said tentatively. "You've got my attention. So how do I help my dad?"

"Tsk, tsk, tsk. Well, I can't just *tell* you, can I? What would be the fun in that?"

That didn't sound promising. "What do you mean?"

"Simple. You play me at bingo. If you win, then I put you on the path to helping your father."

Her phrase "on the path" didn't exactly sound like she was going to hand me a glossy brochure titled "How to Save Your Dad's Life in Three Easy Steps." But seeing as how I didn't have any other leads on deck, I was willing to consider anything.

"That's all?" I asked. "We just beat you. At bingo."

"That's right."

Grimsby gave me a thumbs-up. "Why not? I'm strangely good at games involving nothing but complete, blind luck. If there's no skill involved, then I'm your guy."

I stared at Granny V for a long moment. "Okay, we're in."

"Wonderful!" She smiled, then reached across the table to shake on it.

When our hands touched, I felt a tiny spark against my palm. I jerked my hand out of hers in surprise. I turned my palm up, but it looked completely normal. Static electricity? I started to apologize but then realized she was already talking again.

". . . let you have one of my boards and a dauber to mark your squares."

I shrugged it off, then met Grimsby's eyes and whispered, "You're sure you can do this?"

He nodded and pretended to brush off his shoulder. "I've got this. No problem."

Granny V extracted a bingo card from her bag and slid it across the table to us along with a red tube that I assumed was the dauber. She then pulled a Mary Poppins and reached down into her bag with both hands. Like *allll* the way down to her shoulders. When her head disappeared into the bag, I looked under the table to make sure there wasn't a hole or something underneath it. There wasn't. I had a bad feeling she had more than just a spoonful of sugar in there.

When she re-emerged from the bag, she was holding a stack of what must have been twenty bingo cards. She proceeded to arrange them neatly on the table in front of her.

"Okay, now there *may* be a problem," Grimsby said, rubbing his chin nervously.

Then Granny V went on another spelunking mission into her bag.

"Don't worry," said Grimsby, rallying a little. "There's no way she can possibly keep track of all those cards at once. I mean . . ."

Then our geriatric friend popped back up with a pair of what looked like giant neon-pink oven mitts. As she pulled them on, I half expected her to reach back into her bag and retrieve a tray of piping-hot snickerdoodles next. On the bottom of each mitt were clusters of colored circles that looked suspiciously like . . . daubers. As if to confirm, her hands flashed over the array of bingo cards and left little colored dots on the free space in the middle of each card.

Grimsby's mouth fell open. "The oven mitts"—he turned to me with wide eyes—"of *doom*."

"Yeah," I said weakly. "And instead of cookies, she's about to serve up a steaming tray of bingo beatdown."

The little old lady in front of us rolled her shoulders and jerked her head side to side with a popping noise to loosen up her neck. "Ready, dears?" she said sweetly. "Don't forget your free space."

"Whoa" was all Grimsby managed. He looked down at our lonely bingo card and put a single red dot in the middle.

Right then Gwynn emerged out of the haze and flopped into a chair next to us. She hugged a book titled *Latin for Everyone* to her chest, and her unicorn backpack had returned. "Hey, you two, I've been looking everywhere for you. I thought we were going to meet—" She froze as she took in the scene. Us sitting there with our bingo card. The quietly humming Granny V arranging her collection of cards across the table.

"What's going on?" she asked with a nervous edge to her voice.

"What do you mean?" Grimsby said. "We're just playing a round of bingo. With this, uh, nice old lady across the table. Her name's Granny V."

"You're playing with her?"

"Well, not *with* her, exactly," I said. "She says if we beat her, then she'll give us some sort of clue about helping my dad."

"Did you shake on it?" Gwynn's voice had taken on a hint of panic. I was suddenly wishing I'd listened to my intuition earlier.

"Yeah. Why?" I said, remembering the sting of the electric shock.

"You guys get information if she wins, right?"

We nodded.

"Did she tell you what she gets if you lose?"

Grimsby and I looked at each other. Guess we'd forgotten to ask about that. "Nooo," I said, drawing out the word. "Why? What does she get if we lose?"

Gwynn put her face into her hands. She spread her fingers and stared back at us with a stricken look. "Your souls."

# CHAPTER 13

# B-I-N-G-O

Before we could unpack this little bomb, a screech of static filled the room. "Testing, testing," a man said into a microphone that stood on a small raised stage at the front of the room. "Okay, everyone, please take your seats. We'll begin in just a moment."

Next to the man was a small table with a clear plastic cube on top of it. The cube was filled with what looked like Ping-Pong balls with letters and numbers on them. After waiting for the clatter of chairs and conversations to subside, he flipped a switch on the side of the cube. The balls began bouncing wildly around inside it like angry bees trying to escape. After briefly reminding everyone of the rules, he pushed a button, and one of the balls shot up a little shaft on top of the cube. He turned the writing toward himself and read it aloud.

"B4!"

Granny V's hands shot across her bingo boards, leaving little colored dots in their wake. We all studied Grimsby's board hopefully, but he shook his head. Nothing.

I motioned to my two friends, and they huddled their chairs in closer.

"Hold on," I said under my breath to Gwynn. "Maybe there's something funny in the smoke here, but it sounded like you just said 'our souls.'"

"Yeah," she whispered back. "I did. If you lose, she gets your souls."

The caller announced the next ball. "G51!"

"That's nuts," hissed Grimsby as he triumphantly marked the first space on his card. "How can she take our souls?"

"Well, you said her name is Granny V, right? Did you ask her what the 'V' stands for?"

"No," I said. "I just figured it was short for one of those old-people names you don't hear much anymore, like Vivian or Violetta."

"Or Verisimilitude," Grimsby added.

We both stared at him. He put up his hands. "What? It's a name."

Gwynn rolled her eyes. "How about 'V' for 'Valkyrie'?"

"But you're a Valkyrie," I said. "And you're not trying to take our souls."

"Or *are* you?" added Grimsby, his eyes narrowing.

"O62!" boomed over the speaker system.

Gwynn ignored Grimsby and said to me, "Yeah, but she's not like me. Granny V, or whatever her real name is, is a *dark* Valkyrie. They don't follow the same rules. Normal Valkyries like me take the souls of fallen heroes to the afterlife. Dark Valkyries are also known as soul hunters. But they don't wait until you're dead. Sort of like how a big game hunter keeps trophies—heads, furs, and other stuff like that—dark Valkyries keep collections of living souls. For eternity."

"Well, my soul is Jewish, so she can't have it anyway," Grimsby said.

"That's not how it works, numbskull. Anyone who accepts a challenge from a dark Valkyrie agrees to the same rules."

"You're sure?" I said, eyeing Granny V. "She still looks like one of those grandmas who hand out lollipops on their front porches."

"Don't you think I'd be able to spot another Valkyrie?"

"N32!"

"Okay," I said. "There must be some way to get out of this, or, you know, void our agreement. I mean, it's not like she gave us a written contract with all the rules spelled out."

"Yeah," Grimsby chimed in. "You're a Valkyrie. Can't you talk her out of it?"

Gwynn shook her head. "It doesn't work like that."

"So what do we do?" I asked.

She shrugged her shoulders sadly. "You win."

*Or you're both goners*, she didn't say. I suddenly couldn't breathe, and not just because the room was full of smoke.

"Hmmm . . ." said Grimsby. I couldn't tell if he was thinking or bemoaning our bad luck. We looked at him, but he was busy studying Granny V's bingo cards with interest.

"Got an idea?" I asked.

"Maybe. What you were saying just a minute ago. You know, about the rules? That got me thinking. And I may have a way to, if not *win*, exactly, then at least not *lose*." He turned toward me. "But, full disclosure: It's kind of a long shot."

"It's better than anything I've got," I said. "Do you think she'll still help us with my dad too? Maybe she even has an antidote or something."

"Oy vey. One thing at a time. I'm just trying to make sure we live past seven o'clock."

"Why, what happens at seven?" said Gwynn.

"That's when *Jeopardy!* comes on. And I'm pretty sure wherever dark Valkyries keep your soul has terrible TV reception."

I was up for anything that gave us even the smallest sliver of hope. "Okay, what do we do?"

"I need you to make a distraction," he said.

"Like what?"

"G46!" the caller announced.

"I don't know," Grimsby said. "Fake a case of mad cow disease. Pretend *you're* a mad cow. Whatever. I just need Scary Poppins's attention off her cards for a minute."

"A distraction . . ." I said, looking around the room for inspiration. My eyes landed on Granny V's dog, Skol, lying peacefully at her feet, and an idea started to form.

I leaned toward Grimsby. "Hey, do you still have any of those dough ball things in your pocket?"

"Yeah . . ." His hand moved automatically to guard his pocket. "But it's my last one."

"Really?" Gwynn asked. "You're willing to trade eternal doom . . . for a *doughnut*?"

Grimsby stared at her for a few seconds. "Fine," he said at last, and reluctantly plucked a ball of dough from his pocket and plopped it into my hand.

I gagged a little at the feel of the greasy lump in my palm. It's a good thing dogs will eat anything.

"N33!"

Grimsby's bingo card was still woefully short on hits. But Granny V had a handful of cards that looked like they could be winners any second. We had to hurry.

Pretending to tie our shoes, Gwynn and I ducked under the table. I waved the doughnut in the air, trying to get the dog's attention.

"Maybe if you try blowing on it to waft some of the scent to the dog?" Gwynn suggested.

I inhaled and blew like I was trying to put out the candles on a hundred-year-old's birthday cake. A fleck of lint lifted off the top and settled to the floor. No response from the dog.

"Can't you blow any quieter?" hissed Gwynn.

"Sorry," I shot back. "I've never blown on a *doughnut* before."

"Here, let me try."

I held the doughnut toward her. She cupped her hands around her mouth and blew in Skol's direction. Suddenly his head perked up, and little dark eyes peered at us from beneath his mat of fur. Gwynn's eyes turned triumphantly toward me, like "See?"

"That's right," I said softly to the ball of fur. "Good doggie. Want a little treat?"

A small twitch of his tail gave me hope that this might actually work. The dog got to his feet and inched tentatively toward us. I expected Granny V's hand to shoot under the table at any second. But she was probably so focused on crushing Grimsby that she didn't notice. So far so good.

"Okay, what's the plan?" asked Gwynn.

"Once the dog gets close enough, I toss the doughnut across the room. The dog chases the doughnut. Instant chaos." I pantomimed an explosion by clutching my hand in a fist and then flicking my fingers out for dramatic effect. "Doughnut grenade."

Gwynn didn't look convinced.

But Skol continued to inch forward, his little black nose sniffing the air.

Grimsby's head was suddenly under the table with us. "You guys gonna do this today? I'm getting murdered up here."

"Sorry, yeah, almost there," I said.

A little farther. A little farther. Just as the dog opened his mouth to grab the treat, I snatched my hand away and, in the same motion, stood and flipped the dough ball underhand across the room. Or at least that's how it went in my head. It turns out that trying to throw a slimy, partially mashed wad of dough isn't the same as tossing, say, a golf ball. Instead of flying across the room per my plan, it only rolled wetly off my hand and landed with a plop in Granny V's bag on the other side of the table.

Gwynn smacked her forehead. "What was *that*?"

"Sorry! It was supposed to—"

Before I could complete my sentence, Skol barked, leapt up

onto the table, and dove into the bag. The bag toppled over under the weight and fell off the table. With a yelp and the sound of clinking glass, both dog and bag crashed to the floor.

A dozen snow globes rolled out of the bag and scattered across the floor. So that's why her bag had been so heavy. One of them struck a nearby guy with a walker and toppled him like he was a bowling pin.

Suddenly Granny V was on her feet. There was a stampede of people running to help the fallen senior citizen, everyone was shouting, and the bingo game screeched to a halt.

"Not bad," said Gwynn.

I shrugged casually. "All part of my plan."

A pair of snow globes rolled to a stop near my feet. One said "Elvis Presley" on the label and held a miniature of a man dressed in a white suit with rhinestones on it. The other snow globe was empty other than the swirling snow, like it was missing something. The label on the snow globe's base read "Abby Beckett."

I gasped and turned to Gwynn. "You said dark Valkyries keep collections of souls. I'm going to spend eternity . . . in there?" We looked at each other with wide eyes.

As quick as lightning, Granny V retrieved the scattered snow globes, slid them back into her bag, scooped up the dog, and deposited him in her lap. His fur was now polka-dotted blue, green, and red from her bingo mitts, like the animal from that book *Put Me in the Zoo*.

"Wow, that was fast," said Gwynn.

I gave Grimsby a questioning look. "I just hope it was enough of a distraction."

He gave us a thumbs-up as he covertly slid something I couldn't see into his blazer pocket with his other hand. I looked for an idea of what he'd done but couldn't spot anything. I had to trust he knew what he was doing.

Soon after, the older gentleman with the walker was returned to his feet, and the game resumed. Grimsby's bingo card still looked mostly empty. But Granny V was only one square away from bingo on several of her cards. I didn't see any way we could win short of a miracle.

"B14!"

Granny V's hands flashed over her cards, then paused, and her eyes flicked back and forth like she was confirming. "BINGO!" She leapt up from her seat and spiked an oven mitt on the floor like she'd just scored a touchdown.

My stomach instantly dropped into my shoes. We'd lost. Game over. Literally.

The caller motioned to someone, and a younger man walked over to check Granny V's winning card. His eyes jumped back and forth from her card to a notepad in his hand as he reviewed the numbers she'd marked. I held my breath, hoping she'd made a mistake. Finally he raised his head and nodded to the caller. The win was confirmed. Our fate was sealed. Granny V's smile lit up her whole face.

As the checker started to turn away, though, Grimsby said, "Huh, that's weird . . ." a little too loudly. He was intently studying Granny V's winning card.

"Sorry?" said the checker, pausing in midturn.

"I mean, something seems odd about"—he reached out and swiped his thumb across the 14 in the winning B14 square. The 4 smudged—"that 14." Grimsby held up his thumb, now smeared with black ink, toward the checker.

The checker frowned down at the card. Where before there was a B14, there was now a B11. He turned a grim gaze on Granny V, then straightened and announced loudly to the room, "Clearly this player has doctored her card and therefore forfeits." Staring directly at her again with disgust, he continued, "For *all* cards." With a sweep of his arms, he gathered up all her bingo cards and stalked away.

"How did you . . . ?" I whispered to Grimsby, gesturing to where the cards were.

"Easy. I used to help with bingo setup as part of, well, after-school detention. One day I sort of broke the B14 ball. Long story. Anyway, I noticed the new ball we got to replace it seemed to pop up a lot in games. It must be slightly lighter than the other balls or something."

Gwynn nodded, impressed. "So you doctored her card to look like it said B14 . . ."

"Exactly." He shrugged. "I figured it was just a matter of time until—"

A muffled cry of rage came from the other side of the table, and we all turned. Granny V's face contorted from confusion to disbelief. To burning rage. When she turned her gaze on us, I could have sworn there was a flicker of orange flame in her eyes.

"Okay, yeah, *now* I see the dark Valkyrie," Grimsby said. I turned toward him as his hand went into his blazer pocket and the tip of a black pen disappeared out of sight.

"You . . . you . . ." sputtered Granny V.

"I think the word you're looking for is 'won,'" said Gwynn. "Well, not technically, but since you forfeited, that means they beat you. Now you have to keep up your side of the bargain. Tell us how to help Abby's dad."

Granny V stared icily at each of us, her gaze flicking from face to face. I tensed, thinking maybe she was going to stuff us all into snow globes anyway. "Fine," she breathed at last through clenched teeth.

She plunged her hand into her magical beach bag and fished around in its voluminous depths. When it emerged, her fingers clutched a small rectangular object. She tossed it onto the table unceremoniously. It spun once and skidded to a stop in front of me.

"Huh?" said Grimsby, furrowing his eyebrows.

I picked it up to study it more closely. It was an age-yellowed index card, its once-sharp corners rounded and creased from use. Random sequences of numbers were stamped onto it in different colors. I flipped it to the back, but the other side was blank.

"I don't get it," I said, looking up in confusion. "How will this help my dad?"

Granny V swept to her feet. "As the great Mick Jagger once said, 'You can't always get what you want.'" With that, she scooped up her dog, turned on her heel, and disappeared into the haze of cigar smoke.

# CHAPTER 14

# THE BOTANIST'S JOURNAL

"I can't believe this!" I said, stomping angrily to my feet and dropping the card onto the table. "I was an idiot to think she might actually be able to help my dad."

Grimsby cracked his knuckles with a loud pop. "Want me to go after her? Give her a little shakedown maybe?"

Gwynn raised an eyebrow. "I don't think that'll be necessary."

He turned to her, looking a little relieved. "Why not?"

Without answering, she plucked the card off the table and held it in front of her. "You guys really don't know what this is?"

Grimsby and I exchanged a look. "No," we said together.

She pointed to a series of letters and numbers typed along the top of the card. "Here's a hint. See this? That looks like a call number."

"Ohhhh . . ." I said excitedly, making the connection. "Duh, I should have recognized it! It's one of those cards libraries used to keep track of which books were checked out before computers, right?"

"I think so," Gwynn said.

I took the card from her and inspected it more closely. "It's been a long time since I've seen one of these. So you think the clue is a book, then?"

Grimsby rubbed his chin. "Okay, that could be a little more helpful. Depending what the book is, I guess. Maybe *Chicken Soup for the Dark Valkyrie's Captive Souls*?"

Ignoring Grimsby, I asked Gwynn, "Does Vale's library still use these?"

She shook her head. "Not anymore. But I work there as an aide sometimes, and occasionally I'll come across a really old book that still has one in it."

Grimsby peered over my shoulder. "What are all these other numbers? 06.10.78 . . . 10.31.45."

"I'm pretty sure those are due dates," Gwynn said.

"Hmmm . . . that means 06.10.78 would be, what? June 10, 1978?" He frowned at the card. "Wow, so the last time this book was checked out was in 1978? How do we even know it hasn't crumbled to dust by now?"

Gwynn checked her watch. "Well, hopefully it can last one more day. The library is already closed for the night."

"Okay, so let's meet in the morning and visit the library before class," I said. "I really should check on my dad right now anyway."

I left the bingo hall with my spirits slightly improved but still with the feeling that whatever the book was, it wouldn't be an easy fix. *Just keep hanging on, Daddy. I'm trying.*

\* \* \*

The next morning I met Grimsby and Gwynn outside a pair of large doors with the words "F. J. Feola Library" stenciled over them.

"How is your dad?" Gwynn asked, laying a hand on my arm.

I pictured the dark circles around his eyes. The way his cold hands lay curled in his sheets as if clutching desperately to this world. "The doctors keep reassuring me he'll pull through. But I can read the worry in their eyes. They've taken blood samples, run brain scans—all the usual stuff and then some. But nothing seems to make any difference. It looks like it's going to come down to unlocking the secrets of the svefnthorn."

She squeezed my arm. "And you? How are you holding up?"

I reached back and massaged a kink in my neck; the wooden arm of the chair I'd been sleeping on by my dad's side seemed to have dislocated one of my vertebrae. "I'll make it. Just hoping whatever we find in the library sheds some light on any of this."

When we entered the library, I was awed by the sheer number of books. Shelves stretched nearly to the ceiling in countless rows around a central study area and along each wall, alternating occasionally with arched stained glass windows that threw soft blue and red geometric shapes across the floor. A balcony ran along the outer walls to provide access to the books higher up. The whole scene—the scent of ink on paper carrying to us like incense, still forms bent over open pages as if in prayer, the pregnant hush of expectation—made it seem like we were entering some lost temple of literary wonders.

"This way," said Gwynn, motioning us deeper into the stacks.

"Does the call number give you any idea what the book is about?" I said.

Gwynn walked past more bookshelves, studying the numbers on them as she passed. "I'm not a hundred percent sure, but I think it's somewhere in the botany section."

"Botany?" asked Grimsby. "So maybe it's like a book on herbal remedies for obscure ailments?"

Gwynn stopped and ran her forefinger along the spines at the end of one shelf. "I'm not sure. But if it's here, then it should be right about . . ." She knelt and continued to the next row down. "Oh . . ."

"What's wrong?" I said.

She looked up at us over her shoulder. "It should be right here, but the numbers skip past the one we're looking for. It's possible it was mis-shelved." She double-checked the surrounding books and the shelves above and below. "But if so, it could be anywhere in the library."

Grimsby snorted loudly, stepping back to take in the expanse of books around us. "So you're saying we have to search this whole place for one book? Talk about a real needle in a haystack."

The excitement that had been steadily building in my chest all morning suddenly fizzled out as I studied the ocean of books around us.

"Maybe not," Gwynn said. "Let's check with the circulation desk first and see if they can help."

She led the way across the room to a large, waist-high oak desk behind which a woman stood tapping on a keyboard.

The woman looked up and smiled as we approached, the delicate chains draped from her eyeglasses giving off a soft tinkling noise when she moved her head. "Oh, hello, Gwynn. What can I do for you?"

"Hi, Mrs. Mallo," Gwynn said. "This is my friend Abby Beckett. Yesterday was her first day at Vale. And I think you know—"

"Mr. Grimsby," said Mrs. Mallo, finishing with an audible sigh.

Grimsby chuckled awkwardly. "I swear that book was like that when I checked it out."

Gwynn rolled her eyes before continuing. "Anyway . . . we were hoping you could help us with something?"

Mrs. Mallo noticed the card in Gwynn's hand. "Oh my, I haven't seen one of those in quite some time. Where did you get it?"

"It's sort of a long story." Gwynn gave me a quick look. "But actually, this is what we need help with. We tried to find this book on the shelves, but it doesn't seem to be there."

"Hmmm, well, let me take a peek and maybe I can find something."

Gwynn handed the card across to Mrs. Mallo, who studied it for a few seconds before placing it on the desk next to her keyboard and typing in the call number. She frowned, typed a few more keys, and then her frown deepened.

"Is something wrong?" Gwynn said.

"Not exactly," said the librarian, still studying the screen. "This book appears to be on reserve."

"Oh no," said Gwynn. "So we can't check it out?"

Mrs. Mallo looked up at me then. "I'm sorry, dear, what was your name again?"

"Um, it's Abby. Abby Beckett."

"And this is just your second day at Vale?"

"That's right," I said.

The librarian nodded and looked back at her screen. "Normally new students don't appear in our system for ten days. But the name on this hold"—she looked back at me—"is Abby Beckett."

Gwynn and I stared at each other. *Huh?*

"That's weird," said Gwynn, turning back to the librarian. "So someone put a book on hold in Abby's name?"

"That's the other odd thing about this one. Normally holds expire if not picked up within fourteen days."

"Oh," I said. "Then . . . when was this one placed?"

Mrs. Mallo peered at me over her glasses. "Nearly four years ago."

While we waited for the librarian to return with the book, I stared at the floor, feeling a tight knot forming in my stomach.

"Four *years*?" said Grimsby. "How did someone put a reserve on this book for Abby four years ago?"

Gwynn reached out and put a hand on my arm. "Abby, are you okay? You look like you're going to be sick. Did something happen four years ago?"

But I continued staring at the floor without answering. There was no way. It had to be a coincidence. Because I knew exactly what had happened four years ago. That was when my mom had died. Had she placed a book on reserve for me right before then? No, that seemed . . . impossible. But still. *Some*one had reserved it for me. And if not her, then who? And how had a dark Valkyrie happened to get her hands on the book's library card?

Just then Mrs. Mallo returned. She handed a thin book to me across the desk.

"Here you go, Abby. Please be careful with it. As you can see, it's a bit fragile."

The book felt brittle, with a cracked leather binding that was way older than the 1940s.

"Thank you, Mrs. Mallo," said Gwynn. "Guys, let's grab a table and get a closer look at this."

I took a seat at a nearby study table and laid the book in front of me, feeling reluctant to open it. The cover had no title, only three symbols etched in dull gray.

Grimsby leaned over the table. "Backward seven, letter 'Z,' upside-down 'Y.' Huh?"

"I think those may be Norse runes," I said.

Gwynn nodded. "Exactly what I was thinking." She pointed toward each one and recited, "Laguz, for water or renewal. Eihwaz, for the tree of life. And this one . . ." She broke off. "Well, it looks like Algiz, for protection, but I've never seen it upside down like that."

The knot in my stomach squeezed tighter, and I said quietly, "I have." And I told them about my encounter with the dark shadow in my home in North Carolina, when my pendant had burned red with the same symbol. "I think upside down it means danger. Or even death."

Grimsby's eyes widened, then, recovering, he said, "Hmm, well, you said this was a book about plants, right? So . . . renewal. Tree. Death. Maybe it represents sort of the circle of life. You know, hakuna matata . . . something like that."

"That's actually not a bad suggestion," Gwynn said.

I gingerly opened the cover and started to flip through the book. Its pages were dog-eared and yellowed with age, and they looked like they might disintegrate if handled too enthusiastically. A spidery handwritten scrawl and rough ink sketches filled the pages.

"It looks like some kind of journal," I said.

Gwynn studied the pages over my shoulder. "All the entries seem to be from the early 1800s. Mostly descriptions of rare flowers and other exotic plants." She pointed to one entry and read aloud, "'V.H. greenhouse damaged by late winter storm.'"

"V.H.," Grimsby said. "That's probably Vale Hall. So you think this is a journal of some plant enthusiast who lived here back in the 1800s?"

"That'd be my guess," I said as I continued flipping through more pages. "Maybe a botany teacher or—"

"Hold on," Gwynn said excitedly. "Go back a page."

"What is it?" I said. I stared down at the page she was pointing to, trying to make out the spidery script as I read aloud: "'10 June 1826: svefn. cultivar . . . shows particular sensitivity to sunlight.'" I jerked my head up in surprise. "Wait. Svefn—do you think that's . . . ?"

"Yeah," she said, her eyes lighting up. "Dr. Swenson called it a svefnthorn. That's kind of a unique name. What other plant could this be?"

"Sniffin . . . what?" said Grimsby as I scanned farther down the page.

"Svefnthorn," I said. "It's the thorn that caused my dad's coma." Then I read the next line in the journal: "'Bloom appears to counteract toxin in common harvest mouse. Law of Similars.'" Below that was a rough sketch of a plant with wicked-looking thorns interspersed with tiny pale flowers.

"Law of Similars?" I asked, flipping to the next page, but it only had an entry for another plant. "What's that?"

Gwynn nodded enthusiastically. "I've actually heard of that before. It's a concept that's been around for a long time in natural medicine. The idea that the same thing that makes you sick can also heal you. Or basically 'like cures like.'"

An electric thrill shot through me as I made the connection. But I mentally squashed it down, not ready to let myself get too excited about something that might turn into a dead end. "So what you're saying is that somehow this same plant that poisoned my dad . . . can also make him better?"

Gwynn held up her hands in a cautioning gesture. "Maybe. All we have to go on right now is a vague entry in this old—"

"Details," Grimsby chimed in, waving his hand dismissively. "So where do we find this plant?"

"The journal mentioned a greenhouse here on campus," Gwynn said.

Grimsby frowned. "Vale has a greenhouse?"

"No, I don't think so. Not now, anyway. But this was written almost two hundred years ago." She thought for a minute. "I think I remember there being a collection of old maps and photos here in the library showing Vale's campus at different times in history. Why don't you two look for any other mentions of the greenhouse in the journal, and I'll see if I can find those maps."

Twenty minutes later, Gwynn returned with a few rolls of paper tucked under her arm. "Find anything?"

"Nada," Grimsby said. "He only mentions the greenhouse one other time but doesn't say anything about a location."

"How about you?" I asked, eyeing the rolled papers hopefully.

Gwynn held them up as she moved toward the table. "I managed to find some surveyor's maps of the campus from the early 1800s. I figured we might be able to locate the greenhouse on them."

She unrolled one map and spread it across the table, pinning down the corners with books as the three of us crowded around to study it.

"What language is this?" I asked Gwynn after trying to decipher the unfamiliar characters on the map.

She shrugged. "Maybe some surveyor's shorthand? I've never seen it before."

After a minute, Grimsby pointed to a small rectangle at the top right of the campus. "Here it is."

"How do you know?" Gwynn asked.

"Well, look at the little scribble there. Doesn't it look like a plant? I bet they used that to indicate the greenhouse."

I squinted at the tiny sketch he was pointing to. It did sort of look like a plant. "Where is that?"

Gwynn's face fell. "It looks like it's right around where the swimming pool is now. They must have demolished it at some point to make way for the expanding campus."

"So I guess we're not any closer, then," Grimsby said.

I looked up at them. "Well, at least from the journal we know the plant probably exists. And it was even grown here at some point. That's *some*thing. Maybe they moved the plants somewhere else when the greenhouse was torn down?"

Grimsby grabbed the botanist's journal again and quickly riffled through the pages.

"Careful with that!" said Gwynn. "It could fall . . ." She trailed off as a page fell out of the book onto the table. "Apart." She glared at Grimsby. "Great, now look what you did."

He plucked the page off the table. Its paper looked different from the rest of the journal, like a piece of lined notebook paper folded in half. He unfolded it and scanned the page, a grin spreading on his face.

"'My dearest Eunice,'" he read aloud. "'I can hardly wait until our next . . .'"

I reached across and snatched it out of his hands.

"Hey!" he said.

"Don't read that out loud," I said as I quickly perused it. "This is a *private* message. Probably two star-crossed but secret lovers exchanging notes hidden in library books."

"That's so romantic," said Gwynn.

Grimsby made a fake retching noise. "Spare me. And anyway, *Eunice*? Whoever it was, it was a *looong* time ago. I don't think they'd mind."

"Why don't I just hold on to this for safekeeping," I said, and slid the note into my blazer pocket.

"So what's our next move?" Grimsby said.

Gwynn sat on the edge of the table. "Well, let's review what we know. There's a mention of a plant—possibly the svefnthorn—that was grown in a greenhouse—"

"Yeah," Grimsby interjected, "that was apparently demolished to make a pool so Chase Lodbrok can win even more sports medals."

"Where is this pool?" I said. "I mean, I know the greenhouse isn't there anymore, but maybe we'll find something that could help anyway."

A bell chimed overhead, signaling five minutes until first period. Gwynn shrugged. "It's worth a try. Should we meet at lunch and check out the pool?"

"I'll bring the fish tacos," said Grimsby.

I groaned. "Is food all you ever think about?

He spread his hands. "What, do people in North Carolina eat fancier stuff, like octopus sushi? But anyway, fish tacos . . . because it's a pool. And fish swim in . . . Oh, never mind."

# CHAPTER 15

# THE SEA MONSTER WITH A WICKED BACKHAND

I anxiously sat through my first-ever class with Mr. Wendel, watching the clock make its painfully slow march toward lunchtime. The day's topic was genetics, and by halfway through the class the whiteboard was full of boxes demonstrating how combined traits from parents like blue eyes and brown eyes typically resulted in brown-eyed kids.

On the bottom of my notes, I scribbled, "Aesir mom + non-Aesir Dad = ?" If I were an Aesir, maybe I'd be smart enough to figure out how to help my dad. Or maybe I'd even have been able to help us avoid this whole mess in the first place.

But the jury was still out on me. And this jury was in danger of dying of old age. Sort of like the skeleton hanging in one corner of the science classroom, which was probably a former student who'd died waiting for one of Mr. Wendel's tedious lectures to end. When the bell finally rang, I leapt out of my seat and headed for the door.

"Don't forget," Mr. Wendel announced over the sound of zipping backpacks. "Your midterm is at the end of the week. And remember, it will count for a full half of your grade."

I stopped at Gwynn's desk. "Midterm?"

"Yeah," she said. "But I'm sure Mr. Wendel will give you more time."

"Ha!" said Grimsby, coming up behind us. "That totally doesn't sound like him."

I sighed. "Great. Well, I'll worry about that later. Which way to the pool? I want to see if we can find anything there or if it's a dead end."

"This way," said Grimsby, frowning. "But maybe don't say 'dead end.' Remember that death rune from the journal's cover?"

"Sorry," I said. "Bad choice of words."

He led the way around a corner into another hall filled with athletic trophies. "So what are you hoping to find? A surviving specimen of that svefn-thingy?"

I shuddered, remembering the wicked-looking thorn Dr. Swenson had showed me. "Isn't it funny how you'd never suspect something so deadly looking would be able to heal too? Almost like it has a secret double identity."

"Yeah," said Grimsby, sliding his gaze toward us. "Sort of like two normal-looking sixth-grade girls who happen to be a harvester of souls and a Viking assassin?"

Gwynn laughed. "Fair point." She narrowed her eyes, looking at Grimsby. "So what's your deep, dark secret?"

He looked away quickly, mumbling something I couldn't quite understand.

Our route continued outside through an open atrium. Grimsby reached out and rubbed his palm on the head of a statue as we passed by. It was a bronze figure of a man wearing a billowing fur-lined cloak. His arms were outstretched over a small pool of water where a fountain burbled softly. The top of his head was shiny as if it had been rubbed frequently.

"What's that?" I asked.

"What's what?" Grimsby said absently, turning to follow my gaze. "Oh, you mean the statue? That's the famous Bellyflop Bjarni."

I recognized the name from Doc's mention the previous day in class. "The Viking who saw North America first? Why Bellyflop?"

"I guess because it looks like he's about to do a belly flop into the pool. The dude had the amazing fortune of finding a whole new continent completely by accident, so everyone rubs his head for good luck."

I laughed, then jogged back and reached out to rub his smooth head. I needed a little extra luck right then.

Minutes later we re-entered the building through another hallway. Overhead a light buzzed, went out, and struggled to come on again. Ahead a door stood slightly ajar onto a dark room. *Cue the horror movie music*, I thought.

I pushed through the door, and immediately we were enveloped in a damp chlorine haze. The silence inside was so intense that I winced at the squeak of our shoes on the tiled floor. The room was nearly pitch-black, the only illumination coming from a couple of dim mercury vapor lights high up in the rafters and a faint blue glow from the pool. Large, shadowy shapes were obscured in the far corners of the room like hulking things waiting to pounce. I shuddered instinctively.

After the door settled shut behind us, the place was as quiet as a tomb, other than a faint dripping noise coming from somewhere in the shadows.

*"ACHOOO!"*

I nearly jumped out of my flannels. *"Shhhhh!"*

"Sorry," whispered Grimsby. "Chlorine always makes me sneeze. Anyway, why do we have to be quiet? It doesn't look like anyone's here."

"Doesn't this place give you the creeps?" I said, peering into the gloom.

"Only because it reminds me of my first time seeing Mr. Bost in a Speedo," he said with a shudder.

"Who's Mr. Bost?" I asked.

"PE teacher."

"I'll go find a light switch," Gwynn said as she disappeared farther into the room.

I slid my runestone out of my shirt and examined it.

"What's that?" Grimsby said.

"It's that necklace I mentioned earlier. The one that lit up with the upside-down Algiz rune when I had my run-in with that intruder in my house in North Carolina."

"Oh. What's it doing now?"

I turned the stone's blank face toward him. "Nothing."

"See? Like I said. Nothing to worry about."

"Yeah, you're probably right."

As we waited for the lights, Grimsby suddenly said, "Oooh!"

"What is it?"

Without answering, he shuffled toward a small table nearby. He returned with a pair of Ping-Pong paddles. "Want to play?"

"In the dark?"

"Glow-in-the-dark balls," he said, holding up a ball that glowed with an almost-alien light. "Anyway, got anything better to do?"

"Okay." I shrugged. "But I haven't played in forever, so I'm probably a little rusty."

"Don't worry, I'll take it easy on you."

He took up position on the other side of the table, then . . . *WHACK!* Something whizzed by within inches of my head.

"Hey!" I said, ducking for cover. "What gives?"

"Oops, sorry. Just, um, warming up."

I could hear the *tick-tick-tick* of the ball as it bounced away from us on the tile floor and then a wet *plip* as it dropped into the pool.

"It was a bad idea to put the Ping-Pong table so close to the pool," Grimsby said.

"You think?" I gave him a look that was probably wasted in the dark. "Hold on a sec. I'll go grab it."

I trotted toward the edge of the pool and peered down. The ball should have been easy to spot even in the dim glow of the underwater lights. But I couldn't see it anywhere. That was odd.

Suddenly some sort of sixth sense—maybe my new internal weirdness alarm—went off. Something wasn't quite right. As I gazed into the pool, there was an almost-imperceptible movement along the bottom. I squinted, trying to make it out. What I initially took for the translucent green floor of the pool seemed to be . . .

I gasped and rapidly backpedaled away as a giant green tentacle shot out of the pool with a loud splash.

*SMACK!*

It slapped wetly against the concrete where I'd been standing seconds earlier. My heart raced wildly while I watched the tentacle slide back into the pool. What was that . . . thing in the pool? And where had it come from?

"Abby?! What happened?!" Gwynn shouted with alarm.

Just then there was a loud metallic *THUNK*, and the lights started to come on. A side door opened, and a group of swimsuit-clad students poured out of the locker room. They were led by a shockingly pale, overweight man wearing nothing but a Speedo and a whistle. The kids were talking and laughing, headed right for the pool, oblivious to the danger.

Not sure what to do, I panicked and shouted the first thing that came to mind: "Sea monster!"

Everyone stopped in their tracks, and twenty heads turned toward me. We stared at each other for a few seconds.

"In the, uh . . ." I said, stumbling over my words and pointing toward the pool. "A sea monster. Or giant octopus. Or something like that."

A couple of the guys burst out laughing. I recognized one: Chase. Oh, great.

"Oooh, sure, a sea monster in the pool," said Chase. "I'm *soooo* scared." He trotted over to the pool to look in. Suddenly his smirk froze. His face instantly lost all its color when a long tentacle launched out of the pool and wrapped around his torso. It dragged him clawing and screaming toward the water.

"HELP!" he cried in pure terror. "Get me out of here!"

Instant pandemonium. Suddenly kids were running around yelling, aimlessly bouncing around the room like yesterday's bingo balls in a blind panic to get away from the monster. Another tentacle shot out of the water and narrowly missed flattening a girl as she ran past.

I looked to the teacher, Mr. Bost, but he was only running around in circles blowing his whistle uselessly. As much as it pained me to help the one guy who seemed determined to make my life at Vale miserable, I knew we had to do something to save Chase. Fast. I whipped my head around, looking for a weapon or anything that might help.

Glancing down, I remembered the Ping-Pong paddle in my hand. I shrugged, then hauled back and chucked it at the tentacle dunking him into the pool.

But another tentacle erupted from the water and curled around the paddle's handle, plucking it out of the air. I ducked, half expecting the paddle to come flying back at me. Instead, the scaly arm waggled the paddle in the air.

Grimsby apparently noticed this too from under the Ping-Pong table, where he'd retreated for safety. "What's it doing?" he shouted at me.

"I don't know," I shouted back.

Chase had one arm around a pool ladder, and his free fist beat wildly at the tentacle that held him around the waist.

Grimsby cocked his head to one side with a strange look on his face. "I think the sea monster, uh, wants to play a round of Ping-Pong."

"What? Seriously?"

He shrugged and grabbed another ball, tentatively slapping it toward the pool with his paddle.

The tentacle holding the paddle launched into action, swishing toward the bouncing ball. With a loud crack, its paddle connected with the ball. I had just enough time to flop onto the floor as the ball came rocketing back toward us. Rolling to my belly, I followed Grimsby's awed gaze to where the ball was now embedded in the far wall of the gym.

"Try it again!" I shouted over the screaming kids. The monster seemed to have temporarily forgotten about Chase.

"Are you nuts?"

"Hit the ball again! Try to distract it while I figure out how to save Chase."

Grimsby nodded and reached for another ball. He swatted it

toward the pool as hard as he could, then immediately ducked for cover back under the table. It worked. The ball came zooming back toward us like a comet. For a sea monster, it sure had a wicked backhand.

"Again!" I shouted, making a circular motion with my hand. "Keep it up!"

While Grimsby kept the creature distracted, I scanned the room looking for anything that might help.

"Abby!" Gwynn called from across the room. I saw her standing well clear of the pool holding a long pole used for rescuing swimmers. She made a few stabbing motions toward the pool with the pole, and I caught her drift. We could poke at the monster on the pool's bottom. That might annoy it enough to let Chase go. And maybe get it to come out of the pool and into the open.

That could be bad. But, well, we'd figure that part out when it happened. One thing at a time.

Gwynn pointed over my head, and I turned around. There on the wall behind me was a similar pole with a net on the end. I grabbed the pole off the wall and turned back to face her. Signaling a thumbs-up, we both cautiously approached the pool from opposite sides, careful to watch for other tentacles.

Silently I mouthed, "One, two, three . . . NOW!"

We both stabbed into the pool, trying to get as far as we could toward the bottom. But I only connected with water. The poles weren't long enough. I ducked as the tentacle holding the Ping-Pong paddle suddenly stopped and swept toward me. A forest of tentacles blasted out of the water and waved around wildly. We may have missed, but we'd gotten its attention. More screams erupted from the terrified kids all around us as they dodged the slimy green arms. We'd been trying to irritate the thing. Mission accomplished.

I retreated like any sane person would. But Gwynn made a barbaric battle cry and leapt into the air toward the monster. She splashed into the water headfirst and disappeared, her battle cry cutting off abruptly when her head went underwater. I called out in alarm and ran toward the water, battling back scaly arms. I frantically scanned the water for any sign of Gwynn. Then a tentacle shot out of the water, dangling her by one ankle. She furiously pummeled it with her fists.

"Gwynn!" I shouted in horror. "What are you doing?!"

"Don't . . . worry . . . about me," she grunted as she flailed at the writhing arm. Despite her heroic efforts, it looked like we might all soon become sea monster food.

"Abby!" shouted Grimsby.

"Kind of busy right now," I yelled in exasperation while beating back tentacles.

"No, listen," he said. "Remember when you guys distracted the monster?"

"Yeah?" I slapped a tentacle away from my ankle. "What about it?"

"Well, another Ping-Pong ball fell into the pool. But then it disappeared. The ball, I mean. I think the creature, um, ate it."

"Ate it? But why would it eat a Ping-Pong ball?"

"I don't know. Maybe it thinks they're eggs or something."

I delivered a hard karate chop to a tentacle that was trying to wrap around my arm. It recoiled but continued to hang menacingly in the air. "But then why would it hit them back at you?"

"Beats me. Likes to play with its food, maybe?"

"Hmmm," I said, an idea slowly taking shape. "How many more balls do we have?"

He peered down into a five-gallon bucket next to him. "Lots. This is almost full."

"Okay, this may be a ridiculous idea, but the balls are full of air, right?"

"Uh, right," he said, a confused look on his face.

"So if the monster eats enough of them, then all that air should make it float toward the surface. Then we can attack it with the poles."

"You're right. That's a pretty ridiculous idea." He grinned. "But it might work."

"Hope so. But it could take a while." I looked toward Chase, Gwynn, and the others still running around the room. "And I'm not sure we have that long."

Grimsby looked down again at the bucket. "Leave it to me. Just keep that thing busy."

"Okay," I said. Then I shouted toward Gwynn, "Grimsby says to keep it busy! He has an idea!"

"No . . . prob—" she grunted back as the tentacle dunked her headfirst into the pool. She emerged seconds later sputtering, her long hair plastered across her face.

I started to take another run at the pool with my makeshift weapon but skidded to a halt as a loud howl suddenly filled the room.

"YAAAAAAAAAAAAHHHHHHHH!"

Everyone stopped running around and screaming for a minute and turned toward the noise.

It was Grimsby.

He hoisted the bucket of Ping-Pong balls over his head and gave another primal yell. Then he charged toward the pool and everything went into slow motion. Framed in the white glow of an overhead light. Skinny legs and loafered feet churning. A determined snarl fixed on his face. He blew right past the "NO RUNNING" sign without even flinching. It was a charge worthy of the greatest Viking heroes of old.

Then, just as quickly, it all started to fall apart. As he neared the water's edge, one of his loafers flew off. He stumbled. Tried to catch himself but slipped and fell forward. Together Grimsby and the bucket slammed against the tile floor. A hundred Ping-Pong balls exploded out of the bucket and bounced into the pool to a staccato of *plip-plip-plip-plip*.

Silence. Nothing happened for a minute. Then, with a slurping noise, the balls started to disappear from the pool's surface like they'd been vacuumed underwater. The room was quiet as everyone held their breath, waiting to see what would happen. After what seemed like an eon, Grimsby rose on all fours and crawled closer to the pool, peeking over the edge to see what was going on.

Just then the water erupted in a geyser as the creature blasted upward, buoyed by the feast of Ping-Pong balls it had eaten. I felt my insides turn to water as a giant, glowing yellow eye rose above the pool's surface. But in the next instant, the monster exploded. Pool water and particles of wet, slimy goo flew everywhere, knocking me flat on my back and covering me with filth.

As I lay there stunned, the silence was broken by the sound of someone spitting and gagging. To one side of me lay Gwynn, wiping guts out of her eyes. By the pool Chase was on all fours, coughing and trembling but apparently unharmed. Then I spotted Grimsby at the pool's edge, completely covered in slime from head to toe. I didn't know if it was the sight of him, or relief after the fight for our lives, but I started giggling uncontrollably, finally letting go a full-belly laugh.

"What was that . . . you were saying earlier . . . about octopus sushi?" I said between gasps of laughter.

Grimsby looked down at himself covered in slime, and then his shoulders started heaving in laughter too. He held up a surviving Ping-Pong ball and said, "That's a spicy meatball!"

We both burst into more laughter, but suddenly Grimsby's laugh turned to a strangled gagging noise. I looked to see what was wrong. He was staring back at me with his mouth open in surprise.

"What is it?" I said, quickly looking down at myself, thinking maybe I'd sustained a terrible injury I hadn't noticed yet.

"The journal . . . look!"

He pointed past me, and I whirled around to see what he was looking at.

Not far away on the floor, apparently jostled out of my backpack in the fight with the sea monster, the journal we'd found in the library lay partly covered with sea monster guts. But there was something strange about it. It almost seemed to be . . . glowing.

I cautiously crawled toward it and wiped the muck off the cover. That's when I saw what it was.

"The water rune," gasped Gwynn, who had silently come up beside me. "It's like it's on fire!"

As we watched in wonder, the rune grew brighter and brighter, soon turning white-hot before emitting a brief flash of light and then subsiding to a deep blue color while the other two runes remained a dull gray.

"What do you think it means?" I said.

"You said it's the Norse rune for water, right?" said Grimsby as he joined us. "You don't think . . ." He trailed off as he turned to survey the puddles of pool water that were now everywhere.

"That we just conquered some sort of water test?" I finished for him.

"Then what about the other two?" Gwynn said, still wringing water out of her hair. "Tree . . . and death? What do those mean?"

Before anyone could answer, the sound of squeaking wheels cut through my thoughts, and the school janitor entered through a door on the opposite side of the room, pushing his familiar garbage can–and–mop bucket combo. He looked from the piles of sea monster guts to his little mop and frowned, evidently wishing he had a much bigger mop. I cringed, feeling bad about being involved in two messy cleanups in the same number of days, even though neither one was one hundred percent my fault.

But it seemed like a perfect metaphor for the mess my life had become in just a few short days. And it was sure going to take an epic mop to clean it all up.

# CHAPTER 16

# A LINEAGE OF BLOOD

Not able to focus in class, I spent the rest of the afternoon hiding out in the library, trying to answer all the questions spinning through my brain.

First, there was the sea monster. That was nuts. I mean, come on. Sea. Monster. For real?

Then there was the journal. Was it some sort of magical map? And if so, to what? To finding the svefnthorn and helping my dad? That would be amazing. And that's what Granny V had suggested. But whoa: from a murderous dark Valkyrie who'd just tried to steal my soul? That made me wonder, even if it led us to the sleep thorn, what was the catch?

And finally, who was the mystery person who'd left the journal for me in the first place? *Four years ago.* My mom? Did she somehow know she was in trouble and leave me a trail to follow in case something happened to her? I was so torn, because I wanted that too.

When the bell rang to signal the end of the school day and I'd made exactly zero progress, I was ready to pull my hair out. So I decided it was probably a good time to give my brain a rest and go back to spend some time with my dad.

Bare trees threw long black stripes across Vale's campus as I trudged through the snow, headed toward the hospital. Snow was the worst. I already despised the stuff. I kicked a clump of it in frustration, sending icy white fragments exploding in every direction.

"Abby!"

I looked around, spotting Gwynn and Grimsby jogging toward me. I stopped, waiting for them to catch up.

"Where have you been?" Gwynn said as they came nearer.

Grimsby stopped by a large oak tree and leaned in to study it closely, looking it up and down. He moved to the next tree and stuck his face right up to it, squinting his eyes and rapping on it with his knuckles.

"Hiding," I said, turning toward Gwynn. "Mostly. Trying to figure out what any of this means."

"Find anything?" she said.

"Not really, but . . ." I looked past her at Grimsby, who was actually sniffing a tree. "Okay, what's up with you and the trees already?"

He turned toward me and said innocently, "Oh, nothing, just a little research of my own."

Gwynn laughed. "That's what we were trying to find you about. The second rune—you know, Eihwaz? I did some more digging and found out it's often used not to represent just any tree, but *the* tree." When she saw I wasn't following, she added, "You know, Yggdrasil?"

I looked at her like she was nuts. "Wait. The mythical tree from Norse mythology that connects the nine worlds? *That's* what you think we have to find? As in, right here somewhere on Vale's campus?"

She nodded. "Well—"

"We don't even know for sure what the runes are. Clues? Guideposts leading us to . . . what? A cure for my dad? A greenhouse that doesn't exist anymore? Or maybe even our own deaths? Or . . ." I stopped, realizing my voice had been steadily rising as all my frustration boiled over to the point that I was almost shouting.

Gwynn bit her lip, looking a little hurt. "Sure, well, when you put it like that . . ." She shrugged, turning up her palms. "But remember, for the first rune we had to fight a sea monster in the school's swimming pool. And do you really think it was a coincidence that the water rune changed after we, well—"

"Blew up the sea monster?" Grimsby finished helpfully.

I pressed my fist against my forehead. "Sorry, I didn't mean to jump all over your theory."

"That's okay," said Gwynn. "You're dealing with a lot right now. I get it."

I smiled. "So then how does that explain why Grimsby's going around sniffing trees?"

"Oh, that." She rolled her eyes. "It's because Yggdrasil is supposed to be an ash tree." She raised her voice a little louder to be sure he heard. "Which I keep telling him doesn't mean it smells like ashes."

"Abby!" a voice called behind me.

I turned and saw Doc striding across the lawn toward us.

Apparently everyone was looking for me. He'd exchanged his gray cloak from yesterday for khakis, rubber boots, and a maroon hoodie with "VALE KNATTLEIKR" printed across the front.

"I've been trying to find you," he said, stopping in front of us. "First, to apologize for the way we dumped all that news on you yesterday."

I dropped my gaze to the ground. "Thanks. I've sort of been hiding."

He rubbed his chin. "I'm sure this has all been really hard on you. And I know people say this all the time, but if there's anything you need, just say the word. Really."

"Thanks," I mumbled. I looked up at him and opened my mouth to say that I'd be okay, but instead what came out was: "Actually, you can. I'm tired of all this. Tired of feeling like I'm in the dark all the time. Tired of no one knowing how to help my dad. Even tired of having to thoroughly dry my hair every morning so it doesn't freeze to my skull on the way to school. In the past week, I've been attacked, shot at, and humiliated by the Viking governing council. So what I really need is for someone to stop treating me like a little kid and tell me what's really happening." I stopped, my eyes wide in surprise that those words had simply poured out of me.

Doc's eyebrows had steadily risen as my tirade continued, and now he stood speechless in front of me, evidently as surprised as me. For a few seconds we just stared at each other.

Then he looked away and cleared his throat before saying slowly, "Given the circumstances . . . I think that's fair." He nodded once as if making a decision, then turned back to me. "It's time you knew more about your Viking heritage. Come with me. I need to show you something."

"Right behind you," Grimsby said, moving to follow our teacher as he turned to go.

"Ah, Mr. Grimsby . . ." Doc said, looking back over his shoulder.

Grimsby stopped in midstep. "Oh. You meant just Abby. Roger that. We'll be, um, right here. Well, probably not *right* here, but . . ." He waved his hands in circles. "Around. You know, somewhere on Vale's campus. Like—"

Gwynn slugged him on the shoulder to get him to stop talking and then waved at me. "See you later."

I laughed. "Bye, guys."

Fifteen minutes later, Doc led me into a field house that sprawled low across the back half of the campus. Everything at Vale seemed to come in only one size: enormous. And this building was no exception.

"Is this your first visit to the longhouse?" Doc said.

I nodded. "As in Viking longhouses?" I knew from my studies that in early Scandinavian society, Vikings had constructed enormous longhouses that were the centers of community life.

"Precisely," Doc said.

Inside were thousands of alternating maroon and gold plastic chairs arranged in concentric rings around a glass-enclosed playing field. Dozens of divisional, regional, and state championship pennants going back over a century hung from the rafters overhead. I absorbed it all in a sort of daze while still processing Gwynn's idea that we had to somehow find Yggdrasil. That seemed impossible. My brain sought desperately for any other way we could help my dad but so far was coming up empty. If a team of scientists couldn't help him, then what could I hope to do?

We turned down a long hallway, and Doc gestured to a door that said "Coach Ruel" on it. "Let's talk in my office."

I entered a small but neat office. The door clicked shut behind me, and Doc slid into a large leather chair behind the desk.

"Have a seat," he said, motioning to a pair of wooden chairs in front of the desk. The backs of the chairs were inlaid with intricate carvings of what looked like depictions of Norse myths. In one scene Thor stood with his hammer, Mjölnir, raised high above his head.

"I do a little wood carving when I have the time," Doc said, noticing my inspection.

*Wow*, I thought, *he* made *these?* I looked around at the trophies and medals crammed onto every flat surface around the room. "Pretty impressive."

Following my gaze, he said, "Indeed, knattleikr has a long and rich legacy here at Vale." He leaned forward a little and interlaced his fingers on the desk blotter. "But for now I'd like to focus on another legacy. Yours." I turned to him. I wasn't sure what legacy he was referring to. My humongous failure resulting in my dad's coma? Or the disbandment of the Aesir and everything I'd spent my life working toward? "Yeah, some legacy so far," I said, and shook my head in frustration.

"Well, as you will undoubtedly discover as you grow older, things aren't always what they seem. But let's start from the beginning, shall we?" He steepled his hands in front of his mouth and frowned down at his desk, considering where to start. "You're of course familiar with the major Norse gods, such as Odin and Thor?"

I nodded.

"Although we call them gods, they weren't actually gods as we use the term today. Rather, they were part of an ancient race of superhumans. Stronger. Faster. But still mortal. In fact, they were the very first Aesir."

I leaned back in my chair, frowning. "So . . . Beowulf didn't start the Aesir order?"

Doc shook his head. "No, he only endowed them with the specific commission to protect the human race from Grendels. The Old Norse name for the Aesir translates roughly to 'shadow warriors' because Grendels were associated with shadows and darkness. The Vikings coalesced as a warrior class around these shadow warriors, who at their peak numbered in the hundreds. That number has waxed and waned over the centuries commensurate with the need to protect humankind."

"Sooo . . ." I said, drawing out the word as my brain struggled to keep up. "Then where did Grendels come from? And why didn't my mom ever mention any of this?"

"Normally this knowledge is reserved for when a Viking is initiated as a warrior. But under the circumstances, I thought it important that you learn it a bit early. Now, to answer your first question, you're familiar with the story of Loki, I assume?"

"Sure. He was the brother of Thor, right?"

"That's right. The two had another brother named Balder who was known as 'the most beautiful and beloved one.' Everywhere Loki went, it was always Balder, Balder, Balder. Everyone despised and avoided Loki. But they'd throw big parties in honor of Balder's beauty. It was during one such party that went on for many days that Loki finally had enough. His jealousy boiled over . . . and he killed his own brother."

Doc peered at me through his large glasses. "Does that remind you of anything?"

I thought about it for a minute, then made the connection. "The partying, the outsider driven to murder—it sounds a lot like the story of Beowulf."

"Exactly. Loki's punishment was to be cast out and subjected to a serpent's venom that hideously deformed him, transforming him into the very first Grendel. The story of Beowulf is just the most recent in an ancient cycle pitting the fractured halves of the human family tree against each other. Light against dark. Brother against brother." He paused and reached out with one finger to spin a small globe resting on the corner of his desk. "With the very fate of the world in the balance."

As I watched the globe spin, it seemed to match the swirl of thoughts in my head. It occurred to me for the first time that I'd never thought about what Grendels really were or where they came from. Or why it was so important that the entire Aesir order was formed to stop them. "This is . . . a lot to take in," I said.

"It always is, when you see your own life set against the sprawl of human history. Realizing that since the dawn of time, the Vikings have been the final bulwark against a darkness that seeks to overcome and destroy humanity. And the Aesir have the most important role of all. Because Grendels are the direct descendants of Loki himself and masters of dark legions of trolls, goblins, giants, and many other nightmarish creatures. If the Aesir were to fail in their task of stopping them . . ." He paused, considering the right words. "Well, simply put, it would mean the end of humanity as we know it. The earth would be overrun by the armies of eternal night."

As we sat staring at each other wordlessly, the air seemed almost charged, like the seconds before a lightning strike. Suddenly I realized I'd been holding my breath. I looked away and ran a hand nervously through my hair. "But that hasn't happened yet . . . right?"

Doc blinked and shook his head as if emerging from a dream. "No." He shuffled some papers absently on his desk. "No, it hasn't. After the time of Beowulf, the cycle went dormant."

"Because Grendels were finally defeated, you mean." The back of my neck prickled as I remembered the argument with Unferth. "But I really did see a Grendel. You believe me, right?"

Instead of answering directly, Doc smiled and said, "I think I told you that I knew your mother in her time here at Vale? We were actually good friends. But we had heated arguments on the subject of Grendels. She was firm in her conviction that the danger was still very real, even after all these years. I'm afraid I disagreed with her, and now I regret that I didn't do more to defend her against detractors who claimed her obsession bordered on mania toward the . . . end. It wasn't until more recently that I started thinking she may have been right."

I perked up at this. "Why do you say that?"

He got up and walked over to the door, opening it briefly to look outside, then making sure it was firmly shut before turning back to me. "Because a few years ago, we started losing contact with your fellow Aesir. One by one, all over the world, communications were going dark. The rest of the Grey Council didn't think anything of it. But when I looked into it myself, there seemed to be a pattern emerging. A pattern that led me to one unavoidable conclusion: Someone—or something—was systematically wiping them out."

What was left of my lunch churned in my stomach. "You mean, like . . . the hunters became the hunted?"

He nodded grimly. "Exactly. So, you see, the recall of the Aesir to Vale wasn't entirely for the reasons you were led to believe. When I presented my findings to the council, we knew that immediate action was necessary. Yet they still refused to believe Grendels could be involved. And then the attack on your home . . . Well, we knew we had to bring you in. To protect you and your dad before it was too late."

My mind leapt back to the dark shadow. The eyeless giant on the motorcycle. Maybe the hunters *had* found us after all. Then I suddenly recalled the lack of communication from my aunt and gasped. "But my aunt Jess? What about her?"

Doc shook his head. "We lost touch with her a few days ago. A team has been dispatched to investigate. But so far . . . nothing."

My head throbbed. All this information. It was too much to process all at once. "What about the other Aesir? If they're being recalled too, then where are they?"

Doc looked down for a minute. When he raised his head, he had that same thousand-yard stare from the previous day. "I'm afraid that you and your aunt"—he drew in a long breath—"may be the last Aesir left. I'm so sorry we—I didn't see it until it was too late."

And if my aunt didn't make it, he didn't say . . . I'd be the last hope. It felt like all the air had gone out of the room. I wanted to run and scream and curl into a little ball all at once. Because if the survival of the Aesir depended on me, then we were all as good as dead.

". . . but I don't know what it was." I realized Doc was speaking again, but my ears must have temporarily checked out.

"Sorry?" I said.

"I was just saying, I've come to believe that the whole chain of events ties back to your mother somehow. Perhaps some discovery she made or . . ." Doc studied me for a long moment, as if reading my thoughts, then said, "I know."

I could feel my face turn hot. He knew? Wait . . . he knew what, exactly?

"Your mom and I, and then later your dad, kept in touch about your progress. Any signs of special abilities blossoming as you grew up. Your dad most of all has felt the pain of being the weak link in your genetic makeup that's held you back from what you've wanted most. To be an Aesir. To carry on your mom's work. Her legacy."

Tears pricked my eyes as I thought of my dad blaming himself for this. "He . . . he has?"

Doc chuckled. "In fact, I think he sent me a photo of every A you ever got on a report card. Every medal or ribbon you ever won. In his eyes, you are the most special thing in the world, Aesir or not."

My heart ached with love for him and at the same time with the painful feeling that he was wrong. That I wasn't special at all. "But what if I'm not? What if I'm just . . . normal?"

Doc adjusted his glasses. "I've met a lot of people in my time. And you know what I've found? It isn't where you're from. Or what you know." He tapped on his chest. "The true measure of who we are is what's in here. And whether your Aesir abilities develop or not, I can tell you have the heart of a warrior. Just like your mom."

I turned my head away, taking all this in. Just then I heard talking and a burst of laughter from the locker room outside. Doc shuffled his papers into a neat stack and started to rise.

"Wait," I said, "you mentioned earlier you thought my mom had something to do with everything that's happened to the Aesir. Why?"

He glanced toward the door. "Not now. We'll have to finish our discussion later."

*Wait! My mom! I need to know!* I wanted to scream.

But Doc was already digging through a box on the floor full of what looked like jerseys. "Just be sure that what we talked about stays between the two of us. It's important for now that you keep acting as if nothing has happened. As far as anyone else knows, you're just a normal kid adjusting to a new school."

Just a normal kid? That's exactly what I was worried about. But right then, I'd have given anything to be dealing with nothing worse than too much homework and maybe a bad case of acne. "But if I'm the last"—I glanced toward the door—"you know, shouldn't I be doing something?"

"Indeed." Doc extracted a maroon jersey and held it up in my direction. "There we are. Number 27. Powerful to the Vikings as a multiple of nine. For now, we go into a different sort of battle."

He tossed me the jersey and I caught it in midair. I stared at him blankly before making the connection, then shot a nervous look in the direction of the playing field. "You mean I . . . What, right *now*? I don't have time for this. What about the whole Grendel thing? The Aesir being hunted out of existence? My dad?"

"You probably wondered why we gave you a knattleikr scholarship."

Oh, right . . . that. Dad had mentioned that it required me to actually go to practice and games or risk losing it. And if I lost the scholarship now on top of everything else . . . "Well, yeah, it crossed my mind."

He nodded. "It's because the game brings together all your years of training into a cohesive whole. It may not seem like it at first, but as you learn to play, you'll see how natural it all feels. And if what I fear is happening comes to fruition, you'll need to quickly master those skills to weather the storm."

*A storm. A storm is coming.* The words echoed in my mind again, sending a tremor all the way down to my toes.

As he moved to open the door, Doc added, "Don't worry. It's no big deal."

# CHAPTER 17

# KNATTLEIKR

Call me paranoid, but I've noticed that when adults say stuff like "no big deal," it generally means it's a pretty big deal. Just a few days ago, my dad had said the same words to me about driving, and now he was lying in a coma. So you can't blame me for being a teensy bit nervous as Doc led the way out onto the field ten minutes later.

"Knattleikr was a favorite game of the early Vikings," he explained. "We've modernized it a bit, but it's essentially the same rules. Success takes a combination of strategy, planning, and brute physical strength. Not unlike going into battle."

I chased after him, trying to balance a three-foot-long heavy wooden stick with a curved openmouthed dragon head carved into one end. And simultaneously to jam a plastic helmet onto my head while not getting twisted up in my oversized jersey. Like everything I'd been through recently, it all felt way bigger than I could handle.

We exited the tunnel onto a large rectangular playing field covered with artificial turf and lined by glass walls. On either end of the field was a goal about six feet wide. About a dozen other players were already on the field tossing a small brown ball or stretching to warm up.

"So they had arenas like this?" I asked, looking around and taking in the whole expanse.

"No, early Viking games were generally played outdoors, sometimes on frozen lakes. And, of course, they occasionally resulted in the deaths of some of the players."

I was sure the color drained from my face at this. I turned to see if he was joking. He wasn't.

"But not to worry. We play an updated version. We've had a few broken bones and sprained ankles. But no deaths." Doc gave me a wry smile. "Same basic rules as the original Viking version, but since there are no out of bounds, the play is much quicker. Five players on each side plus a goalkeeper. Think of it sort of like a giant game of pinball, only with human bumpers."

A set of knuckles rapped on my flimsy plastic helmet, and I turned to see Grimsby stuffing another ball of dough into his mouth. "You look like a bobblehead in this thing," he said as he chewed. "I had one of those once, but its head kept falling off." As an afterthought, he added, "But I'm sure that won't happen to you."

"Thanks for the pep talk," I said.

A horn blared. The players stopped practicing and moved into their positions on the field.

"Ready?" Doc asked me.

"As ready as I'll ever be." Or in other words, not at all.

"Good. We're going to warm up with a little scrimmage. I've separated the players into maroon and gold squads. I have you playing charger for the maroon team. That means you can go any-where on the field. It's a lot of work, but it's important because you set the tempo for your team." He jogged off the field, followed closely by Grimsby. They closed a door in the glass behind them. It felt a lot like being sealed into a gladiator's arena.

Grimsby took a seat in a row of metal bleachers next to the glass and started a one-person wave. "Gooooo Abby!" Somewhere he'd found a giant foam finger, which he waved encouragingly.

I looked for Gwynn, wondering where she'd gotten to, but she was nowhere in sight. I raised my stick toward Grimsby in acknowledgment, then turned back to the field. And nearly ran right into a player on the gold squad.

"Sorry," I said. "I—"

Oh, great. It was Mr. Fuzzy Pants himself. Chase Lodbrok—the self-appointed king of the school, and world history class.

I was expecting at least a thank-you for saving his life from the sea monster. Maybe even a fist bump. But instead when he saw me, an evil grin spread across his face. "Hey, brah," he said, borrowing Hawaiian lingo even though there wasn't a palm tree in at least a thousand miles. "If it isn't my close, personal friend Abby Beckett." He nudged the guy next to him with his elbow. "Hey, drop me a beat."

The guy cupped his hands around his mouth and started beat-boxing, both he and Chase bouncing like they were part of a rap crew as Chase opened his mouth:

*"Her name is Abby Beckett.*
*Now everybody check it.*
*They say she got game, but she just gonna wreck it.*
*And get herself owned when she don't expec' it."*

My face flamed hot and my fingers tightened around my knat-tleikr stick. I felt a hand grab my shoulder.

"Hey, don't listen to them."

I turned and did a double take. Under a plastic helmet of her own, I recognized Gwynn's face smiling at me. So that was where she'd gotten to. She was wearing an oversized jersey tied around her waist to hide her wings.

She glanced at Chase, who was high-fiving the small posse gathered around him, then back at me. "They're only trying to get in your head. Let's bury them on the field instead."

I slid her hand off my shoulder. "No, I've got this."

Then I turned to Chase. "You really want to go there?"

His eyebrows shot up as he regarded me with a smirk.

"A rhyme battle with the daughter of an English PhD?" I said. "Okay, then try this on:

> *"Hey, y'all, my name is Chase.*
> *I got a pretty face*
> *But in between my ears*
> *All I got is empty space."*

"Ohhhhhh," one of the guys said, and thumped Chase on the back. "You just got *burned*."

As the small crowd of guys laughed, Chase's eyes smoldered. He was no longer smiling. Was it a smart move to escalate the little war between us? Probably not. But it sure felt good.

Gwynn gave me an impressed look, then jerked her head

toward the center of the field. We jogged into position, and I looked around at the huge arena, once again feeling very out of my depth.

She held out a gloved fist. "Take no prisoners."

I took a deep breath before bumping her fist with mine. "Right. No prisoners."

"What's wrong?" she said. "You look like a deer caught in the headlights."

There was just the small problem that I had no clue what I was doing. "No, I-I'm okay." The quaver in my voice didn't sound at all convincing.

As if reading my thoughts, she winked and said, "Follow my lead. I'll teach you everything you need to know. Catch the ball in the dragon's mouth." She pointed toward the dragon head carved into the end of my stick. "Then fling it in the goal down there." She indicated the other end of the field, then with a sidelong glance added: "The ball, not the stick. Easy as that."

"Ball. Stick. Goal," I repeated. "Got it."

On the sideline, Doc was busy positioning what looked like a toy cannon, aiming its muzzle into the air. "Ready?" he called.

Chase and Gwynn raised their dragon sticks to indicate they were. I wasn't so sure, but I lifted my stick anyway.

"Okay, standard rules apply. Five points per goal. The ball stays in play unless it travels outside the glass enclosure or the ball carrier becomes incapacitated." My heart gave an extra-wobbly beat at this. "First team to fifty wins."

Based on the size of the cannon, I was expecting a fun little popping noise, sort of like a toy cork gun. So I naturally ducked for cover when a teeth-rattling explosion launched a small brown ball high into the air over the field.

*Ball. Stick. Goal*, I repeated to myself, pushing off the ground before anyone else noticed. Easy.

I jumped and reached for the ball with my dragon stick. But with my feet still in the air, another stick swiped the backs of my legs. Hard. I flipped, my feet going up into the air as my shoulders crashed into the ground. I've heard artificial turf is supposed to be safer and all, but to the back of my head, it felt a lot like fuzzy concrete.

I lay there for a few seconds, waiting for the whistle from the sidelines. I mean, that had to have been a foul. Maybe even enough for a yellow card or even an ejection. But the whistle never came.

"Abby! Get up!" Gwynn shouted as she sprinted past me.

I rolled onto my stomach with a grunt, but it was already too late. Chase was running down the field in the other direction with the ball. As he approached our last defender, he jerked his wrists to launch the ball against the glass wall. Then, with a spin move, he was around the defender and expertly met the ball where it ricocheted off the wall. With a smooth arcing motion, he launched the ball toward the goal. The net jumped. A horn sounded. Five points for the other team.

Chase came running back toward me. "Some superstar," he said with a sneer. "Had enough yet?"

With a scowl, I got back to my feet. *Okay, if that's how we're going to play, then get ready for war*, I thought. "Bring it on," I fired back.

Gwynn jogged back and slapped me on the shoulder. "Hey. Stay focused. It's only one goal."

We played several more rounds, the gold squad racking up goal after goal as we fell behind thirty-five to ten. The maroon squad seemed hopelessly outmatched, with Gwynn the only one able to get any points on the board. I was sweating, frustrated, and on the verge of quitting. As messed up as it was, only Chase's taunts kept me from hurling my stick and walking off the field. I had an unexplainable need to prove myself to this guy.

Then the cannon fired again, and the ball was back in the air. Chase jumped and snagged it. He ran toward the sideline, angling for an open shot. But this time I was right behind him. As he dodged around one of my teammates, I darted in for a body check. Time for some revenge. Instead, out of nowhere, another body crashed into me at the last minute, sending me sprawling against the glass wall face-first. Grimsby's eyes widened as my nose and cheek mashed like Play-Doh into the glass right in front of him.

And the guy wasn't done with me yet. With a nasty laugh, he shouldered my face even harder into the wall.

"Get *off* me," I seethed with my lips pressed into the glass, my arms swinging uselessly behind me in an attempt to fend him off. Finally the pressure let up, and I crumpled to the ground in time to see Chase expertly flip the ball toward the goal again and to hear the horn sound. Another five points.

Gwynn's concerned face appeared above me. "Are you okay? Maybe you should sit out the next round. You know, just watch and learn?"

I lay there on the ground, hurting all over, when suddenly I was overwhelmed by the image of my dad lying in a hospital bed not far away, slipping toward death. And that was an even worse pain, knowing that I couldn't think of a single thing I could do about it.

"Hey, Beckett." I heard Chase's voice again, snapping me back to the present. "Need a spatula to scrape yourself off the field?" He and Beatbox Guy erupted into laughter and gave each other high fives.

"No thanks," I growled to Gwynn as I pushed myself off the turf. "I can do this."

There was another boom from the cannon. I crouched, ready to jump for the ball, but I felt a hand on my shoulder pushing me out of the way.

"I've got this," Gwynn said. "Go long."

I took off in a dead run. When I looked back over my shoulder, she gracefully leapt into the air to snag the ball in her dragon's teeth. She dodged a swipe from a defender and planted her feet. Then in one fluid motion she hauled back and heaved the ball in my direction.

I flung out my stick and leapt for the ball, the muscles in my shoulders and arms straining to reach it. With a sudden rattling noise, the ball settled into the dragon's teeth. I had it! I fell to the turf, rolled, and came up facing the goal.

Only one opponent stood in my way. Chase Lodbrok.

That's when everything went into slow motion. In a split second, an eerie focus came over me as years of training gelled into this one moment. A dozen possible paths to the goal sprang into my mind, then were evaluated and discarded until only the best remained. And as soon as I had it, my body was in motion. I charged toward Chase, feinted to the left, then ran *up* the glass wall, my feet catching air as my body flipped end over end. Using the momentum of my somersault, I whipped the ball toward the goal with everything I had, feeling all my frustration, fear, and anger explode into that single forward motion.

The ball rocketed across the field. The goalie dove, but he was too late. I watched in disbelief as the net jerked. Then, with a sharp crack, the glass wall behind the goal disintegrated in an explosion of tiny shards. My throw had carried the ball all the way through not just the back of the net but the wall behind it too. The horn blared again. Score.

When I overcame my initial shock and turned around, everyone stood frozen, staring at me. Some had their mouths open in shock. Others eyed me warily. "Um, sorry," I said awkwardly, feeling suddenly self-conscious, like I'd just done something horribly wrong.

Gwynn was the first to move, uncertainly at first but then

jogging across the field toward me smiling. When she passed Chase, she nudged his gaping chin back in place with the tip of her gloved finger. "Looks like someone got owned when he didn't *expec'* it."

Doc clapped his hands for attention at the sideline. "I think that's enough for today. Let's have everyone hit the showers." He headed across the field in my direction.

Gwynn stopped in front of me and held out a gloved fist. "Wreck-It Beckett. Has a nice ring to it. You practice that move a lot?"

I bumped my fist against hers. "Uh, never, actually. It sort of just . . . happened."

She nodded appraisingly. "Well, maybe you can just happen to teach it to me sometime." She took a last glance at the shattered wall, then back at me. "Catch up with you after we get cleaned up?"

"Um, yeah. See you then." I bent in half, breathing hard and still wincing from a brutal blow to the ribs from one of the dragon sticks.

Doc regarded me with an unreadable expression as he approached. "What did you think?"

"I think even my bruises have bruises," I panted. "But I might have gotten the hang of it at the end there."

"Yes, in my fifteen years of coaching knattleikr, I can't say I've ever seen a move like that. You caught a more experienced defender off guard, and look what happened. I think what you discovered is that it's not enough to only use your body. You have to use your brain too." He tapped his head to emphasize his point.

"Yeah," I said weakly, tapping my head in reply and wincing at even this light contact with my skull. "Ouch."

"Viking warriors once used this game to train for battle because they also knew that relying solely on brute force nine times out of ten results in a one-way ticket to Valhalla. But enough lecturing for now. I think you've earned a hot shower."

In the hallway leading to the locker rooms, I spotted Chase talking with an older man who had his back turned to me. The man slapped him on the shoulder, and Chase jogged off to the locker room. As I drew closer, the man turned, and his piercing gray eyes were unmistakable. Unferth. I also recognized the similarity of features to Chase for the first time, and a lightbulb came on in my head. They must be father and son. Chase Lodbrok. Unferth Lodbrok. One doing his best to ruin my social life. The other destroying everything else that mattered to me.

I felt the anger boil up in my chest as I made a beeline for him. Words piled on top of words as I marched toward him, ready for my emotions to explode like hot lava. But as I neared him, my resolve started to crack under the intensity of his gaze. Before I lost all my nerve, I quickly blurted the first words that came to my mind: "Why did you hate my mom? What did she ever do to you? Maybe expose you as an incompetent hack?" Ugh. Did my voice sound as whiny to him as it did in my head?

His face underwent a sea change from shock, to confusion,

to anger. When he spoke, his calm voice belied the steel in his eyes. "I saw you leave Coach Ruel's office earlier. What did he tell you?"

I looked at him with confusion, not following where he was going with this. He stepped in front of me, blocking my path to the locker room. I backed up a step, felt the back of my leg depress a lever, and suddenly heard water running. When I turned, I saw I'd backed myself into a small alcove with a drinking fountain. Trapped. The anger seeped out of me like the water gurgling down the fountain's drain to be replaced by a tight feeling of foreboding as I realized my tactical error.

Mr. Lodbrok's eyes regarded me coldly when I looked back toward him. "Did he say you were brought here for your protection?" he said. "Something like that?"

"I . . . um . . ." I glanced to both sides, looking for help or a way out.

"And what would we do, exactly? Surely you know from the Beowulf legend that a Grendel cannot be defeated by steel alone. No, Grendels are protected by an ancient curse that both deforms them and shields them from mortal wounds. Only a sword crafted by the forges of old can harm them. But the last one of those was destroyed, its blade melted by the blood of the Grendel that Beowulf killed."

I opened my mouth to speak, but nothing came out. Was all this true? Why hadn't Doc told me, then? "Yeah, so why are you telling me this?" I finally choked out.

"You wanted to know the truth," he said. "Here it is: We are not engaged in a child's game. You can forget about any so-called protection. *If* your mother was correct, and a Grendel still lives"—he paused and glared hard at me—"then there is absolutely *nothing* that you—or any of us—can do to stop it."

He held me with his glare for a few seconds, then spun on his heel and strode back toward the field and out of sight.

# CHAPTER 18

# IGGY

The bitterly cold air caught me like a slap to the face, momentarily driving the breath out of my lungs when I burst through the rear doors of the arena and into the late afternoon. I couldn't remember ever feeling as lost and alone as I did at that moment.

I hurtled across the snowy field, intending to run until I couldn't run anymore, but soon pulled up short at a steep embankment. The stream that bisected Vale's campus barred my way. That struck me as the ultimate irony: Among all my other failures, I couldn't even succeed at running away.

I stamped my foot in frustration. "Aaaahhhhhhh!"

"Aaaaahhhhhh!" came a cry from behind me.

I whirled around.

A few yards behind me, Grimsby fell toward Gwynn, who caught him as she came up behind him. He pointed at me accusingly with the giant foam finger he'd been wearing earlier. "Maybe warn a guy next time you decide to practice your Viking battle cries, eh?"

"What . . . ? Where did you guys even come from?" I said.

Gwynn gestured back toward the arena. "We saw you run out the back doors of the longhouse. Figured something was up."

"Yeah," said Grimsby, "we've been following you like halfway across campus calling your name."

"Oh," I said. "Yeah. There's sort of a few things on my mind."

"Anything we can help with?" said Gwynn.

I sighed. "Well, it's a long story."

"Does it look like we're busy?" Grimsby said, holding the giant finger to the side of his face like he was thinking.

So I filled them in on my conversation with Doc and the ensuing encounter with Chase's dad, leaving out only the part where we were all going to die grisly deaths at the hands of an army of mythical baddies.

"I can feel something building," I finished. "First there were the attacks on my dad and me. Then there's this weird journal that leads us to a sea monster in the school swimming pool. And now I find out there's someone hunting the Aesir. I wish I knew where it was all leading. Or even who . . . or what is behind the scenes, pulling the strings. But I can't put all the pieces together."

Gwynn stared at the ground, deep in thought. "Well, someone wanted you to have the journal. Seems like whoever it is wanted to help you."

"Help?" said Grimsby with a snort. "*Help?* Thanks, but I don't need the kind of help that ends with us being sea monster food."

Gwynn spread her hands. "But we didn't. That's the point. I think it's more like some kind of test." She looked at me. "You know, to prove that you're worthy of the truth. Or something like that."

I nodded slowly. "That kind of makes sense. So what do you think the next test is?" My whole body shivered, but not completely due to the cold.

She shrugged. "Only one way to find out."

"You mean find this world tree or whatever it is?" Grimsby said. "If you remember, we're sort of stuck on that one. It's not like there's a blinking neon sign somewhere that says 'This Way to Ye Olde World Tree.'"

We all fell silent, probably thinking the same thing: dead end.

I raked my hands through my hair in exasperation and turned around, staring helplessly at the frozen stream. Wait. The stream . . . the stream . . . Why did that remind me of something? Then a flash of inspiration hit me. I looked both directions up and down the stream's course.

Then I spun around to face my friends. "Maybe not a sign, exactly, but the next best thing. Gwynn, do you still have that old surveyor's map we found in the library?"

She swung her backpack off her shoulder and started to rummage through it. "I have it somewhere . . . Yeah, here it is." She slid out the map and handed it to me. "Why?"

I quickly unrolled it and held it out in front of myself, my friends crowding in to look too. "Because I thought I remembered . . . Yeah, there it is. See that symbol we thought was the greenhouse earlier? Notice any recognizable landmarks around it?"

Grimsby gave a little grunt of recognition, then stabbed at the map with his foam finger. "Sorry." He slid the finger off, then traced the curve of the stream. "The stream seems to run right past it."

I turned back toward campus, holding the old map out in front of me at arm's length. "But something doesn't seem right. According to this map, Vale's main hall should be over there." I pointed in the opposite direction, toward where the soccer fields were now located.

Gwynn slapped herself on the forehead. "Of course! I can't believe I forgot. The original campus was moved a long time ago. Something about the ground underneath being unstable."

A tingle of excitement shot through me as I turned back to follow the line of the stream to where it disappeared into the forest behind Vale. "So if we just follow the stream . . ."

Grimsby was nodding. "We find ourselves a world tree."

Overhead, dark clouds billowed across the sky, threatening an incoming storm. An icy breeze tugged at my hair and clothes.

Seeming to read my thoughts, Gwynn said, "We'd better get going if we don't want to be caught outside in this storm."

We jogged along the bank of the stream, soon arriving at the tree line, where dense undergrowth blocked our progress.

"Are there any trails that run close to here?" I said.

Grimsby scuttled down the embankment and first tried pressing one toe onto the ice, then his whole foot, and finally his entire weight. "Seems pretty solid to me. Makes as good a trail as anything, don't you think?"

Gwynn and I looked at each other, then shrugged and scrambled down after him and followed him onto the ice. If I was careful and slid my feet, I found that I could walk on the frozen stream without too much trouble.

As we entered the forest, the treetops overhead swayed ominously in the increasing wind. I turned up my collar against chilly gusts that gave me the eerie feeling of ghostly fingers sliding across my neck, grasping and hungry.

We stared around as we walked, looking for anything that resembled a world tree. But they all just looked like normal trees. Venturing deeper and deeper into the forest, my earlier feeling of frustration slowly crept back. It occurred to me that even following the stream we could very easily walk right past the tree, and with it what was probably the only chance to cure my dad. A solitary snowflake jerked and twisted toward the ground in the wind like a lone sentinel at the front of an army of white.

Grimsby froze suddenly, waving for us to stop. He cocked his head to one side. "Do you guys hear that?"

My heart raced as my eyes darted around. What had he heard? Was someone following us? I froze, but all I could hear was the wind. The creaking of the swaying trees. The . . . Wait, what was that? I stood as still as a statue. The sound was very faint, but when I strained my ears to listen, it sounded like . . .

"Is that someone singing?" Gwynn said, her eyes narrowing.

Grimsby cringed. "If you can call *that* singing. It sounds like one of those tone-deaf *American Idol* contestants."

"What do you think?" I said. "Should we go check it out?"

Grimsby stared ahead into the darkening trees. "Creepy forest. Three kids all alone. What could go wrong?"

Gwynn shook her head and stepped past him. "Did anyone ever tell you that you have an overactive imagination?"

As we followed Gwynn along the streambed, the singing grew louder. I still couldn't recognize the song, but the voice sounded distinctly male. There was also a dim light up ahead now. Had we circled our way back to the main Vale campus?

Suddenly we stumbled out of the trees into a large clearing that seemed to be illuminated with its own soft glow. The singing immediately went silent, like we'd tripped some sort of switch as we'd left the trees.

In the center of the clearing stood an enormous tree—so large that the stream split in two and circled around its base. The wind had died, and when I looked back, there was a distinct line where the stream magically transitioned from a block of ice to a happy burbling flow like it was the middle of summer. We all craned our necks upward, looking into the tree's canopy, which was so high we couldn't see the top from where we stood.

Grimsby whispered, "Just a wild guess, but I think we may have found the world tree."

I looked around the clearing. But where was the mystery singer?

"Hello?" I called.

*Hello?* I winced as my own voice echoed loudly back to me. I guessed it had something to do with the acoustics of the clearing.

I knelt down next to the stream, letting my fingertips skate across the surface of the water. It was surprisingly warm. My frozen fingers prickled as they thawed, and then the warmth continued all the way up my arm. In my reflection in the water, my eyebrows pressed together in confused wonder as the feeling spread throughout my body, filling me with a peaceful, golden glow.

Suddenly there was a movement in the reflected shadows above me. An almost-imperceptible shift. I spun around, craning my neck upward, my heart racing.

Nothing. The branches overhead were empty.

"See something?" Gwynn whispered, kneeling down next to me.

"Is someone there?" I called out, my voice cracking.

*Is someone there?* echoed back.

*This is silly*, I thought. I'd only seen a leaf stir in the wind or an animal scurrying through the branches.

"Silly!" I said out loud, as if trying to convince myself.

*Silly!*

It occurred to me that it was strange how my voice echoed back to me like this. If anything, it seemed like the dense forest around me should absorb my voice, not echo it.

"You guys feel that too, right?" Grimsby said, shuddering like he'd just seen a spider crawling across his hand. "Like there's someone watching us?"

I walked to the other side of the clearing to get a better look around, but all I could see was the giant tree. I gestured to Gwynn to circle around the other way. Maybe someone was hiding on the other side, sneakily keeping the tree between us and them. We met on the other side. Nothing.

"Where are you?" I tried, teetering on the edge between panic and morbid curiosity.

*Where are you?* The echo used my words, but somehow now that I was listening more closely, it didn't sound like my voice.

"Are you copying me?" I asked, turning in a slow circle to listen for the direction of the reply.

*Are you copying me?* This time it was accompanied by a little giggle. It seemed to come from behind me, but when I turned, there was still only the tree.

"Cut it out!" I said.

*Cut it out!*

Grimsby held out his hand. "Hold on. My little sister likes to play this game all the time. There's only one way to get her to stop." He paused, looking around, then said, "Cinnamon has no synonym. Try that five times fast."

*Cinnamon has no synonym.* After the fifth time, all was quiet again.

Grimsby frowned appraisingly. "That was pretty—"

*Six sticky skeletons.*

He turned to us with his eyebrows raised questioningly.

"I . . . think it's a challenge," Gwynn said. "Let me give it a try." She repeated the line perfectly five times, then pumped her fist in the air. "That all you got?"

"Here," I said. "I've got one: The stump thunk the skunk stunk."

*The stump thunk the skump. The thump . . . Ugh, I can never get that one.*

"Ha!" I said. "Who are you? Stop hiding and show yourself."

There was silence for a few seconds, then: *My name is Iggy.*

We all looked around. Nothing.

"But where are you?" Gwynn said.

*I am the tree, and the tree is me.*

Grimsby frowned. "Very funny. No, really. Where are you?"

*You mean you've never talked to a tree before?*

I thought for a second. "Okay, fine," I said to the tree. "If you're the tree talking to us, then do something, uh, tree-ish."

I heard a rustling noise from above, then a swirl of leaves fell to the ground at our feet. Looking down, I saw that the leaves formed a picture of a face with its tongue sticking out.

"Noooo wayyyy," we all said together.

I jerked my head back up toward the tree. "You *are* talking!"

*What is it the kids say these days? Well, DUH . . .* There was the sound of a throat clearing, then in a deep, resonating voice, the tree continued, *I am the mighty, all-knowing world tree, supporter of the heavens and the earth. Also I like tacos. You don't have any, do you?*

We all stared at each other, then back at the tree, and slowly shook our heads. No tacos.

*Cat got your tongue? Penny for your thoughts? You have vanquished me in the time-honored battle of the twisting of the tongues. So now you may ask me something. Anything.*

"Well . . ." I said, slowly edging away as I remembered that in Norse myths the world tree was protected by a giant angry squirrel. "I'm kind of stuck right now. But I'm not sure it's exactly something you can help with." I shook my head. Was I really talking to a tree?

*Maybe something about . . . your dad?*

I froze. "Wait. You know about my dad?"

*Uh, maybe you missed the part about the all-knowing world*

*tree? You know, from, like, two seconds ago? Stay with me, kid. Of course I know about him. I even know where you need to go to help him.*

Gwynn and I exchanged a startled look.

"You do?" I nearly shouted. "How? I mean, where?"

*Easy. Your answer lies in the Well of Weird.*

"The Well of Weird? No, seriously."

*Really. It's a well. And,* boy, *is it weird.*

I looked back at Gwynn and Grimsby, but they only shrugged and shook their heads. I narrowed my eyes. "Okay, then how do we get there?"

*Well, I can't exactly just draw a map for you. That would be against the rules. Also, I don't have any hands.*

I spread my hands. "What rules? How am I supposed to find it, then?"

*I guess I could . . . hmmm . . . Yeah, I think it would be okay to give you a clue. Let me think. Yeah, how about this?*

The ground started to vibrate. I threw my hands out to steady myself and stared down nervously. Earthquake? But then I recognized what it was. The tree . . . seemed to be humming. Then out of nowhere it sang:

> *In order for your dad to save*
> *A secret from beyond the grave*
> *You'll need to find, then hold your breath*
> *And you will surely conquer death.*

I ground my teeth in frustration, realizing this was some sort of riddle. Why couldn't someone just give us a straightforward answer for once?

The tree warbled out the last line in an out-of-tune falsetto. Apparently we'd found the mysterious singer with the awful voice. I waited, expecting more. Fifteen seconds ticked by. A minute.

I closed my eyes and slowly mashed my fist against my forehead. "That was . . . it? That was the clue?" I didn't see how that helped with *any*thing.

*Pfft, I'm all, "Best clue ever! Hashtag winning!" and she's all, "Duuude, that was it?"*

I repeated the lines to myself, trying to make sense of what they meant. What did it mean by "a secret from beyond the grave"? I looked up at the branches. "Why should I believe you about any of this? I mean, no offense, but you're a . . . tree."

*Look, bro. Can I call you bro? A wise tree once said, "Sometimes to see clearly you just need to change your perspective." Spoiler alert: That wise tree . . . was me. You might be surprised what you can see from up here. Anyway, on to the reeeaaallly important stuff. Can you do something for me now?*

"Uh, sure?" I said.

The ground started to vibrate again, and this time I recognized the vibrations as bouncy guitar chords I'd heard somewhere. I looked around in surprise as out of nowhere a piano joined them. Then the tree launched into Elvis Presley's "All Shook Up."

"Wait! Hold on!" I shouted, lowering my hands from my ears as the tree stopped singing.

*What's wrong? I was too pitchy, wasn't I?*

I raised an eyebrow. It struck me as ironic that an all-knowing world tree had no clue it was a terrible singer. "No, not at all," I lied. "It sounded, um, fine. Really."

*Well, thank you. Thank you very much*, the tree said, doing its best Elvis impression.

"I'm sorry," I said, throwing my hands up in frustration, "but I don't see how what you said helps me at all. Can you give me any other clues?"

But if the tree heard me, it didn't bother to answer. It was busy practicing its Elvis impression.

"Excuse me, um, Iggy?" Gwynn tried. "Iggy!"

*Thank you very much. Thank YOU very much . . .*

"Abby?" came Grimsby's voice. But I was too busy trying to get the tree's attention.

"Um, ABBY?" Louder this time.

"WHAT?" I whirled around.

Grimsby shot out his hands to protect himself and then pointed at my backpack, which lay on the ground a couple of feet away.

I dropped my gaze. In the surrounding gloom, I could see the bag glowing with a faint greenish light. I ran across to it and yanked the zipper open, pulling out the journal. On its cover the second rune looked like it was on fire. The tree rune.

"We did it!" Gwynn said. "We found Yggdrasil."

Grimsby nodded slowly. "Or Iggy, I guess."

I wanted to feel excited that we were only one more step away from helping my dad. If that really was what this was all about. But instead I felt more frustrated than anything. "Only . . ." I looked back up at the tree. "It wasn't exactly what I was expecting."

*THANK YOU VERY MUUUUUCH*, the tree said.

Actually, not at all what I'd expected. A flash of light brought my gaze back to the journal. The new rune settled into a deep green color.

"That leaves only one more to find," Grimsby said with a weak smile. "The final rune."

"Maybe final in more ways than one," I said.

I stared into the night, where I could see snow swirling beyond our protected glade, anticipating what lay ahead for us out there but not wanting to name it.

Somewhere out there was the final test. The one that would lead us to death.

# CHAPTER 19

# LODBROK'S CONFESSION

Asgard's village square was crowded with families eating and laughing together, as if there was nothing unusual about a Viking community living underneath suburban Minneapolis. Nearby a little girl sat across from her dad. She giggled as a long string of gooey cheese stretched from her slice of pizza. I silently wished it could be me and my dad. *Soon*, I told myself. *We'll sit right there and share a pizza. With pineapple for Dad's half, just how he likes it. Really soon.*

Grimsby clutched his stomach. "What's the rune for cheese fries? I'm starving!"

I shook the snow out of my hair and brushed off my jacket. "What, do snowstorms make you hungry too?" Outside, the wind and snow had escalated into a full-on blizzard.

"I think eating makes him hungry," Gwynn said. "But since it's dinnertime, it's probably not a bad idea to get some food and talk about our plan."

I turned to scan the shop fronts, wondering if anything could jump-start my appetite. It felt like I'd barely eaten anything since we'd arrived at Vale. But between worrying about my dad and struggling to figure out how I could possibly fulfill the promise I'd made to my mom, somehow I just hadn't been hungry.

Suddenly my heart froze. I ducked behind one of the huge timber pillars that supported the ceiling.

"Everything okay?" Grimsby said, looking up from where he was sitting nearby, trying to knock snow out of his loafer. He turned to follow my stare. "Ohhhhhhh."

Only ten feet away, Mr. Lodbrok waited in line for coffee, his foot tapping impatiently while he repeatedly glanced down at his watch.

"I don't think he saw me," I said.

Gwynn started to move toward him. "Want me to—"

"NO!" I said, clutching at her sleeve, then lowering my voice. "No. Thanks. I'm not sure I'm ready to face him again yet. Or maybe ever."

The barista slid a cup across the counter to him.

"Does that look like my name?" he growled, pointing at the cup. "Or does Vale not teach reading anymore?"

"Really?" I said, my fingers curling into fists as I watched the girl scramble to find his order while attempting to fight back tears.

She handed him a new cup, and I ducked out of sight when Mr. Lodbrok turned toward us, steam obscuring his features as he sipped his coffee. He strode by without noticing us and continued across the square, looking like he had something urgent to do.

It occurred to me that I didn't know what his role was in the

Viking community. If Professor Roth ran the school, and Doc taught and coached knattleikr . . . then what was Mr. Lodbrok's role, exactly? I mean, other than chief jerk. He was up to something. And he was tied up in all this business somehow; I just knew it. And what was his deal with my mom? And me? There was only one way to find out.

Then, my feet moving almost before my brain had made the decision, I started after him.

A hand caught my arm. "Abby . . ."

I spun toward Gwynn. "What?"

She stared at me, her eyes narrowing in concern. "I see that look in your eyes. What are you planning to do?"

I shot a look over my shoulder. It took me a minute to find Mr. Lodbrok disappearing into the crowd. If I didn't go now, I'd miss him. "Nothing. Just . . . I'll be right back."

She let go of my arm and glanced over at Grimsby before turning back to me. "Need any help?"

"No, I've got this. You guys get some dinner. I'll only be a minute. Really."

"Okay, just don't do anything stupid."

Well, I couldn't guarantee that. I sprinted in the last direction I'd seen Chase's dad heading, feeling the flame of anger I'd felt earlier building with each step. Had I already lost him? I jumped up onto a chair and jerked my head from side to side, scanning the crowd. There he was, disappearing down a corridor on the opposite side of the village square. I leapt down off the chair and raced after him.

The hall was empty and quiet when I arrived, the noise of the crowd quickly falling away. I crept forward slowly now past doors and more hallways on both sides, worried I wouldn't be able to find him in this maze. What else was down here? The garage Grimsby had speculated about, with tricked-out vehicles and possibly some warships? Maybe a Viking workout room? I imagined a bunch of huge dudes playing catch with telephone poles or bench-pressing small cars.

". . . are we going to explain this?"

I froze, recognizing Mr. Lodbrok's angry voice coming from inside a door just up ahead. I snuck closer and pressed my body against the wall outside.

"Yes, sir. I'm sorry, sir. It won't happen again." It was a second male voice, which I didn't recognize.

"The sea monster, or octopus, or whatever it was"—Mr. Lodbrok paused—"was meant to kill her."

My heart nearly stopped. The sea monster was supposed to kill *her*? Was supposed to kill *me*? Had Unferth Lodbrok just confessed to attempted murder?

"Now we have to try to make it look like the whole thing never happened," he snapped. "Do you think you can handle that much?"

Then the other voice again: "Yes, sir, I will. You can count on me. Like it never happened, sir."

"Good. See to it, then. I can't have this getting out." I heard his voice getting nearer, and I frantically looked around for somewhere to hide. But there was nowhere. Then Mr. Lodbrok strode through the door and down the hall away from me without even a glance in my direction. He pressed his palm flat against a panel next to a door. It slid open and he disappeared inside.

I stood there pinned against the wall, stunned. Whatever I'd thought he was up to, murdering me wasn't even remotely on the list. His earlier words came back to me: *If a Grendel still lives, then there is absolutely nothing that you—or any of us—can do to stop it.* If he believed that, what would he do? Would he go so far as to join the Grendel to try to save his own life and his son's? It made sense, now that I thought about it. I mean, how else could someone track down the Aesir so easily unless someone on the inside was helping track them down? Had he sent the Grendel after me in North Carolina?

The sounds of angry muttering cut off by the door next to me slamming closed jerked me out of my thoughts. I blinked and shook my head, then eyed the door down the hall where Mr. Lodbrok had disappeared.

*No*, I thought even as the idea started to form. *That's ridiculous.* But . . .

If I wanted to prove the Grendel was real—that we were all in grave danger—and if Mr. Lodbrok was somehow in league with it, then continuing to tail him seemed like my best chance. Either for finding the Grendel or speeding up my inevitable death.

Or both. I wasn't sure.

I looked both ways. The hall was empty. Now was my chance. If I thought too long about it, I'd chicken out. I crossed to the door, and my hand hesitated over the touch pad for only a second before I pressed it.

The door slid open to blackness. A stale breath of air wafted from the room. An image of walking into the gaping maw of a giant flickered through my head.

*Your mother was a fool.*

I set my jaw. *And her daughter is here to wipe that smug look off your face.*

I stepped inside. The door slid shut behind me, plunging me into blackness. I stopped. What now? I closed my eyes and let my other senses explore the room like I'd learned in my training. Silence. No sounds of movement. The faint smells of steel and cleaning oil like my training space at home.

A tingle of foreboding somewhere deep in my brain made me hesitate just as I was about to step forward. Was it possible that Mr. Lodbrok could be lying in wait for me in the dark? No. That was silly. He hadn't seen me. Probably. *Okay,* I told myself, *now you're being ridiculous. You're not going to bail out just because of a little darkness.*

I ventured farther into the room, and a row of lights flickered on along one wall. Motion sensors, I guessed. From what I could now see, the room looked like some sort of training gym. A row of Viking helmets and swords lined the illuminated wall alongside what were either battle training machines or exotic torture devices. Mr. Lodbrok was nowhere in sight. There must have been another exit from the room.

I crossed over to the display of helmets. They were either pretty great replicas or real Viking helmets, with rounded iron caps and nose-bridge guards, many of them bearing the marks of actual battle. None of the silly horned helmets that most people mistakenly associate with Vikings. I'd had a plastic version that I used to wear around everywhere as a kid. It's amazing how fast other kids get out of your way on the playground slide when you're coming up the other way wearing a helmet with pointy horns.

I lifted a helmet off the rack and carefully slid it onto my head. Then I turned toward a nearby mirror. Not to brag or anything, but I looked pretty awesome. I growled at my reflection.

Next I examined a row of swords. They were a variety of sizes and colors, and it felt kind of like picking a ball at a bowling alley. I chose one with an intricately designed silver handle and pulled. With a metallic *hisssk*, it slid free of its sheath. The blade was as black as coal and gleamed faintly in the dim light. I took a practice swing, stumbled, and almost fell. *Real cool, Abby.* It was a little heavier than the wooden training swords I was used to. But it wasn't like there were numbers on these like on bowling balls to help you pick the right size. It occurred to me at that point that I'd let these cool toys distract me while I should have been looking for Mr. Lodbrok.

But right as I was about to put the sword back, somewhere above me a chime sounded. Then the room went completely black.

# CHAPTER 20

# THE VIKING QUEEN

I froze. Even my heart stopped beating for a second as a shiver of dread shot through me. What. Was. Happening? I'd been so distracted playing dress-up that I'd forgotten about the possibility of danger.

That's when I heard the drums. Initially I thought it was my own heart thumping in my ears. A rhythmic pounding noise. Faint at first, then growing steadily louder. But it wasn't my heart.

A gentle breeze stirred against my face, carrying with it the unmistakable scent of salt air. This was getting weirder. Had the air-conditioning just kicked on?

Then the floor seemed to heave gently and sway. I attributed this to my overactive imagination until a particularly sharp jerk made me stumble. Fortunately, I caught myself before I sprawled on my face. Along with the steady pounding noise, I could now hear a complaining creak and groan of wood each time the floor rolled. Then a seagull's cry.

A faint light shone behind me. I turned. A fiery crimson sun broke over a horizon, illuminating a forest of at least a hundred iron helmets around me, all glowing bloodred. A small cry of fear escaped my lips as I stared into the grizzled, battle-scarred faces of a horde of Viking warriors.

With the aid of the dawn light, I could now see what the pounding noise was. Each warrior was thumping his sword hilt, staff, or club in unison onto the floor. No, not a floor. A deck. A shadow loomed over me as the deck rolled again, and I cowered instinctively. Looking up, I saw a dragon-head prow staring menacingly back at me. Then came a sharp snapping noise, and I turned as a massive white sail with the silhouette of a raven painted on it in black bellied in the wind. My breath was coming in shallow gasps as all the sensory overload threatened to overwhelm me. But as much as my brain refused to believe it, there was no denying—I was on a Viking raiding ship. It was like I'd been dropped into the middle of an IMAX movie. How was that possible?

*Okay, okay*, I told myself. There has to be some rational explanation for this. Only a minute ago, I'd been in a training room and— That's when it hit me. Yes! This had to be another sort of illusion. Like the fires in the sconces. The moving tapestries. I backed up another step, tripped over something, and began to fall. A strong hand grabbed the front of my shirt and hauled me forward before I pitched over the ship's edge into the heaving waves.

That shouldn't be possible in an illusion. Right?

"Don't be too anxious, child," the Viking said, grinning at me through a mouth of missing teeth. "There'll be plunder enough for us all."

Plunder? *This isn't real*, I told myself. *This isn't real. This isn't—*

The wail of a horn pierced the air somewhere behind me. I spun around. Across the waves, a small village of mud-and-straw huts clustered not far from the shoreline. People in medieval-type clothing screamed and ran in panic. A stream of humanity flowed toward the walls of a gigantic stone castle in the distance.

The sights. The smells. The sounds. My brain screamed that this was all too real as I fought to hold on to the last shred of my sanity. I was somehow at the front of a Viking raiding party. And we were about to land.

With a splash and a grind of protesting wood, the ship jerked to a halt ten feet from the shore. Two men scrambled to drop a wooden ramp into the water. I flinched as a chorus of battle horns blasted in my ear. Then I was jostled forward as warriors began to advance all around me with loud cries and savage screams. Carried along by the invaders, I stumbled down the ramp and felt freezing water soak my boots as I stepped into the ocean. The shock of the cold water was exactly what I needed to jerk me back to reality before I was trampled to death under a wave of horsehair boots.

I shook my head and took off at a jog, splashing through the remaining water and up onto the beach. All around me, Vikings stormed onto the shore and into the village, yelling wildly and smashing in the doors of the simple dwellings as they set fire to their thatched roofs. The acrid smell of smoke preceded the heat of flames, which seared my face as a roof nearby exploded into a fireball. I was relieved to notice that all the villagers seemed to have escaped behind the castle walls by this point.

As weird as it seemed, I was actually starting to get into the whole scene. Or at least the adrenaline rush was switching over from "Run for your life!" to "How sweet is this?!" After all, the holograms I'd seen earlier were pretty impressive. This *had* to be another of them. There was no other explanation that made sense. It was like dropping into the world's most realistic video game. So I shoved aside the little part of my brain that still screamed danger and instead, with a barbaric yell of my own, joined a band of raiders heading for the castle.

As we neared the open field surrounding the fortified walls, a row of defenders armed with pitchforks, shovels, and rusted plow blades stepped forward to block our way. They clustered tightly together and raised a mismatched collection of iron pot lids and wagon wheels like shields to form a human barricade. The invading Vikings formed their own tight phalanx, raising their shields into a battering ram. I found to my surprise that I was wearing a shield on one arm, so I raised it too and ran ahead at full speed.

With a mighty crash, we smashed into the defenders. For a few moments their line held. I pushed with all my strength, close enough to smell the rancid breath of my opponent on the other side and be sprayed by spit from his labored breathing. Then their line broke, and we plunged into chaos as Vikings and defenders clashed in hand-to-hand combat on all sides.

Stinky Breath Guy, thin, red-faced, and in a dented helmet

that resembled an overturned cooking pot, charged at me with pitchfork raised. I lifted my sword just in time to block his blow. The loud clang of metal on metal reverberated through my arm so badly that I almost dropped my weapon. Then a burly Norseman slammed into him from the side, and with a grunt both of them went down.

Nearby someone shouted, "To me! To me! Take the castle!"

My eyes searched the melee for the source of the cry. A tall Viking with long flaming-red hair stood atop an overturned wagon, waving an ax in the air. A woman. She seemed to be the leader, because the others swarmed to her call. I leapt over the struggling men at my feet and ran after the tall Viking as she jumped down from the wagon and sprinted toward the castle. We rushed up a small rise to a stone bridge that ended at the castle gate. The defenders hadn't had a chance to fully close the gate yet. To give the men inside more time, a fresh group of soldiers swarmed out from behind the wall.

The tall red-haired Viking turned directly toward me. "Take my back!"

Suddenly I couldn't move.

I recognized the Viking queen. It was my mom.

The battle around me seemed to go into slow motion, the sound of the clashing weapons quieting to a murmur. How . . . how was she here?

Years of emotion welled up in my chest. Feelings I hadn't realized I still had until now. I'd always told myself that I was okay. That I'd gotten past the pain of losing her. But now I realized the truth: Her death was still a hot, painful wound that remained open even after all these years.

The ring of steel nearby snapped me back to the present. I ducked just in time to avoid a sword aimed right at my head. I felt a small sting as the *whoosh* of metal narrowly missed making me permanently a foot shorter. I reached up to touch my ear, and my hand came back bloody.

But instead of fear, I only felt anger. Anger rising in me like a searing flame. I charged into the defender with a roar and catapulted him over the side of the bridge. He fell into the moat below with a yelp and a splash.

My mom glanced over her shoulder at me appraisingly and grinned. I was fired up now. I pressed my back to hers, and we fought through the throng back-to-back. The solidness of her shoulders and the muscles in her torso as she swung her battle-ax in great arcs made me feel invincible. I stabbed and swung my sword in a frenzy, warding off defenders with a fury I hadn't known I possessed as we battled our way toward the castle gate.

In a few short minutes, we were on the verge of breaching the gate. I was on a high that said no wall or gate could stop us now. Then, out of nowhere, tiny white gaps began to appear and grow in the scene around me, like I was looking at a tapestry being eaten by a thousand moths. With a gasp, I spun around in time to see my mom's form slowly dissolving into the blank whiteness.

Her hand reached toward me, and for a second it seemed that her eyes focused on mine. "My little Grendel hunter . . ." she breathed, then faded into nothing.

"Mom! No!" I screamed as I reached for her. But she was gone.

I was back in the training gym. Alone. I fell to my knees and let my sword clatter to the floor. As high as I'd been seconds ago, I felt that low now. Crushed. A combination of sweat and tears streamed down my face. It had been the most alive I'd ever felt, fighting back-to-back with my mom.

And now she was gone. Again.

Somewhere off to one side, I heard a door open and the sound of running feet.

"Abby!" someone yelled. Footsteps sprinted toward me. "Oh no! You're hurt!" It was Gwynn. She gasped, evidently having spotted my bloody ear.

Without raising my head, I said in a rough voice, "It's just a nick. I'll be fine."

She knelt and tentatively touched my ear. "You're lucky that's all it is. The simulation was set to 'berserker.' That's basically Viking for 'insane.' No one has ever tried that level. It's amazing you even survived."

"So it wasn't real after all?" I still clung to the image of my mom even though I knew it was just that. An image. "But I could smell the ocean. Feel the"—I winced as I lifted my sore arm—"the defenders pounding on me. How is that possible?"

"We call it VIC." She pronounced it with a long "i" like "bike." "Short for Virtual Immersion Chamber. And yeah, it's very realistic. That was your mom's goal."

I jerked my head up, searching her eyes for a minute before I made the connection. "You mean she . . . she built this?" I choked on the words, then stared at the floor again and put my hands over my face. "I saw her . . . in there."

Gwynn placed a hand on my shoulder. "I know. Yes, she came up with the idea for this training simulator. She programmed many of the simulations using actual warriors as models for realistic human movement, like they do in movies and video games. She was a brilliant scientist."

I bristled a little at the word "was," even though I knew Gwynn didn't mean anything by it. "How did I . . . I mean, what happened just now? If this VIC thing is so deadly, shouldn't there be some sort of password or something? Or at least a sign on the door? 'Warning: Potential death or dismemberment' or something like that?"

"There are . . . or were, at least." She looked back the way I'd come in. "That door is never left unlocked. How did you even get in here?"

I suddenly remembered the reason I'd come into the room in the first place. I gripped her hand. "Mr. Lodbrok! I have to tell you . . ." I trailed off, glancing around the room for any sign of him. But my least favorite member of the Grey Council was nowhere in sight. Had he lured me in here to finish the job he'd failed to do with the sea monster? Could he be somewhere listening right now? I decided I couldn't risk letting him know I'd overheard him.

I looked back at Gwynn. "I'll have to tell you later. Anyway, how'd you find me?"

Gwynn shrugged. "The whole Valkyrie thing, remember? Sensing people in danger? And just in time too," she teased, punching me in the shoulder. "Before you . . ." She drew her finger across her throat.

"What do you mean?" I protested. "We were just about to take the castle!"

"What you missed, hero, was the giant vat of boiling tar the defenders were just about to pour on your little raiding party. I hear it's a natural remedy for all sorts of things. Warts . . . toe fungus . . . *living*."

I went wide-eyed and shuddered at the thought. "I do like hot showers, but that's a little extreme." Then I remembered. "'My little Grendel hunter . . .'"

Gwynn frowned. "Sorry?"

"In the simulation. Right before my mom disappeared. That's what she said. 'My little Grendel hunter.' There was a split second there when I was sure she recognized me. Like she was talking right to me. I mean, that's what she used to call me. It was . . . weird."

We sat in silence for a few seconds while Gwynn bandaged my ear, then I finally shrugged and looked at her. "It's not the first weird feeling I've had since I got here. To Vale, I mean. To grow up a Viking myself and have no idea any of this even existed. All this stuff I never knew about my mom, I guess because she died when I was still so young, and I never asked my dad because it's still hard for him to talk about her. My head literally hasn't stopped . . ." I trailed off and narrowed my eyes. There was something off about Gwynn's expression. "Speaking of weird feelings, I'm picking up one from you now. Is something wrong?"

My back pocket buzzed. I slid my phone out. Four missed calls. Several new text messages. My stomach gave a little lurch.

Gwynn studied my injured ear and fiddled with the bandages. "Are you sure you're okay? Maybe we should have you—"

"Gwynn." I grabbed her wrist. "I'm fine. What is it? What happened?"

She sighed. "We need to go to Asgard's medical clinic."

"But I told you. I think I'm okay."

"No, it's not that." I could tell she was trying to find the right words. The way she averted her eyes seemed anything but good. "I've been looking for you everywhere. There's been some news. About your dad. Something's . . . wrong."

# CHAPTER 21

# A GRIM PROGNOSIS

We burst through a pair of doors in Asgard's medical wing labeled "ICU." Unlike "VIC," this abbreviation I knew all too well: intensive care unit. The place people go when they're in serious trouble.

"Wait, why are we here?" I said. "I thought we were going to visit my dad. You know, in the hospital?"

Gwynn bit her lip as she looked back over her shoulder at me. "He was moved here an hour ago. I guess the facilities are—"

My gasp cut her off. Through a window, I'd spotted my dad's still form lying on a bed among a coil of wires trailing from machines.

I ran to his side. Staring down into his pale face, my eyes blurred with tears. In just the space of time since I'd last seen him at breakfast, his features had shockingly thinned. His cheekbones jutted sharply against his skin like poles holding up a collapsed tent.

"What . . ." The words caught in my throat. "What happened?"

Gwynn met my gaze across the bed, sympathy filling her eyes.

I reached for his motionless fingers but paused with my hand in the air. "Is it okay? Holding his hand won't hurt him?"

"Of course not," said a voice behind me. I turned and saw Dr. Swenson sweep into the room. "I'm so glad Gwynn was able to find you, Abby. When your father's condition worsened, we knew we had to move him to Asgard to monitor his condition more closely. As you can probably see, the facilities down here are even better than those of the public hospital."

"What happened?" I repeated. "Just this morning he looked fine. Or, well, at least way better than *this*."

The doctor shook her head. "As you know, we've had a team hard at work researching the svefnthorn. From the scant historical evidence we have to work with, we estimated that the sting of one thorn alone is fairly, let's say, inconvenient at most. Its effects might be something similar to, for example, a high-dose sleeping pill."

"But?" I said, hearing a hesitation in her voice.

She nodded and turned to look down at my dad. "But as I mentioned, your attacker was seemingly firing clusters of these thorns at you. Your father was hit by at least a dozen of them. That many at one time will . . ." She paused, searching for the right words.

"Will what?" I asked, fighting back a darkness creeping into my mind. "Just say it. I can handle it."

"Will cause his heart to slow." She gave me a sympathetic look. "Until it completely stops."

My head swam, and the room dimmed around me. Dr. Swenson and Gwynn grabbed my arms and guided me to a nearby chair. I suddenly wished I could take back the words "I can handle it." I couldn't handle this at all. Fresh from just losing my mom again, the thought of losing my dad now was too much.

"I'm afraid, as we're seeing in your father's case," continued Dr. Swenson, "without prompt treatment there comes a tipping point where the venom's effects accelerate precipitously. And with no known cure—"

"Hold on," Gwynn cut in. "We may know one. A cure, I mean. Sort of. At least we think it . . . We just have to . . . find it first." She seemed almost too flustered to put the words together. "Abby, do you have the journal?"

I shrugged off my backpack and slid out the small book, flipping it open to the bookmarked page before handing it to Dr. Swenson. "It's right here. An old botanist's journal that we think talks about growing the svefnthorn somewhere on Vale's campus."

Dr. Swenson studied the page. "Well," she said without looking up, "this would certainly speed up our efforts at deriving a cure if we could extract some of the nectar from the plant itself. Assuming it works as the entry here suggests. We're at best still several weeks away from manufacturing an antivenom on our own."

I clung to her words like they were the last lifeline keeping me from drowning in a cold black ocean.

She closed the book and handed it back to me. "If you can tell me where the plant is, I can have someone take a sample right away." She lifted the receiver from a red hospital phone on the wall and looked at us expectantly. Then, seeing our faces, she put it back in its cradle. "What's wrong?"

I looked at Gwynn, then back at the doctor. "That's . . . the problem. We haven't exactly found the plant yet. We aren't even sure if it still exists." I could almost feel the brief swell of excitement in the room crash and fade away like a wave from the shore.

"Oh," said Dr. Swenson. "I see."

Gwynn, trying bravely to sound hopeful, said, "But we will. We just need some time and I'm sure we'll find it."

Dr. Swenson folded her hands in front of her, then looked down at my dad. "You'll need to hurry. From my estimates, your father only has at best—"

Just then a paging system pinged on and a voice overhead talked over the doctor as it called her to another area of the clinic. But I thought I heard her say "four to eight." Weeks? I guessed.

My desperate brain immediately switched into problem-solving mode. "Okay, that's . . ." I paused and calculated in my head. "At least twenty-eight days. Maybe more. We can find it by then, right? Even if we have to turn Vale upside down."

"My apologies," Dr. Swenson said grimly. "I believe I was drowned out by the paging system. What I said was forty-eight *hours*. And that's a best-case scenario. Based on your father's current rate of decline, I would estimate that if we aren't able to administer some sort of countermeasure by"—she looked down at her watch—"perhaps midnight tomorrow, then I fear it will be too late."

With that, the lifeline snapped, and I was tumbling into the dark waters. Falling. Sinking. "What?!" I gasped. "That's all?"

"I'm very sorry," said Dr. Swenson, "but I have to go attend to another matter at the moment. I promise you, we're doing everything we can to save your father. If you'd like to stay, I'll return as quickly as possible so that we can discuss this more." She encircled my free hand with her own and squeezed. "The important thing is not to give up hope. Not yet. Our best chance is if you can find the svefnthorn. And quickly."

As she turned and rushed out the door, Grimsby's words from my first day at Vale came back to me: *Abandon hope, all ye who enter here*. I hadn't known then how fitting it would be. I slumped farther into my chair and stared helplessly at my dad.

"How are we supposed to find it by midnight tomorrow?" I said to Gwynn, tears brimming in my eyes.

She pointed to the journal. "We found the second rune already. That means we're just one step away."

I waved my hand in frustration. "At least we had some idea what we were looking for then. But the last rune . . . Death? What's that supposed to mean? How do you find *death*?"

I squeezed my eyes closed and felt hot tears slide down my cheeks. Then I felt Gwynn's hand on my shoulder. For a few minutes, we stayed like that without speaking, the only sounds the white noise of activity in the ICU outside the room punctuated by the regular beeping of my dad's heart monitor beside us.

Finally I broke the silence. "I failed him."

Gwynn squeezed my shoulder. "No. You didn't. This *isn't* your fault."

"Maybe not completely," I said. "But I can't help but think that after he basically threw away his life to make sure I had one, what happens? The first time he really needs me, I freeze up. Act like a scared little kid. And now he's dying."

Gwynn didn't say anything, as if she sensed there was more I needed to get out.

"After my mom died, it was just Dad and me against the world. I remember this one time when he pulled up to drop me off at school. It was a drizzly gray morning." I nodded slowly, remembering it like it was yesterday. "She'd been gone for more than a year. But I was still in a dark place and getting worse, somehow not able to get past it and move on. Angry at the world, you know?

"Anyway, on the radio the intro to 'YMCA' starts playing. And Dad loves his oldies. But this one? It's one of his favorites. He stares at the radio for a minute like he's thinking, then suddenly he cranks up the volume and throws his car door open. I slide down farther into my seat as he comes around to my side, opens the door, and reaches out a hand toward me. And I have no idea what he has in mind, so I just say, 'What?'

"'It's time to start living again,' he says.

"Of course, we're sitting practically in front of the school's front doors, so there are kids all around us. There's 'YMCA' blasting into the schoolyard, and kids' heads are turning to see what's going on. I—"

My breath caught in my throat, leaving me unable to continue. In the background the steady beeping and whooshing noises filled the room.

After I didn't say anything for a while, still lost in the memory, Gwynn finally prompted, "So what happened?"

I shrugged. "I took his hand. And that morning went down in Kleckner Elementary history as the day Angus Beckett led a dance party in the school parking lot. Because the strangest thing was, after the other kids stopped staring at us kicking our feet and spelling Y-M-C-A over our heads like a couple of lunatics, a few of them actually joined in. Then more. It was just like in one of those old musicals where everyone spontaneously drops everything and starts to dance."

I looked back over my shoulder at Gwynn. "That was the first time I was able to shake off the darkness that had eaten at me since my mom's death. I eventually crawled out of that pit. Because of my dad. But I guess that's the kind of person he is. In spite of everything we've gone through, he's always able to find the positive in any situation. It's like some weird happy disease you get when you're around him. If your cup is half-empty, then he's got plenty to share from his own."

Gwynn didn't say anything for a while, then: "So what do you think he would do right now? If that was you lying there instead of him?"

I laughed a little, wiping away a tear. "Probably tell me to get my rear end out of bed already."

Gwynn laughed too. "He sounds like a great dad. But you know what that story tells me?"

"What's that?"

"That he wouldn't give up."

I nodded slowly. "Never."

"And neither should you." She looked at me earnestly. "Not while there's any hope left. You can count on me to help you out." She made a mock grimace and continued, "And Grimsby, I guess. For whatever that's worth."

I laughed through my tears. She was right, of course. There's no way I was giving up. But as I looked up at the clock on the wall, each movement of its second hand matched the beating of my dad's heart monitor as if counting down the final seconds of his life.

# CHAPTER 22

# RETURN TO THE FORGE

In a dream, I ran down a long tunnel that seemed to telescope out farther and farther as I ran. My dad called to me from one end: "This is what you trained for. You *can* do the YMCA." From the other end, my mom's voice floated to my ears: "My little Grendel hunter . . ." I was paralyzed, not knowing which way to go.

Then the scene shifted, and I stood in the middle of the knattleikr field. I was the last Aesir, and the stadium seats were filled with monstrous forms, snarling and taunting me. Among them, a single figure stood, towering over the rest and wearing a cloak that blazed as if made of flames. "Do you really think you can stop me? One little girl?" The fiery figure swept its arms forward, motioning for the horde to attack.

Just as they fell on me in a swarm, I jerked awake. Blinking my eyes, I sat up slowly and took in my dad's unmoving form, his ghostly pale face nearly the same shade as the hospital pillow. No. Is he . . . ? I spun toward the heart monitor. Its display still showed a weak but steady peak-and-valley rhythm. He was still with me. My own heart gave an extra-hard thud of relief.

*My little Grendel hunter.* Again in the dream. Why was that bothering me? Some connection lingered on the edge of my consciousness, just out of reach.

The clock on the wall now read 2:11 a.m. I'd lost more than *two hours.* I couldn't believe I'd fallen asleep studying the journal, desperately looking for a clue that I felt had to be there. A muscle in my back twinged painfully from sitting in one position too long. When I raised my arms over my head to stretch, I heard the whisper of something small falling to the floor. I frowned and looked down. Oh, right. The secret love note. It must have fallen out of my pocket.

As I scooped it up, my chest ached remembering the secret notes my mom and I had exchanged when I was little.

*Abby is the bestest ever.*

*Psst . . . Daddy ate the last cookie.*

Wait.

*My little Grendel hunter.*

Was that it? Was that the connection? The hidden drawer in her workbench had been stuffed full of notes, drawings . . .

Suddenly I sat up straighter. Hold on. The workbench she'd used here looked exactly like the one she'd had back home. Did that mean it also had the same secret drawer? Mom's journal was missing from the workbench shelf here in Asgard. Could she have hidden it there? My thoughts sped through the events of the past few days, rapidly putting things together. Was it possible that her final words in the simulation were a secret message that only I would understand? Pointing me to the one thing that could both prove Grendels still existed and give me the final piece of the puzzle I needed to save my dad?

I quickly scooped the journal into my backpack and shot out the doors of the medical ward, startling a lone night nurse as I passed. Asgard's halls lay silent and empty at that late hour. Only a handful of Vikings still monitored computers in the command center, their faces lit by the white glow of their screens like disembodied heads in the low light. They ignored me as I passed through.

Finally I arrived at the forge Gwynn had showed us on our first visit to Asgard. Now the moment of truth: the iris scanner. Would it let me in? I carefully stepped up to the silent scanner shaped like a dragon head and stared into its dark eyes. *Come on. Come on.* I realized too late that I hadn't thought about what happened when it rejected someone. The sharp teeth looked wickedly sharp. Or maybe a blast of fire from . . .

The eyes blinked green. The door rumbled open.

*Whew.*

For a few seconds, I stood there on the threshold. The forge sprawled vast and quiet in front of me. Here and there thin tendrils of steam still curled toward the ceiling, out of sight amid the scattered orange glow of dying embers. My heart thudded in my ears. It felt like disembarking a spaceship onto some volcanic alien planet.

I forced myself to take a step forward. Then another. I startled as the door slid shut behind me. Which way had we gone? I swiveled my head left and right, trying to remember. Everything looked completely different in the dark. But I thought I recognized a display of throwing knives to the right and headed in that direction.

The forge appeared completely empty as I worked my way deeper into its core. So far I'd seen no one. I guess even Viking blacksmiths had to sleep sometimes. As I walked, metallic ticking noises and occasional shrieks of cooling metal surrounded me like hunting calls from strange and terrifying nocturnal creatures. I kept my feet moving forward, trying to stay focused on my mission.

After wandering for what felt like an hour, I started to notice familiar things. We'd passed that massive bellows, right? And there was the place where Grimsby's backpack had caught on fire. I started to move faster. Then I turned a corner and Mom's workbench lay in front of me, silent and dark. I stopped in front of it and spread my hands palms down on its rough wooden surface as if by doing so I could connect with her beyond the grave. By touching something she had touched . . . Wait a sec. *A secret from beyond the grave* . . . That was part of the clue from the world tree, right? Yes! This had to be it!

I shook my head. *Focus.* Sucking in a quick breath, I slipped my trembling hand under the carved wooden surface, relying on memory to probe with my fingertips for a hidden switch. Where was it? I could feel my last shred of hope hanging by the thinnest of threads. It had to be there. Otherwise I was toast. Out of . . .

*Click.*

I let out a long sigh of relief. The hidden compartment. I shot a look over my shoulder toward the forge, worried that even the small sound had echoed through the cavernous room. Stillness. Nothing. I allowed myself to breathe again.

I turned back toward the workbench. My fingers fumbled excitedly for the drawer and I slid it out. Inside I felt a single object. Something smooth and metallic that I couldn't identify. What? Already half knowing the effort was futile, I poked my fingertips into the back corners of the drawer. The journal simply wasn't there. The brief rocket of success I'd been riding seemed to sputter. I lifted the metal object from the drawer, recognizing its contours in the dim light but not ready to give up hope yet without examining it more closely.

An arm lamp hung over the workbench. Should I risk turning it on? Another loud metallic shriek from the gloom sent an electric spark up my spine. "It's just cooling metal," I told myself quietly. "Stop letting your imagination freak you out."

I swung the lamp lower and clicked it on, then studied the object that lay reflecting dully in the circle of yellow light. It was a simple metal spoon. And not even a particularly nice spoon, its plain handle mottled with the tarnish of age.

I turned it over in the light. This had to be some kind of mistake. But, then, why was it in the drawer? Was it possible that Mr. Lodbrok was right and she'd gone completely off the deep end? Spending her final days working on secret . . . kitchen utensils?

I heard a noise behind me and instinctively slipped the spoon into my back pocket as I spun around. Nothing. I was sure I'd heard something beyond the normal sounds of the forge this time.

"Hello?" I called in a loud whisper. "Is anybody there?" I waited five seconds, the faint echoes of my voice slowly fading. Ten seconds.

Suddenly a shape emerged from the darkness as if part of the shadows had separated and come to life.

"Eeeeeee!" I squeaked, my heart nearly stopping. Then I recognized the blacksmith Gwynn had introduced us to earlier. He still wore his welder's mask over his face, which seemed a little weird. I mean, who walks around with a mask on all the time? There's Darth Vader, and the psychopathic killer from *Friday the 13th*, and . . .

"Oh, sorry!" I said, exhaling a shaky breath. "I—I didn't realize anyone else was down here. Kind of creepy at night and all. Not that *you're* creepy. Nope, you're all right. Totally. Did I mention my name was Abby? I don't think Gwynn officially introduced us. I'm—" I casually slid one quaking hand over my mouth to cut off my nervous chatter.

Through my whole monologue, the giant blacksmith had stood regarding me silently. I could see myself reflected back in the black glass over his eyes, looking tiny and helpless like a trapped mouse.

When he still didn't say anything, I shot my eyes toward the exit and said, "Okay, well, nice talking with you. I have to, um . . ."

As I started to step away from the workbench, I thought I heard him say something that sounded vaguely like "weapon."

I stopped in midstep and tilted my head to the side. "Sorry, what was that?"

"Give me. The weapon." Louder this time. His deep voice echoed eerily behind the welding mask.

Weapon? What was he talking about? Didn't he make weapons for a living? I was silently kicking myself at this point for not picking up an ax or sword earlier. I spread my hands and glanced back at my mom's workbench. "Sorry, I'm not sure what you're . . ."

He gestured toward the open drawer, and suddenly I knew exactly what he meant. And I also had a very bad feeling about this.

"I d-don't know what you're t-talking about," I said, at the same time chastising myself for being such a terrible liar. Even *I* didn't believe me. I started to slide away in what I thought was the direction of the door.

"My master will be pleased when Fenris delivers both you and weapon."

I froze again. Fenris. I assumed he was referring to himself in the third person. Sort of like Tickle Me Elmo's way less popular big brother—Murder You Fenris. In stores everywhere for $19.95. *Stop it*, I told myself as I felt my brain slipping into the jokey detachment that sometimes happened when I was scared out of my mind. I needed all my brain cells focused on getting out of here. Right now.

"My master will reward Fenris muchly," said the hulking giant, cutting into my thoughts.

*My master?* Who was he talking about?

"You made Fenris fail first time," he continued, and raised his hand to the bandage on his bulging bicep. "But will not fail second time." He shifted his bulk so that he was blocking my direct path to the door.

I made him fail? At what? I'd only met him earlier for, like, two seconds. The bandage . . . Waaait a minute. The queasy feeling in my stomach went from bad to worse. Even as he raised his hand to the visor on his mask, I knew in my gut what was coming next. Still, I couldn't tear my gaze away.

In slow motion, the visor lifted. A burst of orange flame from a nearby kiln erupted just then, illuminating a thick, bushy mustache, and above that, a smooth, eyeless visage. It was the giant with the motorcycle.

A scream caught in my throat as bile rose from my stomach, causing me to gag violently. As it turned out, that may have saved my life, because it distracted my brain long enough to return motor control to my arms and legs.

As the giant reached for me, I rolled onto the surface of the workbench, then vaulted over the back of it, praying I wouldn't land in an open flame or on sharp instruments and become an Abby skewer. When I landed on smooth concrete, I blew out a breath I'd been holding for too long. I frantically spun my head from side to side, trying to decide on my best options. Should I try to get back to the command center or go farther into the forge? Fenris sort of had the route closed off back the way I'd come, so that only left one choice.

An enormous bellow sounded behind me, followed by a wrenching noise as Mom's workbench started to lift off the floor. That was my cue. I sprinted recklessly into the depths of the forge, choking on the acrid smoke that seemed to fill every corner of the huge room. More loud crashes and the screech of rending metal followed me. I dodged and weaved deeper and deeper into the maze like a trapped rat, the noise seeming to gain ground no matter how fast I ran.

I quickly realized I was at a disadvantage. Not only did Fenris know his way through the forge, but he didn't seem to be limited to my circuitous route. When something was in his way, he simply went through it. My current strategy was only going to end one way: with me getting a one-way ticket on the Valkyrie Express to Valhalla.

I needed a new plan. But first I needed to hide. Taking a hard left turn, I slid underneath a low water trough that I guessed was used to cool hot metal. I could have used some cool water right then, with the heat of the forge and running for my life leaving me sticky with sweat. The spoon pressed uncomfortably against me in the tight space. Why would this giant possibly want it? Whatever the reason, it wasn't to help him lay into a bowl of Froot Loops. I had to keep it safe until I figured this out.

I scanned the immediate area for a weapon. Anything. Nearby, a tool handle protruded from the top of a waist-high open firepit. Was it an ax?

The noise of his earlier pursuit had gone quiet, and now an

eerie silence again permeated the forge. With one hand, I gripped the back leg of the water trough and pulled myself farther into the shadows underneath it.

Then I waited. And waited. Where was he? Had I lost him? Maybe I should . . .

A gigantic pair of boots silently stepped into the open path next to my hiding place. I jerked reflexively, nearly banging my forehead on the underside of the trough. For a giant, he sure could move stealthily. I held my hand over my mouth to mask the sound of my ragged breathing. The boots paused there for what seemed like an eternity.

*Don't breathe. Don't scream. Don't. Don't. Don't.*

At last he moved on.

I silently counted to ten, then slid into the gap between the trough and the brick firepit that stood next to it. I looked down. Okay, so it was a shovel, not an ax. But it would have to do. The heat of the coals resting in the pit felt almost intense enough to singe off my eyebrows. I turned away and waited, one hand resting on the shovel handle. Was he out of earshot? I turned back to the firepit and slowly . . . silently . . . began to slide the shovel out of the coals.

Then there came a barely audible noise behind me. Without even thinking, I spun. Saw that blank, horrifying face looming out of the darkness. Swung the shovel toward it, along with a scoop of glowing orange coals.

He roared in pain. Direct hit.

I wriggled the rest of the way out of my hiding spot and raced back the way I'd come, following his path of destruction to Mom's now-overturned workbench, then working my way by memory to the entrance. The sound of Fenris's screams grew fainter as I ran, but I didn't bother to turn around until I shot out the doors into the cool of the hallway and heard them rumble closed behind me. As I collapsed on the floor with my lungs burning, a familiar stern face appeared above me.

It belonged to Professor Roth. The leader of the Grey Council.

# CHAPTER 23

# A FIRESIDE CHAT

Professor Roth's eyebrows lifted a fraction of an inch. "Ms. Beckett. Whatever are you doing here? And at this hour?"

I scrambled to my feet. "I . . ." I looked toward the closed door to the forge and backed away, half expecting the giant to come crashing through it at any minute. "I couldn't sleep. So I was just . . . I was looking for . . . Then he tried to kill—" I stopped, realizing I was probably looking and sounding deranged with my breathless speech, wild hair, and my arms and hands smeared with black soot.

Was Fenris a Grendel? No. At least, I didn't think so. He was terrifying, but I hadn't felt the same level of soul-crushing despair as I'd felt back in North Carolina. *My master will be pleased* . . . Was he working for a Grendel, then?

Professor Roth stared at me for a long moment, then slid her hand to a brooch on the lapel of her suit jacket and pressed it. Within about five seconds, two giant Viking guards came at a run from around a nearby corner.

"Check the forge for an intruder," she ordered crisply. "Report to me what you find." They nodded, drew their longswords, and disappeared inside.

She turned back to me, and her expression softened, an almost-imperceptible shift in a slab of granite. "You've obviously had quite a fright. Come with me."

I followed her through the dark subterranean corridors of Asgard, eventually climbing a tight spiral staircase made of cut stones that wound upward for what seemed like an eternity.

I could feel the pressure of each second ticking by, and I didn't have the faintest clue how to save my dad. An image of the wires attached to him curling around him snakelike and slowly strangling the life out of him came unbidden to my mind. I shook my head to clear it. I'd thought for sure that the secret I'd find in my mom's workbench would be what I needed. But now I had . . . nothing. And no idea where to turn next. I touched my back pocket. Nothing, that is, except an old spoon apparently worth killing me over.

"Can I ask where we're going?" I said at last.

But even as I asked the question, we came to a solid wall. The headmaster touched it with her fingertips, and it swung open easily. We stepped through the doorway into an enormous room that felt like a freezer in the predawn chill. As I moved farther into the room, I heard a soft *whump* behind me. I turned and an immediate warmth bathed my face as flames came to life in the giant fireplace we had just passed through. With the light, I quickly realized where we were. Back in Professor Roth's office. So she had her own secret entrance into Asgard. Through the fireplace. Okay, that was . . . sort of awesome.

A clinking noise made me turn to see the headmaster pouring steaming liquid from a small urn into two small teacups. When she was finished, she lifted one of the cups and handed it to me. It was only when my trembling hand reached for it that I realized how badly I was shaking. I managed to take the offered cup in both hands, relishing its warmth against my palms.

"Come. Sit," Professor Roth offered, and gestured toward two chairs near the fire.

One half of my brain wanted to scream, *We don't have time for a tea party!* But to the other, exhausted half, the opportunity to sit sounded . . . really nice. I dropped my backpack next to one of the overstuffed armchairs and collapsed into the seat with a long sigh. Ouch. What was I sitting on? One hand reflexively went to the lump in my back pocket, but in the same moment I remembered. The spoon.

My eyes flicked up toward Professor Roth. She regarded me silently through the steam rising from her cup. "Sorry," I said, "just, um, making sure I'm not injured." That seemed reasonably believable.

I awkwardly looked away and imagined a scenario where I announced, *I have a secret weapon that will save the Vikings!* Then revealed . . . *ta-da!* . . . a spoon.

*Riiiiight.* Not unless Vale was besieged by giant monsters made of banana pudding.

They might just think I'd gone nuts too, like they all thought my mom had. Like mother like daughter. I glanced back at Professor Roth. Should I tell her about overhearing Mr. Lodbrok's confession about trying to have me killed by a sea monster? What if she was in on it too? Could I trust her? I wasn't sure yet.

I lifted my cup to my mouth to buy me a few more seconds while I decided what to do but was surprised when a chocolatey liquid touched my lips. My eyes shot downward. What I'd been expecting was warm tea, but instead in my glass was a thick, mocha-colored liquid that tasted like melted chocolate bars. My taste buds wanted to climb into the cup and do the backstroke through the delicious drink.

"It's a Viking favorite," said Professor Roth, noticing my surprise. "Much thicker and richer than modern hot chocolate."

"It's delicious." I sighed as I eagerly sipped more of the thick concoction and felt it slide across my tongue and down my throat, warming me from the inside out. My lips made an embarrassing slurping noise, and my eyes jerked back up to where Professor Roth continued to study me. I shifted in my seat in the intensity of her gaze.

Her fingers flexed like they were playing invisible piano keys on the side of the cup. "You remind me much of myself at your age."

I stared back at her wordlessly, not sure how to respond. In the firelight and with her long golden hair streaked with gray falling loose over one shoulder, she looked almost . . . human.

A thin smile played across her lips as she turned her head to stare into the fire. "Indeed, when I was a young girl, the thing I wanted most was to be an Aesir. To join the elite class of Viking warriors nobly hunting our greatest enemy." She paused and made a small noise that might have been a sigh. "Alas, my special abilities never materialized. I was . . . devastated, to say the least."

I dropped my eyes to the floor, silently wondering if that would be my fate as well.

"But eventually," she continued, "I learned a new truth. That I didn't need to be an Aesir. That I could do great things regardless of, or perhaps in spite of, my lack of any special gifts. And eventually I would come to be master of all this." She spread her arms, indicating, I guessed, not just the school but the sprawling Viking city under our feet. "I would bring order to a disorganized Viking community and return it to its glory as one of the most powerful forces on the world stage."

Professor Roth stood and slowly approached me. I shrank back into my seat and glanced around nervously, wondering what was happening. But then she simply bent, lifted the urn at my side, and refilled my cup with more of the syrupy chocolate.

"I suppose you're wondering why I'm telling you this?"

I shrugged like the thought hadn't crossed my mind at all. But . . . yeah.

The headmaster pivoted toward me so that I could feel the full weight of her stare. "It's because I see the same enormous potential in you. To do great things. Amazing things. But to get where I am, I first had to give up something. I had to throw off the past—a legacy born in darkness, when words like 'magic' and 'monsters' were used to explain things we didn't understand." She reached out her hand and gently encircled mine with her long, elegant fingers. "Abby, you too need to put aside your past. To stop blindly chasing fairy tales and realize your full potential."

I squirmed uncomfortably and finally jumped to my feet and began to pace, unable to sit still any longer, a thousand different emotions pinballing through me. What she was saying made a lot of sense, but . . . I spun toward her, my agitation easily readable in my face and body language. "But I *saw* a Grendel. In my kitchen in North Carolina. It was right in front of me."

The headmaster waved her hand dismissively. "You saw what someone wanted you to see. What you were programmed by your years of training to see. A child's nightmare. It's only when you let go of the foolish traditions of the past that you can begin to see clearly."

My blood boiled. "No! I *know* what I saw. Why won't anyone believe me?"

"Abby." She stared into my eyes. "You've been under a lot of pressure lately. Sometimes life asks us to take on adult challenges earlier than we'd like. And now you need to prepare for the possibility that you may soon have to make decisions that you're not feeling entirely prepared to make should your father . . ."

She didn't finish her sentence. She didn't need to.

I clenched my hands into fists and strode angrily across the room to stand looking out through one of its tall windows, unable to process all this at once. The warm chocolate churned in my stomach. If only my mom were still here. She'd know what to do. At least she'd believe me.

Outside, the sun was just sliding above the horizon, its golden rays imbuing Vale's campus with what felt to me like a false promise of endless possibility. Dawning on what could be my dad's last day among the living. Before I could speak again, I heard a polite cough and realized someone else had entered the room at some point during our conversation. Looking over my shoulder, I saw one of the Viking guards from earlier approach Professor Roth and speak quietly to her.

She said a few sharp words in reply, then stepped toward me. "Ms. Beckett—Abby—I'm afraid my duties call me away. We will continue our conversation soon, I promise you. Until then, I urge you to strongly consider my words. The choices you make now. Your next actions. Even now you are shaping your future, and whether you rise to greatness . . . or are consumed by the shadows of the past."

As she started to walk away, I called out to her. "Wait. In the forge. What . . . what did they find?"

Professor Roth turned back and studied my face for a few seconds. "Nothing. Nothing at all."

Then she turned and led the guard out the door, leaving me standing alone in the flickering firelight. I turned back toward the window, feeling lost and confused.

Then I gasped.

There in the courtyard several floors below stood the statue of

Bellyflop Bjarni that I'd seen earlier. His arms were stretched in a V over his head. The angle of the morning sun cast his shadow toward me across the circular pool of water at his feet . . . exactly in the shape of the upside-down Algiz rune.

The death rune.

# CHAPTER 24

# THE WELL OF WEIRD

*You might be surprised what you can see from up here.* Iggy's words echoed in my mind. And it was true. I'd never have noticed it unless I was looking down from above, just like now. Could the pool below actually be the mysterious Well of Weird that the tree had mentioned? Was it somehow connected to saving my dad?

A bubble of excitement swelled in my chest. I spun around, temporarily shoving aside the grim symbolism of the final rune as I snatched up my backpack, and then sprinted from Professor Roth's office and down the stairs, taking them three at a time. Almost breathless, I hurtled into the crowd of students arriving for the start of the school day, swinging my head left and right, searching for Gwynn and Grimsby.

"Abby!" someone shouted over the noise.

I whirled around. My friends were there, picking their way through the hall toward me.

I grabbed Gwynn's hand and started to pull her in the direction of the pool. "Come on!"

"Huh?" Gwynn said, one eyebrow going up. "Where are we going?"

"Just follow me. I'll explain on the way."

While we jogged through the hallways, I gave them the highlights of my return to the forge and the unsettling chat with Professor Roth afterward, finishing with the discovery of the upside-down Algiz rune.

Gwynn frowned, silently processing this new information. "So Fenris is somehow mixed up in all this?"

I shrugged. "Yeah. I don't see how everything is connected, but there must be something we're missing."

Grimsby panted, trying to keep up with us. "Wow," he said to Gwynn, "you have absolutely horrible taste in guys."

"Hey," she shot back, "grown-ups talking here." She looked back at me. "And you're sure he was the same guy who attacked you on your drive here?"

I nodded. "Positive. Unless you know any other eyeless giants. The funny thing is, I never would have given the spoon a second look if he hadn't tried to kill me to get it."

We all went silent for a few seconds, clearly with the same thought on our minds: What about it was worth killing for?

The sound of tinkling water came from around the corner ahead. I slowed to a walk as we turned and entered the grotto with the statue standing over a small pool. The reappearance of the upside-down rune earlier had me spooked, and I wasn't ready to rush into danger this time.

Grimsby studied the pond as we approached. "Okay, then what do we do now? Toss a penny in and the ghost of Elvis rises from the water holding this thorn we're looking for?"

"Don't you think it's a little too coincidental the way it all fits together?" I said. "The tree's riddle did mention 'hold your breath,' and when do you hold your breath? In *water*."

"Yeah, let me just remind you, it also mentioned *death*." He looked down into the serene pool. "So then . . . what? You're thinking we go for a swim? Who knows how deep that is?"

"Well," Gwynn said, "the tree specifically said 'you will surely *conquer* death.' But it does still worry me that the rune's shadow was upside down. That makes me think if the cure for Abby's dad is somehow down there, then it's not like it's going to be a pleasant dip in the pool."

I gave an involuntary shiver as I studied the mirrorlike surface of the dark water, wondering what dangers lay beneath it. Again I wondered if maybe both my quests—my dad's cure and the Grendel—were somehow intertwined. And if so, was there something important I was missing? Some critical connection that might prevent me from leading us blindly toward our deaths?

Gwynn paced slowly back and forth, thinking. She absently kicked a loose pebble into the pond. Suddenly her head tilted to one side and she leaned closer, peering into the glassy surface. "Weird."

"Weird? Well of Weird?" I said. "Ha ha, very funny."

But Grimsby was nodding his head too and stepped closer to the water. "No, I heard it too. The pebble made a little plop when it fell in, then that was followed by some sort of faint rattling sound."

"So? It just landed on the bottom," I said.

"No, it wasn't that." He quickly searched the area around the pool and plucked a small stone off the ground. He dropped it into the water. There was a plop, then several seconds later we heard a faint clattering noise. If the water had slowed its descent, it shouldn't have had such a noisy landing.

Grimsby was perched precariously on the very edge of the pond now, squinting down into its depths, his curiosity evidently having overcome his skepticism. "There seems to be . . ." He trailed off and squatted down closer, stretching his arm out over the pond.

"Careful!" Gwynn said, taking a step forward and reaching toward him.

But at the same moment Grimsby lost his balance. He somersaulted into the pond headfirst with a cry of surprise cut off quickly by a splash.

"GRIMSBY!" Gwynn and I shouted at the same time.

We rushed to the side of the pond, but he was gone. I frantically peered down into the dark water, but all I could see was my own reflection in the smooth surface. It was as if he'd been swallowed without a trace.

"Abby!" Gwynn said, looking around agitatedly. "We need to find a pole, or stick, or . . . or something. Quick!"

But her words barely registered as I stood there on the edge of the Well of Weird, gripped by an old, paralyzing fear. My mind flashed back to my five-year-old self. Perched on the edge of the high dive. My toes curled around the edge of the board, feeling its rough, stippled surface on my bare feet. A drop of water rolled down my nose and dangled precariously on the tip before plunging an impossibly far distance to where it plopped into the water below. Like then, I could hear my heart beating rapidly in my ears. *Thumpthumpthumpthump* . . .

Present-day me took a deep, steadying breath. I wasn't that little kid anymore. This time there was no backing down. No scrambling down the ladder and running, crying to my mommy.

"Abby! Wait!" Gwynn shouted, evidently reading my intent on my face.

But I ignored her. I closed my eyes, took a deep breath. And jumped.

There was an initial shock of icy water. I decelerated as I plunged downward. Then, just as suddenly, I was somehow falling out of the water and picking up speed again.

Confused, I opened my eyes right as my feet connected with a hard surface and my legs crumpled under me. For a few seconds I lay there on my back in the nearly complete darkness, stunned but relatively unhurt. I looked up, then blinked, rubbed my eyes, and looked again. The water simply stopped in midair several feet above me, like I was looking upside down at the pond's surface, still rippling slightly from my passage. I reached up toward the blue glow of the water, still not believing what I was seeing. *Hold your breath* . . .

A large, dark shape appeared above me. Then a splash. My

brain realized what was happening at the same instant that Gwynn crashed down through the water and landed right on top of me.

"Abby!" Gwynn said in surprise, then rolled and stared upward in awe at the water above us. She reached toward it and her fingertips brushed the water's surface wonderingly. "It's so . . . beautiful."

I lay on the ground, clutching my stomach where she'd landed. "Why didn't you just use your wings instead of my body to break your fall?"

"Oh, right, um, sorry!" She knelt next to me, her eyebrows knitted together in concern. "Are you okay?"

"Yeah," I grunted. "I didn't need those ribs anyway."

She peered around in the dim blue glow. "Where's Grimsby?"

"Grimsby!" I exclaimed, suddenly remembering. I sat up with a grunt of pain and studied our surroundings. But I didn't see him anywhere. "What happened to him?"

We both scrambled to our feet and did a quick search. And I mean quick because we were in a small chamber, not much bigger than, say, your average living room. It looked like either it was a natural cave or it had been hand-carved, because its walls were rough and uneven rock.

"Nothing," I said in exasperation as we met back in the middle.

"Me either. Where could he have gone?"

"Grimsby!" I shouted.

I heard a faint "Over here!" in reply.

The echo in the underground chamber made his voice sound like it had come from everywhere and nowhere.

Gwynn tipped her head to the side, listening as he called out again. Then she stepped toward one wall. "This way. I think."

We approached what looked like a solid wall, but then I felt a faint coolness stir around my ankles and crouched down, exploring with my hands in the semidark. "I think there's an opening here. But it's tight."

I wriggled through headfirst on my stomach with just enough room. Emerging on the other side, I saw with relief that Grimsby was standing there. His grin was lit up from below by a small object cupped in his hands that was glowing a soft white.

"What's that?" I asked as I stood and brushed myself off.

"Grimsby!" Gwynn said as she shimmied out of the tunnel behind me and ran to give him a hug. Then she stepped back and admonished him, "You need to be more careful! It's a good thing you probably fell on something you don't use very often. Your *head*."

He glanced at Gwynn, then back at me. "When I was looking down into the well, I thought I saw something glowing. So, of course, then I, you know, wasn't exactly paying attention to where the edge was. And fell in. Anyway, it turns out what I saw was this." He held it up so we could get a better look. It appeared to be a single flower petal. "I think it may be from that sniffle . . . you know, the flower we're looking for?"

"The svefnthorn?" I asked. "How can you tell?"

He stepped back and tilted his chin upward. "Take a look for yourself."

"Whooooaa . . ." said Gwynn.

I followed their gazes up to the roof of the chamber, about ten feet above us. A tangle of thick vines with nasty-looking thorns completely covered the ceiling. I reached up in wonder, my eyes suddenly brimming with tears of joy. Among the thorns, tiny, glowing white flowers peeked out at intervals, giving the illusion of looking at a night sky filled with stars.

# CHAPTER 25

# A THORNY SITUATION

"No wayyyyy," I said, looking around with awe. "It's all over the place. We should have way more than we need here." My heart raced, already picturing the blush of health returning to my dad's face.

Gwynn scanned the chamber, looking thoughtful. "I guess the svefnthorn survived the demolition of the greenhouse by working its roots downward into this underground cave, where it grew untouched all these years."

"I'm amazed the plant survived this long," I said. "When the botanist said it doesn't like light, he wasn't kidding. It's almost like it thrives without any light at all."

"Yeah, and makes some of its own," Grimsby added. "Kind of creepy."

"But how do we get to it?" Gwynn asked, looking around the chamber. "We need a ladder or something to get up there."

"What do you mean?" I said. "You've got wings. Why don't you just fly up there and grab some?"

"Well, you know, it's dark, and I'm not sure I—" she hedged.

"What?" Grimsby cut in. "You need a lighted runway for take-off or—"

"No, it's not that. I—"

"Come on, I don't get it," he said. "Just fly up there, then."

She balled her fists and glared at him. "Okay, fine, you want to know the truth? I can't. I'm the *one* Valkyrie in the *history* of Valkyries who can't fly. Not even a little. I don't know why. Why do you think I'm studying to be a doctor? Because who needs a Valkyrie who can't fly? So I figure if I can't help people *after* they die, then maybe I can save them from dying at all. Are you happy now?"

She dropped her head and turned away.

Grimsby's eyebrows shot up as he looked at me, then at Gwynn's back. An uncomfortable silence filled the cavern. Then he walked over and put his hand on her shoulder. "Sorry, I didn't mean . . . I didn't know."

She sighed. "It's not your fault. I guess it's sort of a sore spot for me." She turned and gave us a crooked smile. "I haven't exactly told a lot of people about it."

"Well, your secret is safe with us," I said. "And anyway, I'm sure we can figure out another way to get a flower."

Grimsby looked up at the ceiling, then back at me, like he was sizing me up. "Yeah, you should be able to hoist me up, and I'll pick some flowers."

"Wait, I'm hoisting *you* up?"

"Yeah, well, I've got the fingers of a surgeon," he said, holding up his long, thin fingers. "Runs in the family, I guess. I'll be able to get a flower without getting stabbed by all those thorns."

"Okay, good point," I said. I turned to Gwynn. "How many do you think we need?"

Gwynn looked up, studying the vines. "I stopped by the clinic and asked Dr. Swenson about that this morning. She said we'd probably only need a single full bloom."

My heart tightened as I realized it had been hours since I'd seen my dad. "Did you see . . . ?"

She nodded reassuringly. "He's still growing weaker, but he's a fighter. Like you."

I nodded and made a quick swipe at my eyes before turning back to Grimsby. "Okay, let's give it a try." I knelt down so Grimsby could climb onto my shoulders. He accidentally stepped on my fingers as he struggled to throw his legs over my back.

"Ow!"

"Sorry, it's dark. Just relax and I'll—"

"Watch it!" I said as he jammed a finger into my mouth. "Do you have to use my face to steady yourself?"

"Sorrrrry . . ."

Finally he was on, and I wobbled to my feet. He was surprisingly heavy for having such a slight frame.

"Can you reach it?" I asked.

"Almost. Can you move over to your right a little?"

I shuffled over a couple of paces. "There?"

"No, *my* right."

"Your right *is* my right. We're facing the same way."

"Oh, yeah, then I mean your *left*, or *my* left . . . You know what I mean. Yeah, right there."

He dug his heels into my sides, stretching toward the vines. I grunted as his loafers poked into my ribs.

"Be careful!" Gwynn said. "The flower may be the antidote, but those thorns probably have enough poison in them to knock out an elephant."

"Almost . . . got it . . . OW!"

"What happened? Are you okay?" said Gwynn.

"Yeah, just nicked myself. This thing is pokier than the little puppy."

"What?" I said.

"Don't tell me you never read *The Poky Little Puppy* when you were a kid."

"No."

He looked down at me. "What rock did you live under?"

"Hey, it's not my fault. Bedtime stories at my house were about Viking heroes wrecking man-eating monsters. Not cute little puppies. Anyway, can you grab the flower already? I think I might have dislocated my shoulder."

I saw Gwynn smiling to herself as she watched us.

"What?" I said defensively.

"Oh, nothing, you two are just like Tweedledum and Tweedledee."

"Okay . . . got it!" Grimsby called.

I thought I saw a tiny sort of pulse ripple along the tangle of lighted vines when Grimsby plucked the bud from among them.

"Did you see that?" I asked Gwynn.

"See what?"

Maybe I was just imagining it. "Never mind. It was probably nothing." Note to future self: Don't ignore strange things that happen in dark, creepy caves.

I knelt down again, and Grimsby hopped off my shoulders.

Gwynn grabbed one of his hands, yanking it closer to take a look. "The thorn didn't break your skin, did it? We don't need you taking a power nap on us."

"No biggie," said Grimsby, pulling his hand away. "I'm fine." He held up the glowing flower triumphantly in his other hand. Its petals were thin and transparent, almost like they were made of crystal. Each petal glowed from some internal light source.

"I wonder how it glows like that," I said.

"Powerful and ancient magic, clearly," said Grimsby.

This earned an eye roll from Gwynn. "Not quite, genius. It's called phosphorescence. There are organisms that live in the darkest parts of the ocean that glow the same way."

"Fascinating," said Grimsby as he tucked the flower safely into the inside pocket of his blazer. "But I'm sticking with magic."

"What's wrong?" said Gwynn, noticing my frown.

I held up the cover of the journal, which I'd had in my backpack since leaving the medical wing. "The last rune. It hasn't changed yet."

She looked around the room uncertainly. "But we found the svefnthorn. What could we be missing?"

"Yeah," said Grimsby. "Right after we blew up the sea monster, the first rune changed color. And then after we talked to Iggy, the second rune turned green. Now we found this death rune and got a flower from the svefnthorn. What gives?"

A shiver of foreboding crawled up my spine. "Unless . . . the last rune wasn't leading us to the svefnthorn, exactly. It *is* the symbol for death, after all."

Grimsby swallowed nervously. "Oh man, I was really hoping it was a metaphor. You know, like going underground is like dying or something?"

"That would be a simile," Gwynn said.

He shot her a look. "Really? Does it—"

"Whatever it is," I interrupted, shoving the journal back into my bag, "I don't really care right now. We have the flower we need to cure my dad. Let's get out of here."

"One small problem," Gwynn said.

Grimsby threw up his hands in exasperation. "What *now*?"

She pointed back the way we'd come in. "We can't go back up that way. The walls are too steep."

"Oh," he said, looking around the cavern. "Then there must be some other way out. But we should get going. This place really gives me the . . . cheese?"

"Um, I think the word you're looking for is 'creeps'?" I said helpfully.

"Shhh! I smell . . ." He paused and sniffed the air.

"Why do we need to be quiet for you to smell something?" I said.

He ignored this. "Yeah, I think I smell . . . grilled cheese." He sniffed again. "Cheddar, if I'm not mistaken." He pointed. "And I'm pretty sure it's coming from that direction."

"He must be delirious," Gywnn said to me. "Maybe one of those thorns stabbed him in the head."

"I guess we don't really have any choice anyway," I said, anxious to get back to my dad as quickly as possible. I couldn't believe we'd run into yet another obstacle when we were at last so close to saving him. "Okay, let's follow your nose."

We followed Grimsby across the chamber, the glowing flowers overhead helping us pick our way through the dark as we discovered a side tunnel. This new tunnel connected to another series of chambers connected by even more tunnels. As we walked forward, peering down long passageways ending in blackness and relying on Grimsby's nose to guess at each turn which way to go, I began to feel the panicky claustrophobia of being trapped underground. I started to imagine I could hear raspy hisses and scurrying noises down several of the side tunnels, and at one point even thought I saw a pair of glowing eyes peering out at us. But when I blinked, they were gone.

"Guys, do we have any idea where we are?" I said, glancing around nervously after wandering for what felt like hours. Where Grimsby smelled grilled cheese, all I smelled was stale air that reminded me of dead, rotting things. Even worse than the feeling of the walls closing in on me was the constricting feeling of running out of time to get the cure to my dad. If we didn't find our way out of this maze quickly, it could be too late.

Gwynn reached out and let her fingertips trail along a rock

wall beside us as we passed. "I remember hearing once about the original tunnels the Vikings built when they first arrived here. Something about the limestone being too unstable, so they abandoned them in favor of the current location. Maybe that's why the original Vale campus was moved too."

"Oh, great. Thanks," I said. "So now I'm worried not only about what might be lurking down any of these dark tunnels, but also about being crushed to death under a million pounds of rock."

"Sorry, I'm sure—" she started.

"I think I see a light up ahead," Grimsby cut in. "We muz be getting close."

I frowned at the slight slur in his words. "Are you—"

"Shhhh!" Gwynn hissed. "What was that? It sounded like a bat screeching, or . . ."

We all froze and listened. I could hear a far-off *drip-drip* of water but otherwise silence.

"Should we try to go back?" I whispered.

"Go back where?" Gwynn said, staring at the twisting maze behind us. She had a point. Either we could turn around and maybe get lost in the tunnels and never be found again. Or we could go forward into . . . what?

"I vo we go forard," said Grimsby, now clearly slurring his words.

Gwynn looked at him with concern. "I think you may have pricked yourself more than you thought."

"'mokay," he protested, one eye lazily drifting shut. He suddenly stumbled and fell sideways into me.

I caught him under the arms and met Gwynn's gaze over his head, our eyes registering our alarm at the rapid turn he'd taken. "We have to get him out of here," I said. "I guess forward it is." I slung one of his arms over my shoulder and helped steady him as we crept quietly toward the light.

Gwynn quickly poked her head around the corner and waved us forward. "Looks like the coast is clear."

If we'd had any doubt about anyone else being down here, the next cavern cleared it up for us. Candles of all shapes and sizes guttered and dripped in several nooks and crannies all around the large space. Growing from what seemed like every other surface were exotic-looking plants of all types. Thick vines trailed up natural limestone columns that supported the ceiling above at several points, allowing this chamber to be larger than the ones we'd seen previously.

"I think we just figured out where the greenhouse went to," I said.

Gwynn pointed a shaky finger toward the center of the room. "I don't suppose the botanist's journal mentions, um, having a pet?"

I followed her gaze. There amid the foliage was what looked like a giant nest constructed of piles of loose straw, torn clothing, and other miscellaneous trash. Whatever had made it wasn't something I wanted to meet. Near the center of the pile lay the crusts of what looked like a grilled cheese sandwich. So Grimsby's nose had been right.

"'spretty," Grimsby slurred. When I turned toward him, he was staring at the svefnthorn bloom in his open palm. It sparkled and seemed to capture the candlelight. "I'mma just be overhere." He stumbled farther into the cave.

"I really don't have a good feeling about this," I said. "We need to find a way out of here. Now."

Gwynn nodded. "I'm with you. Why don't you check that direction and I'll look over here?"

I walked toward a raised alcove where a small object lay next to a sputtering candle. All at once, I recognized what it was. I ran forward and clutched it with both hands, lifting it up into the light. My mom's missing journal. But what was it doing here?

Before I could examine it more closely, Gwynn called from across the room. "Abby, I think you'd better come check this out."

"What is it?" I said, walking over to join her.

She stood staring up at a wall covered with old movie posters: *Swamp Thing. Creature from the Black Lagoon. Return of Swamp Thing.* "Wow, so . . . whoever uses this place really likes old horror movies? That seems sort of weird."

"Yeah," she said, turning toward me with a worried look on her face. "And what do all these remind you of?"

I stared at the posters. I didn't get what she was . . . *Ohhh.*

"Wasn't the Grendel creature in Beowulf described as a sort of swamp creature?" Gwynn said.

I didn't answer right away because the room abruptly seemed to be tilting. I reached out and put my hand on the wall to steady myself. When I looked up, Gwynn's wide eyes must have matched mine. It was the first time I'd ever seen her look genuinely scared.

I stared back at the nest, then at the posters again. "But it's not . . . It's . . . you know . . . dead." Even as I said it, I knew I was only desperately trying to convince myself. It wasn't working.

Mr. Lodbrok's voice echoed in my mind: *There is absolutely nothing that you—or any of us—can do to stop it.* Maybe that's why he was so adamantly opposed to the idea of a Grendel's continued existence. What better way to keep it hidden than to pretend it didn't exist?

Nearby a shift in the chamber's roof sent a small shower of dust to the floor, bringing me back to the stark reality of our situation. I could figure out the Mr. Lodbrok thing later. Right now we had weightier issues. As in a million pounds of rock hanging precariously above our heads.

"Okay," I said. "We need to get out of here before this whole place collapses. And before whatever made that nest comes back."

Gwynn frowned and pointed at my chest. "Are you, uh, glowing?"

I looked down and saw a faint glow beneath my shirt and realized it was my runestone. I dragged it out, and my knees nearly buckled when I saw the symbol etched into the surface glowing an angry red. The upside-down Algiz rune. "Oh no. This happened last time . . ."

Gwynn met my gaze. "Last time?" But then she froze, her head cocked to one side. "There it is again."

"There what is?"

"That strange squeaking noise. Is it rats or something?"

Then I heard it too. A squeaking noise. It seemed to be coming toward us. Suddenly I recognized it. And it wasn't rats.

Then a familiar figure entered the room the way we'd just come in. He was pushing a garbage can and mop pail.

"Hello, Abby."

# CHAPTER 26

# THE DEATH RUNE

The school janitor. I realized it was the first time I'd heard him speak. All hoarse and raspy. Like he'd been smoking for a thousand years. In a word: creeptastic.

"Hi, uh, sir," I said. I was seriously confused, not sure what to make of him appearing out of nowhere in this underground maze.

The janitor coughed a pair of deep, phlegmy coughs, then looked at me again. A large rat crawled out of his trash can. He didn't flinch when it climbed up his arm and perched on his shoulder. He reached out and gave it a small stroke with his finger. Okay, so he had a pet rat. That was normal, right?

"I suppose you wonder what I'm doing here?" he said.

"Well, yeah, to be honest, the thought crossed my mind."

He laughed at this, then doubled over in a coughing fit before finally straightening and continuing. "I've been observing you for a long time, Abby. For many years, in fact. Watching as you've grown up, though I admit I lost track of you for several years. Which is why I'm so glad we've recently been able to become . . . reacquainted."

He'd been watching me . . . for years? Okay, if I'd thought I was creeped out already, then now I really was. "What are you talking about?"

"It's simple, really," he said. "I've been waiting for the right moment to extend you an invitation. You see, I've been looking for someone with your unique qualities for ages. I hope you didn't mind my little game that brought us here together like this. But I thought my journal might prove an excellent test of whether I'd finally found the right individual."

"Wait." Gwynn spoke up. "The journal? That was yours?"

I reached back and retrieved it from my backpack. The final rune flashed white-hot before settling into a deep red color. Then the entire journal started to crumble apart and fall like ashes through my fingers.

"I'm happy to report," he said, "that you passed with flying colors."

I looked up from the remains of the journal on the ground and narrowed my eyes. "Wh-who are you?"

He stared at me intently. I thought I saw a weird sort of reptilian cast to his eyes and then it was gone. Then the raspy voice again, slow and soft: "You know. Deep down in yourself, you know."

That's when I had a second revelation. This wasn't the first time I'd heard his voice. It was the same voice I'd heard whisper from the shadows outside my kitchen in North Carolina when all this started. And with that memory returned the same feeling of utter dread. The certainty that death itself was reaching for me. Grasping. I fought to push back the darkness that threatened around the fringes of my vision. My head swam.

"You're a . . . you're a . . ." My brain wouldn't let my mouth complete the thought.

Gwynn stepped in front of me protectively and finished for me. "A Grendel."

Without looking at her, he said, "Some have called me that." He studied my reaction. "Are you surprised, Abby? Not what you were expecting, am I? How do the stories describe us? Misshapen, hideous creatures with fangs and scales? All lies. Lies to make them feel better about themselves. Why? Because it is so much easier to hate something that is nothing like you. To detest what you do not understand. But after all these years, I am no longer interested in labels and words. I am only interested in stopping this senseless cycle. I grow weary of the battle."

I moved forward to stand beside Gwynn. Even with a voice that sounded like it came from beyond the grave, the Grendel's words were oddly compelling. Almost . . . hypnotic. I found myself wanting to believe that maybe we'd been wrong. And that maybe there was another way out of all this. "So what is this invitation you mentioned?"

"Don't listen to him, Abby," Gwynn said, grabbing my arm. "You can't trust him!"

Her hand on my arm was like a splash of cold water, waking me from a dream. I looked down at her hand, then back at the Grendel, now wary of the siren-like lure of his voice. He continued to ignore her and keep his gaze on me.

"Merely this," he said. "To join me. Like many others have. In fact, it is the same invitation I gave to your mother."

My chest tightened. "My mom? What do you mean? She . . . was working with you?"

He coughed again and lifted the rat from his shoulder, setting it down on the ground, where it scurried out of sight. "She was indeed. And for that she was labeled a traitor. Her legacy tarnished. But you can change that. You can set the record straight."

I was momentarily breathless with shock. My mom working with a Grendel? "I . . . can't believe that. How could she possibly work with you? Her sworn enemy?"

But then, there was her whole secret life at Vale that she'd never told me anything about, and it didn't seem quite as hard to believe. Was there a chance he could be telling the truth?

A tremor ran through the ground, like the earth was shifting. There was a low rumbling noise, and I looked up warily at the ceiling.

"Oh, I think you'll find that adults are full of secrets," he said. "Secrets that accumulate over a lifetime like barnacles on the hull of a ship, slowly multiplying out of sight just below the water's surface. In fact, do you want to know a little secret about the Grey Council? Doc . . . as you know him?" He said the name with derision.

I shifted my gaze from the ceiling back to his face. The candlelight flickered over his features, giving him a frighteningly sinister look despite the gentle face and jumpsuit that he was still wearing with "Glen" stitched on the front pocket.

He smiled. "They didn't bring you to Vale for your protection.

No, you were brought here as one thing." He paused, then spat out the word: "Bait."

He watched my face as I processed this information. This was all happening too fast. I felt something brush past my foot and jerked it back in surprise, but when I looked down, the only thing there was a thin tendril of vapor.

"You see," he continued. When I looked up, he'd taken a step toward us. I automatically took a couple of steps backward.

"The problem is that Vale is full of rats. Enemies that surround the Vikings and even now close in from all quarters. And how do you draw out the rats?" He inclined his head toward me. "You bring in some cheese. The one thing the rats want most of all: you."

The sick feeling was back in my stomach.

"N-no. Doc wouldn't lie to me."

"Oh no? Surely he told you, then, that I cannot be defeated? That my flesh is impervious to harm from mere iron or steel?"

"Well, no, not exactly . . ." I said.

"Surely he told you that our fates—yours and mine—are inextricably intertwined?" As he talked, he pulled a loose thread from the hem of his sleeve. "That as the strength of the Aesir wanes, my own grows stronger? That, in fact, the fate of the Aesir now hangs by a single thread." He held the thread in front of him. "One. Little. Girl." With a sharp yank, he tore the thread in half and let it fall to the floor.

"I . . . I . . ." I staggered backward, suddenly feeling dizzy as the stakes hit me with such stark brutality. So it was true. The

Aesir had been hunted down. Eliminated. And now he was going to kill me too. Unless I joined him.

"Join me now and together we will reunite the thread that was severed so long ago. This is what your mother truly wanted."

*Mother.* I clung to that one word like an immovable stone in the hurricane that swirled inside me. I knew in my heart that she had loved me with her entire self. That whatever secrets she may have kept from me must have been because she was trying to protect me. But was there any way she could have had a secret like this? That she had partnered with a Grendel? Any way at all? Any . . .

"No," I said in barely a whisper.

The Grendel tilted his head slightly. "What did you say?"

"NO!" I shouted. "I don't believe you. And I won't join you."

As my words echoed through the underground chamber, I silently prepared for whatever would come next. If he wanted to kill me, then he would get a fight like . . . Hold on. A thought had struck me, and I clung to it like a final hope.

"And anyway, you were wrong. I'm not . . . an Aesir." There. I finally said it. Finally admitted what I'd known in my heart already for so long.

The Grendel stared hard at me, as if peering all the way into my soul. Was he going to let me live? Even if I failed to stop him now, we still had the svefnthorn. We could escape somehow. Could still save my dad. All wasn't lost yet.

A smile slowly spread across his face. "Then killing you should be even easier than I expected." And he stepped toward us.

Gwynn and I scrambled backward, searching frantically for

a way out. A weapon. Anything to save us from becoming the Grendel's next victims. Then, for the first time, I noticed a strange heat in my back pocket. I slid my hand into it, and my fingers closed around the spoon my mom had made. It was surprisingly warm to the touch. What? I heard Fenris's words in my mind: *Give me the weapon.* If it was some sort of weapon, then this was the moment of truth.

I closed my eyes and yanked the spoon out of my pocket, thrusting it in a trembling fist toward the Grendel. For a few seconds, nothing happened.

"Abby, look!" Gwynn shouted.

There was a sudden hiss from the Grendel's direction. My eyes snapped open to see him cringe away from the spoon like it *was* a deadly weapon. I looked from him to the utensil in my hand and back again. That's when I noticed that if the light hit the spoon at just the right angle, its form seemed to shift. Like it wasn't just a spoon, but something much larger and more dangerous. Its shape flickered between a spoon and . . . a Viking battle-ax.

In that instant, all the pieces seemed to collide in my head with a flash of comprehension. The holograms. My mom's work on the virtual reality chamber. The discovery Doc mentioned. No one ever found out what the discovery was because she'd disguised it as a simple kitchen utensil.

My hands tightened around the ax handle as its warmth seemed to flood through me, burning away my doubts and fear. "My mom," I said to the Grendel. "She was able to re-create the process the ancients used to forge iron. That's why you didn't kill me back in North Carolina. Because you needed my help. To find this." I thrust the spoon-ax toward him. "The one way to kill—a Grendel."

His reaction was all I needed to show me I was right. He shrieked, his once-gentle face transforming into a mask of anger. Then, all pretense gone, he whipped his mop out of the bucket. With a flick of his wrists, the mop end spun off to reveal a wickedly sharp spear.

"You had your chance to join me," he said. "Now I am afraid I am done negotiating."

He hurled the spear, and in the same moment Gwynn crashed into me from the side, shoving me behind one of the limestone columns. I heard her grunt, then the sound of the spear clattering against the floor. I pressed my back against the rock column, heart pounding.

Gwynn sank against the column with her hand clamped over her arm.

I shot a quick look around the other side of the column, then looked down at her arm. "What happened? The spear . . . It hit you!"

She winced. "It's nothing. I'll be okay. But we need to get out of here. Now."

Even as I started to protest, I knew she was right. We had the ax, but the Grendel was too quick. And Gwynn was already hurt. Then I remembered . . . "Okay, but we've got a problem." I pointed. "Grimsby."

She followed my gaze to where our friend lay halfway across

the cavern, crumpled on the floor. "He's not moving. The poison must have finally knocked him out."

I spotted a collection of mops, buckets, and other cleaning equipment to one side of the room. I guessed this was where the Grendel stored his supplies for when he wasn't being, well, a Grendel. Among these were a pair of wheeled trash cans that looked like they had seen better days. That gave me an idea.

"See if you can get Grimsby into one of those," I said. "Then try to find another way out. I'll keep the Grendel busy."

"How? You can't—"

"Don't worry about it. I've got this." *I think.*

Gwynn nodded. "Okay, but be careful. We don't know what he'll do. He's still in here somewhere." She rose unsteadily, then took a deep breath.

"Be safe," we said at the same time.

She smiled. "Jinx. You can buy me a Coke when this is all over." Then she turned and sprinted across the chamber.

I looked down at the weapon in my hand. Somehow now that I understood what it was, I could hold and use it like a real ax. It was up to me. This was the one moment I'd been training for my whole life. I flexed my fingers on the ax handle, counted to three, and spun away from the column to the last place we'd seen the Grendel.

Only the flicker of shadows filled the space where he'd just been. The strange vapor I'd seen earlier seemed to be getting thicker, curling lazily around the floor of the chamber.

"Yes, your mother had the chance to join me." The Grendel's eerie voice came from behind me.

I whirled. Nothing. I stood listening to the echo of his words fade into silence. Limestone columns stretched out in every direction into darkness. Each column's shadow danced tauntingly in the flickering candlelight, making it impossible to detect a real threat.

"But she chose violence. So I gave her . . . violence." Again behind me, but for a second time I spun only to find empty air and echoes. *Violence . . . violence . . .*

I turned in a slow circle on the balls of my feet with my ax raised, ready to spring. Expecting an ambush at any second.

"And now you will suffer the same fate as your mother." *Your mother . . . mother . . . mother . . .*

"What do you mean?" I called. Where was he? I had to keep him talking long enough to find out. I started moving across the cavern, trying to draw him away from Gwynn and Grimsby.

"Oh, my. Do you not remember how she really died?"

There was another bump against my foot, but my eyes flicked downward to see only vapor there. I kept moving.

"She perished protecting you. But look what that got her. Nothing."

I froze, feeling like I'd been clubbed in the gut by a knattleikr stick. My mom had died in a fire. The same one that I'd somehow miraculously survived. But that fateful day was a blank in my mind. Was there more to the story?

"No, I can see you didn't know. Interesting. Your father was very clever. He hid you well. I guessed that poisoning him would be the best way to motivate you to help me in my own quest."

"So Fenris *was* working for you!" I shouted.

A disembodied cackle echoed around me. "Alas, it did not go exactly as I'd planned, but in the end I think it worked out even better than I'd hoped. After all, you hand delivered your mother's weapon to me. However, if you perish now . . . your mother. Your father. Their deaths will have been meaningless. All three of your lives. Meaningless." *Meaningless . . . meaningless . . .*

His voice seemed to come from all around me now. I could feel a slow rage building in my chest. I was done with this game. "Show yourself!" I shouted.

My words rang off the limestone columns.

Silence.

No, not complete silence. From somewhere came a low sort of whispering noise that made the hairs on the back of my neck tingle. What was that?

Just then something slammed into me from the side. I recognized the trash can as it toppled to the floor with a loud clatter. The blow knocked me backward into a nearby stone column. My breath exploded from my lungs with the impact.

In the same instant, a figure leapt at me out of the shadows. I put my hands up in surprise and tried a desperate swing with the ax. But strong hands locked around my wrists.

The Grendel pressed me backward into the column of rock, his face drawing so close to mine that I could smell his rancid breath.

At this distance, I could see that his pupils were little reptilian slits. I tried to work one hand free to swing the ax at him. But instead he slammed my fist against the column so hard that small bits of rock dislodged and fell to the ground. Again and again. But I held on. Because I knew that if I let go, I was dead.

But he was too strong for me. And in that moment, with the Grendel slowly closing his grasp on me, I realized one thing with an aching certainty: I had lost. A parade of faces flashed before my eyes. My parents. Grimsby. Gwynn. Doc. All bearing witness to my lifetime of failure, culminating now in my ultimate failure to stand in the way of this evil that wanted to overwhelm us all. As my muscles strained against the crushing force of the Grendel's arms, tears sprang to my eyes, even as I pressed them tightly closed.

"I'm sorry," I whispered. "I'm sorry . . ."

The Grendel hissed, his raspy laugh mere inches from my face. "It's too late for that now. Now you can die just like your mother: pleading for your life. Just like she begged for yours."

Another image took form in my head. A room lit only by a small lamp. Me tucked in bed, my mom sitting beside me reading the story of Beowulf's defeat of the Grendel: "'Against Beowulf the demon stretched his claw; and swiftly Beowulf laid hold on it. Straightaway that master of evil deeds perceived that never had he met within this world in earth's four corners on any other man a mightier grip of hand.'"

As my mom's words echoed in my head, deep down inside myself I felt a change. Years of emotions—fear, anger, sadness, frustration—combined into a pinpoint of energy.

Through clenched teeth, I said the next line of the story out loud: "'In heart and soul . . . the Grendel. Grew. *Afraid*.'"

My eyes snapped open.

"AAHHHHHHHHHHHHHHHH!"

I screamed and threw him backward, feeling the pinpoint of energy explode through my limbs in a shock wave. In the same motion I slashed across his body with the ax.

He cried out and crashed to the cavern floor ten feet away, wheezing and snarling. A deep red slash oozed across his shoulder. His arm hung limply at his side. His eyes shot downward, then back at me in disbelief. "No. Noooo. How?"

I stood there panting, looking down at him, then at my hands in awe, wondering where that burst of energy had come from. The ax rapidly became white-hot. Too hot to hold. I dropped it to the ground, where it started to sizzle and dissolve from the Grendel's blood, just like in the Beowulf legend.

*Crrraaack!*

The nearest column snapped in half and crumbled to the floor. "Abby!"

I turned my head and spotted Gwynn about twenty yards away, struggling to scoop the limp form of Grimsby into the trash can with her injured arm.

Then a glint caught the corner of my eye. When I looked toward it, my heart sank. The svefnthorn bloom was lying there on the cavern floor. Grimsby must have dropped it. I was such an idiot. I should have held on to it myself. And then I realized that even in this moment of triumph, I had managed to fail.

There was an ominous rumble from the ceiling again. This time little chunks of rock dislodged as the whole thing shivered like gray pudding.

I heard a noise from the Grendel and spun back toward him, both hands reaching for my ax until I remembered I no longer had it.

But he still lay on the ground, alternately laughing and gasping for breath. "What will the hero do now?" he sneered. "Save your friends, and let your father die? Or save the flower, and leave your friends to be crushed to death?" He looked up at the crumbling ceiling. "You don't have time for both."

I balled my fists in frustration, looking back and forth from Gwynn and Grimsby to the flower. I pictured my dad's frail form collapsing against his hospital bed, then saw Gwynn fall to one knee next to Grimsby, clutching her arm. It was an impossible decision. I closed my eyes and felt a tear streak down my cheek.

"I—I know what you'd want me to do, D-Daddy," I whispered.

I opened my eyes and sprinted toward Gwynn. "Hold on to the trash can while I hoist him in."

When I knelt and bear-hugged him from behind to haul him to his feet, Grimsby mumbled, "Juz a few more minutes, Mommy."

A movement caught my eye. In the shadows on the periphery of the room, the vapor seemed to jerk and dance. Dark forms started to materialize out of the mist: countless furry things with long claws and wicked-looking teeth, hissing and screeching as they scurried in our direction. Somehow the Grendel's one pet had morphed into a thousand . . .

"Rats!" Gwynn shrieked.

"Yes, my pets!" cried the Grendel. "Do not let them escape alive!"

I looked at Grimsby hanging limp in my arms, then back at the rats. "Sorry, buddy, this may hurt a little." And I shoved him headfirst into the garbage can. A soft groan echoed from the depths of the can.

"This way!" Gwynn shouted, and ran in the opposite direction from where we'd entered the cavern.

Across the top of the trash can I saw a wave of rats approaching. I spun it around with Grimsby's feet flopping to the side and pushed him and the can after her at a sprint. A chunk of rock crumbled from the ceiling and smashed to the floor nearby. Then more and more rocks started falling all around us. I dodged around one, then stopped and changed course as a column toppled in front of us, nearly losing Grimsby in the process.

"Driver," his voice echoed from inside the trash can, "lemme off at the necks stop."

Ahead, Gwynn appeared out of the darkness. "Are you okay?"

"Fine!" I shouted back.

She waved me onward. "Go! I'll be right behind you."

Rock crumbled everywhere, filling the air with a dusty haze. I glanced back over my shoulder and saw Gwynn slap a rat away as it sprang toward her. A dark wave of fur and teeth spread across the floor behind us like a living carpet. We bolted across the crumbling cavern, barely able to see the way forward. I had no idea if we were even going toward an exit or into a literal dead end.

"Over there!" Gwynn shouted. I saw it too: the distinct rectangular outline in the dark of a door lit from behind. Seconds later I barreled into the door shoulder-first, pulling Grimsby behind me without slowing down, feeling a flare of pain on the impact. But the door gave way into a bright white room.

I tripped and sprawled forward, temporarily blinded by the sudden light. The trash can spun and tipped over, spilling Grimsby onto the floor. He flopped limply into a pile of limbs. Gwynn staggered out on my heels and dropped to her knees by my side, panting.

An enormous *BOOM!* came from behind us, followed by a cloud of dust that blossomed out of the door we'd just come through. The caverns had collapsed.

I waited for a minute to let my ears stop ringing, then pushed myself up on one arm. "Where are we?"

The dust slowly dissipated as I peered around. The door we'd just come through had a sign that read "Supply Closet" to one side of it.

"I think we're in Asgard," Gwynn said with surprise. "The Grendel must have used this as a secret entrance to and from his lair."

A pair of burly Vikings turned the corner and sprinted our way, alerted by the noise. They slowed as they recognized us. One had shaggy brown hair just like my dad.

Dad. I lay my head back on the floor again and felt the tile on my bare cheek. It felt cold. Just like everything inside me. Now there was nothing we could do to save my dad. Absolutely nothing. The only antidote was buried under a mile of rock.

"What's that?" Gwynn's voice cut through the fog in my brain.

But I only lay there on the ground, closing my eyes tightly against the darkness that seemed to be closing in on me. It wasn't until I heard her gasp that I flopped my head to one side to see what she was looking at. Grimsby lay on the floor facedown, snoring like a lawn mower. Near his feet was a small glowing object. Gwynn leaned forward to pluck it off the ground.

I sat up quickly, my eyes growing wide. "How . . . ?"

Gwynn's laugh was choked off by a sob. "He must have had it in his pocket the whole time! The original one he saw that made him fall into the well."

She held it up to the light. It was a single petal from the svefnthorn.

# CHAPTER 27

# INCONCEIVABLE

"There," said Dr. Swenson, extracting a hypodermic needle from Grimsby's limp arm, then pressing one palm gently against his cheek. "Now only time will tell if the serum from a single petal is enough to counteract the thorn's poison."

I sat in the ICU between the unconscious forms of my dad and Grimsby. Dr. Swenson had already administered the same treatment to my dad after distilling what we hoped was the antidote from the tiny svefnthorn petal. It seemed impossible that something so small and fragile could bring my dad back from the edge of death. Would it actually work? My fingers clenched and unclenched nervously as I sat there on the precipice with him, not willing to let the tiny bud of hope in my heart blossom too soon. His body seemed to be in the process of slowly collapsing into the bed, with only the beat of the heart monitor giving any evidence that he still lived.

"Owwwww!" I complained, and looked down at Bryn.

"Hold still for just a sec." She continued cleaning a series of deep cuts on my forearm from where the Grendel's claws had raked my skin. Added to the throbbing ache, the antiseptic she was now applying made the area burn like my skin was on fire. "Given the circumstances, you should be glad this is the only significant injury you sustained. This should heal quickly, but you might want to take a break from knattleikr for a while."

Gwynn stood on the other side of Grimsby's bed and stared down at him. Unlike my dad, he seemed to hover on the verge of consciousness, mumbling incoherently as if he was only in a deep sleep. Occasionally his body would give a sudden jerk or his face would twitch like he was fighting the toxin that coursed through him. But my dad gave no outward signs of life.

"Is it strange that the poison never fully knocked him out?" Gwynn said.

Dr. Swenson nodded, studying Grimsby's face as it briefly contorted into a frown. "At even the minimal dosage he received from pricking his finger, he should have been out cold. He's showing the same resistance to the venom that I'd expect of a much larger adult." She smiled up at us. "An adult grizzly bear, that is."

Gwynn smiled. "Well, he sure eats like one. I've never seen—"

Suddenly Grimsby made a loud snorting noise. He jerked straight up in bed like someone had electrocuted him, his arms flailing. "Get them off! Rats!"

"Grimsby!" I said happily, leaning out of range of his windmilling arms.

He froze, then blinked and turned to look at Gwynn and me. "You guys, I just had the weirdest dream. There was this underground cave. And the *janitor* tried to kill us with his mop. And there were all these rats and . . ." He looked around as if noticing the hospital room for the first time. "Mom? What am I doing here?"

Dr. Swenson smiled and leaned down to kiss him on the top of his head. "I'm so happy to see you awake, sweetie."

My eyes widened. "Wait . . . Mom?"

Grimsby turned his head to me. "Yeah, well, I told you my mom was a doctor, right?"

"Sure, but . . ." I trailed off.

As if reading my thoughts, Dr. Swenson added, "I was already established professionally when I met Jacob's father, so I kept my maiden name after we married." She tucked a stray lock of hair behind her glasses, and suddenly I saw the resemblance in the mass of unruly curly hair.

Gwynn leaned down and gave Grimsby a hug. "Good to see you again."

"Oh. How, um, is your dad?" Grimsby asked over Gwynn's shoulder, noticing the bed next to his for the first time.

"Still with us," I said, searching my dad's face for any sign of recovery. "Dr. Swenson . . . er, your mom said you were only exposed to a small dose of the thorn's poison, and very recently. His dose was a lot larger and had longer to work through his body. So to be honest, we're not sure yet if it'll be . . ." I couldn't bear to say the words "too late" out loud.

I stayed by my dad's side the rest of the day. By dinnertime, Grimsby was feeling well enough to go home under his mom's care, his only complaint an odd bump on his forehead. I didn't think he'd be too happy to learn that he'd gotten it when I'd shoved him headfirst into a trash can, so I discreetly avoided the subject.

As the night wore on, I felt like I was slipping into a half-dream state. My exhausted brain clung to the fact that the forty-eight-hour window Dr. Swenson had originally proposed had come and gone, and my dad was still alive. Even if barely so.

At some point, I snapped awake to find Bryn entering the hospital room to check on him.

"How are you holding up?" she said gently to me. She pointed to an untouched food tray on the table beside me. "You know, going on a hunger strike won't do either of you any good."

I sat up and yawned. "I know. I'll be okay." I plucked a carrot stick off the tray and bit into it, mostly to make her feel better because I had zero appetite. "He'll make it," I said more confidently than I felt. "He's always been so strong." But he looked anything but strong now. So small and frail amid all the wires and machines.

Bryn made a few notes on her clipboard. "I'll let the doctor know there hasn't been any change. Be back in a little while to check in on you guys again."

I nodded absently and took a seat at my dad's bedside. His tape player was making a buzzing noise, indicating it had reached the end of the tape, so I hit Stop and switched it off. Then I slid my hands around one of his. "Hi, Daddy. I don't know if you can hear me, but I'm still here. And I'll be here for as long as—" I choked on the carrot and my emotions, then swallowed hard before continuing. "For as long as you need me." A tear slid down my cheek.

"Do you remember all those times we watched *The Princess Bride*? You said it was the silliest movie you'd ever seen, but I knew you secretly loved it as much as I did. And afterward . . . afterward for days we'd go around the house shouting . . . we'd shout . . ."

Suddenly I couldn't speak, overcome with emotion. My head sagged toward the floor and I pressed my eyes tightly shut, trying to block out the heartache.

"Inconceivable . . ."

The word was barely a whisper. Had it been a figment of my imagination? My head shot up just in time to see a corner of Dad's mouth twitch slightly. Had he just . . .

I leapt to my feet. Ran to the door. "Bryn! Dr. Swenson!"

I ran back to his side, my pulse pounding and the fog falling away from my brain. After watching *The Princess Bride*, we'd go around the house for days shouting the villain Vizzini's catchphrase. And I was pretty sure my dad had just whispered that same word a second ago. It was, well, inconceivable.

His mouth twitched again, then he coughed. His eyes fluttered open, and he stared at the ceiling for a few seconds, blinking in confusion. Then his head turned toward me, a look of surprise on his face. "Abby? Where . . . ?" he said weakly. He shifted his gaze over my shoulder.

I spun and saw Gwynn and Grimsby framed in the doorway with a bouquet of balloons. Their mouths hung open in happy bewilderment. Bryn came rushing in past them, the balloons bobbing in her wake, with Dr. Swenson right on her heels. Grimsby's mom hovered a thermometer over my dad's forehead and quickly checked his other vital signs.

"Well, hello, Mr. Beckett. We're all so happy to see you with us again."

I edged past the doctor and fell on my dad in a huge bear hug, unable to speak. My shoulders shook with silent sobs. Dr. Swenson eventually gently pulled me away, then turned to him.

"How are you feeling? Is there anything I can get you? Pain medication, perhaps?"

Dad lay there blinking his eyes. Then in a dry, raspy voice: "Yes . . . I'm dying for . . . a cheeseburger."

I stared blankly at him for a moment. I didn't know if I wanted to laugh or cry. In the end, I did a little of both, leaning over to clutch him in another tight hug.

"Well, you heard the man," said Gwynn, smiling and poking her head out into the hall. "What's a guy have to do to get some cheeseburgers up in here?"

A surprised-looking nurse scuttled off toward the cafeteria. Ten minutes later, a pair of legs returned with the rest of the body and face obscured behind several bags already turning dark with grease stains from burgers and fries. A grinning face peeked around the edge of the mountain of food. It had a bald head and Coke-bottle glasses.

"Doc!" I shouted, grinning.

"I heard you guys were having a party," he said. "Hope you don't mind me crashing it."

"Sig!" Dad exclaimed with surprise.

*Uh, Sig?* "You two know each other?" I asked.

"A story for another time, perhaps," Doc said. He set the food down on a nearby table, then turned to me with a quizzical look on his face. "You wouldn't happen to know anything about a sea monster in Vale's swimming pool, would you?"

Grimsby, Gwynn, and I all looked at one another and broke down laughing.

"Now, that's a story for another time," said Grimsby, already fishing around in the bags of food and pulling out a fistful of fries.

"How about we hear that one now?" Dad said, raising one eyebrow.

So we sat around his bed, bringing him up to speed on the events since our arrival at Vale while we munched on our food. I kept catching myself reaching out to touch his hand or adjust the hem of his sleeve as if to convince myself he was really alive. That the nightmare was finally over. Every once in a while, he asked us to stop and go back and repeat ourselves because we'd gotten to a part that was just too unbelievable.

When we were finished, Doc studied each of us for a long moment, then said, "I knew bits and pieces of this, but it's indeed eye-opening to finally see the full picture. The Vikings owe you each a great debt of gratitude. Abby. Gwynn. Jacob. Thank you." He turned to Dr. Swenson. "And thank you for letting me con-script your son into service."

I frowned. "What do you mean?"

Doc winked at me. "Well, who do you think assigned Mr.

Grimsby to be your tour guide? I think he comported himself quite well under the circumstances."

"But he's not even a Viking," I said, then glanced at Grimsby, no longer sure. "Right?"

"Not a bit of Viking blood in us, I'm afraid," said Dr. Swenson. "But I prefer to think of us as, let's just say, Viking adjacent."

*Viking* adjacent? *What did* that *mean?*

Doc tapped his chest over his heart as he stood and shrugged his jacket on. "It's as I told you: The true measure of who we are is right here. Mr. Grimsby may not be a Viking, but in the times that I fear may be coming, I feel we should not be so nearsighted as to fail to look for allies wherever they may be found." He put a hand on Grimsby's shoulder. "Your friend here has the heart of a true warrior."

I looked at Grimsby, who grinned at me through a mouthful of fries. I laughed and nodded. "The heart of a warrior."

This was all still so unbelievable. My life had completely changed in the space of a few days. But it suddenly looked like everything was going to turn out okay. My dad was alive. The Grendel was gone. It was over.

Then what Doc had said finally registered. "Hold on. What did you mean by 'in the times that I fear may be—'" I said, spinning around. But Doc had already left the room. I looked down at the half-eaten bag of fries in my hand and set it on the table, my appetite suddenly gone.

# CHAPTER 28
# KNIVES AND DOLLS

"Is this Abby's wittle dolly?" Grimsby teased, extracting a pink-and-white bonneted doll with frayed yellow bangs from one of the moving boxes on my bedroom floor.

It was a week later, and I knelt on the floor of my bedroom, finally getting the chance to take my things out of moving boxes. We'd recently moved into our permanent residence, a two-bedroom bungalow on Faculty Row, right off the main Vale campus. That night in Charlotte when my dad and I had fled north already felt like ages ago. I could hear Bryn humming in the kitchen while she baked a batch of chocolate chip cookies. My dad was slowly improving but still far from one hundred percent, so Bryn was temporarily living with us to help out while he recuperated.

"Give me that!" I said, yanking the doll out of Grimsby's hand and hugging her protectively against my chest.

"Ow!" he said, jerking his other hand out of the box and jamming his finger into his mouth. "Are these things real?"

Gwynn punched his shoulder as she leaned over and looked appraisingly at the collection of Viking seaxes—close-range fighting knives—assembled neatly in the bottom of the box. "Never mess with a girl's dolls . . . or her knife collection."

As I came to a framed photo of me with my parents, I dropped into the swivel chair at my desk and leaned back, studying their faces. At last, I felt like something I'd accomplished really mattered. It felt good. I only wished Mom had been there to see it.

There was the sound of a snort beside me, and I turned my head to see Grimsby lying on his back on my beanbag chair and staring at his phone while he sucked on his injured finger. His entire body shook either with the sudden onset of hypothermia or an uncontrollable fit of laughter. I assumed it was the second one.

"Baby dolphin!" he finally gasped, followed by a squeak of laughter.

Gwynn looked up from the books she'd gone back to helping me organize on a small shelf in one corner of the room. "Anything you want to share?"

When he finally managed to control his laughter, he gestured to his phone. "You remember the sea monster in the pool?"

I shivered, recalling the enormous yellow eye emerging from the water. "Yeah, how could we forget? Did someone get it on video or something?"

"Not exactly. Didn't you wonder how they managed to explain that one? I mean, to all the non-Viking students at Vale? It's not exactly something that happens every day."

"Good point. I guess I hadn't thought about it. Why?"

He held the phone's screen up and leaned forward so we could read it. The top video was titled "Girls Save Stranded Baby Dolphin."

Gwynn raised an eyebrow. "What's this?"

"Just watch." Grimsby thumbed the Play button, and we stared at the video as our fight with the sea monster played out basically how I remembered it. With the exception of a few, um, minor points. Like Grimsby going berserk and slapping Ping-Pong balls around the room like a lunatic and everyone running and ducking to avoid being hit. Oh, and that instead of battling a sea monster, Gwynn and I were rescuing an injured baby dolphin from drowning in the school swimming pool. The video stopped just as Glen, aka the Grendel, came into view with his familiar trash can and mop.

I stared at Grimbsy. "How . . . ?"

Gwynn laughed. "Remember how the VIC simulation convinced you that you were actually in a Viking raid? This sort of thing is a walk in the park for Mr. Lodbrok's team. It's not the first time they've had to use their skills to make it look like something didn't actually happen."

"It's not fair," Grimsby complained. "They made you guys look like heroes, and I just look like a big doof. They even deleted my charge with the bucket of—"

"Hold on," I cut in as Gwynn's words registered. "Did you say Mr. Lodbrok's team?"

Gwynn studied the book spines on my shelf and slid a new book into place. "Yeah, Chase's dad runs what's called the PR team."

"You mean, as in public relations?"

"Basically, yes, but officially it stands for 'proximate reality' because sometimes they have to doctor reality a little to preserve the Vikings' secrets. The rumor is there's sometimes even mind-control techniques involved. I heard he was pretty upset about how this one was handled."

Grimsby snorted again. "Proximate reality? More like purely rubbish."

I could feel my stomach slowly sinking into my shoes. "Ohhhh," I said quietly.

Gwynn shoved another book into place and turned toward me with a slight frown. "That doesn't sound good. What's wrong?"

*We have to try to make it look like the whole thing never happened.* Mr. Lodbrok's words echoed in my mind. "I should tell you guys something. About Mr. Lodbrok. I sort of overheard him talking, and I *thought* he was saying he tried to kill me."

Gwynn rose to her feet. "Mr. Lodbrok tried to kill you?! When?"

I shifted uncomfortably. "By, um, putting a sea monster in the swimming pool."

A look of comprehension dawned on Gwynn's face as I plunged on. "So a few days ago, I told Doc about it, figuring he could handle it since, you know, it's *kind* of a big deal accusing a member of the Grey Council of attempted murder—"

Before I could finish, there was a loud banging on the front door.

"Abby! Could you get that?" Bryn called from the kitchen. "My hands are covered with flour!"

"Just a sec," I said to Grimsby and Gwynn as I swung around in the chair and headed for the front door. Whoever it was, they were banging so hard the hinges rattled. I probably should have taken that as a warning that it wasn't just an overly aggressive Girl Scout selling cookies.

"Keep your pants on!" I called to the person outside. "I'm—"

As I pulled the door open, Chase Lodbrok pushed through the entryway and charged at me.

I quickly backpedaled away from him until I met a wall and my head connected with a light fixture. "Ow! What gives?" I raised a hand to rub my head.

Chase stood there nearly nose-to-nose with me, staring with wild, furious eyes, until I wedged my arms between us and managed to push him away. His normally perfect hair fell limply across his face. We stood in the hallway a few feet apart, glaring at each other like caged animals.

Bryn, drawn by the noise, rushed through the kitchen doorway with a rolling pin raised to attack. She stopped and looked from me to Chase.

"Abby? Is everything okay?" I turned and saw my dad standing in the doorway to his room, leaning wearily against the frame. His face was still pale and gaunt from the effects of the svefnthorn.

"I'm so sorry we woke you, Daddy," I said. "Yes, this is Chase Lodbrok. He goes to Vale. But I don't have any idea . . ." I started to say, but then I realized I actually had a pretty good idea why he was there.

Chase must have seen the realization in my eyes, because he said, "There it is. I guess I was right. It wasn't enough for you to wreck half the school on your imaginary '*quest*.'" He made air quotes with his fingers when he said the word "quest." "No, you had to drag my father into this too." Slowly he clenched and unclenched his fists.

"Abby, what's he talking about?" my dad said.

I glanced at him, then across at Grimsby and Gwynn, who had emerged from my room. "Well, I only . . ." I pressed the heel of my palm against my forehead, trying to figure out the right words to explain. "See, I started thinking there was no way the Grendel was working on his own. So I thought about who could have been helping him. And I overheard a conversation where someone admitted to trying to kill me. Or at least I *thought* that's what I heard . . ."

"Wait," my dad said. He was suddenly racked by a coughing fit. Bryn and I both started to move toward him, but he put up his hand. "I'm . . . okay." He looked back at me. "Why am I just hearing about this for the first time? You said the Grendel is gone. So now someone *else* is trying to kill you? Who?"

Chase gave me a dark look. "According to her—my father."

I turned to my dad. "Sorry, Daddy, I didn't want to worry you because you'd almost"—my voice caught in my throat—"*died*. And I didn't want you to have to think about anything but getting better. You've got to understand how it looked . . ."

Chase's phone rang. He looked down at the caller ID, then

thumbed it on. "Yes, sir. Okay, ten minutes. I will." He ended the call. "That was my father. The Grey Council requests our presence in Professor Roth's office."

The air in the room suddenly seemed colder. The last time I'd had an audience with the Grey Council, my whole life had basically been turned upside down. I turned to my dad for reassurance, but he seemed visibly shaken. I wasn't sure if it was from the news of someone out there who possibly still wanted me dead or the summons by the Grey Council, or both. He drew in a deep breath and said, "I'm going with you."

He took a step away from the door and nearly fell. I rushed to catch him and help him back toward his room. "No. I've got this. You need to stay here and rest."

# CHAPTER 29

# AN UNEXPECTED VISITOR

Ten minutes later, Chase and I walked down the oak-paneled corridor in an uneasy truce under the now-familiar withering gazes of past headmasters. I felt dizzy from the lack of oxygen to my brain. Why were we being summoned to an audience with the Grey Council? When we neared the open door to Professor Roth's office, I could hear the sound of raised voices and people arguing. I tapped lightly on the doorframe and the voices immediately cut off.

Professor Roth strode smoothly across the room to greet us with the same half frown that she always seemed to wear. She extended both hands to take mine in hers. "We're so pleased to hear your father is recovering. How is he feeling?"

"Pretty good," I said, "given the circumstances."

"The circumstances, yes," said Professor Roth. "Exactly what we have called you here to discuss." She looked over my shoulder at Chase still standing in the doorway. "Mr. Lodbrok, if you will excuse us now."

The elder Lodbrok's voice traveled across the room. "Actually, I asked him to join us. I thought he could serve as a character witness."

I could guess whose character he meant. Mine.

Professor Roth and Chase's dad exchanged a quick look, then she gestured us toward the table where Doc and Mr. Lodbrok waited, their gray cloaks around their shoulders.

My eyes lingered briefly on the empty chair between the two men. I thought I saw a flash of sadness in Doc's eyes as he followed my gaze, then blinked and looked away toward the fire. Chase and I took seats across from each other, putting as much distance between ourselves as possible.

When we were all seated, Professor Roth nodded. "Very good. We have everyone here now. I think the first order of business we need to discuss is the matter of a rather serious accusation that has been made."

The air in the room seemed to crackle with electricity as I flicked my eyes toward Mr. Lodbrok, then down at the table, feeling my face flame red. Given what I'd recently learned about his role, it looked like he probably hadn't done anything wrong, unless you counted being a jerk. Had it been a mistake to report him to Doc? Maybe I should have just kept my mouth shut.

But the problem still nagged at me. Why had he assumed the sea monster was meant to kill me? And if Mr. Lodbrok hadn't let it in the pool, then who had? Or had the Grendel really been working alone at Vale, completely undetected for apparently over a hundred years? There was Fenris, of course, but I assumed the help more likely came from someone with an IQ slightly higher than a meatball's.

"As to that," continued Professor Roth, "I have taken into consideration the evidence presented concerning certain events of the past weeks." She judiciously avoided saying any names out loud. "But having spoken with the accused party at length, I see no reason to continue this line of inquiry at this time."

"I'm very sorry," I said, glancing at Chase. "Really. I didn't mean . . ." I wavered, trying to decide whether to voice my nagging fear. "But here's the thing: Do we really think the Grendel could have lived for so long among the Vikings without anyone's knowledge?"

Professor Roth turned toward me, her face unreadable. "An excellent point, Ms. Beckett. Indeed, how could such an enemy have lived hidden among us for so long?"

I leaned forward with a mix of excitement and fear. "So you agree? I mean, that there was someone helping the Grendel?"

"Not exactly, no," she said.

Suddenly I had a feeling like I was missing something. "What do you . . . mean?"

Mr. Lodbrok spoke then, not taking his eyes from his hands, which were folded on the table in front of him. "You see, when our excavation team finally managed to make their way through the rubble to investigate your claims, well . . ." His gaze was frigid when he looked up at me. "They could find no trace of a Grendel."

My insides instantly turned to water as I spun toward Doc, who had so far remained silent. But he was still staring into the fire.

"No . . . trace? But there were thousands of pounds of rock. There's no way he could have escaped. Maybe they were looking in the wrong place or . . . ?"

"It's certainly within the realm of possibility," said Professor Roth. "Abby, I personally have no reason to doubt your claims. And we'll of course continue our search. But until we have irrefutable proof, I'm sure you understand the difficulty of my situation. As the leader of the Vikings, I can't afford to risk spreading rumors that could shake Asgard to its core."

Mr. Lodbrok grunted dismissively. "Well, I, for one, find your story frankly difficult to believe."

I felt a swell of anger boil up in my chest as I surged up out of my chair. "What?! You think I'm . . . lying? That I just . . . What? Made all this up? Why would I do that? What would I possibly have to gain from pretending I uncovered a Grendel's plot to bring down the Vikings?"

Mr. Lodbrok slammed his palm on the table as he rose to meet me, then inhaled sharply through his nose as he visibly fought to control his emotions. When he spoke, there was a strained edge to his words. "Those were my questions exactly. And do you know what I think? I see a scared little girl. A girl who would do anything both to prove herself and to salvage the false memory that she holds of her mother."

I seethed, remembering my earlier encounter with Mr. Lodbrok in the longhouse and determined not to back down from him this time. "Maybe I was right about you after all. Even if you didn't have anything to do with the Grendel, it's fools like you who allowed one to live right under the Vikings' noses despite all the evidence."

"Oh, do you want to talk about evidence?" he shot back. "Then let's talk about this botanist's journal you mentioned that conveniently . . . What was it? Disintegrated into dust? Or the magical spoon-ax only your mother knew about, which supposedly melted upon contact with the Grendel's blood. Or how about this so-called secret lair that's now buried under a mountain of rock? Where exactly is this *evidence* you speak of?"

"I . . . I . . ." I stammered, so shocked and incensed that I couldn't speak, but suddenly I realized he was right. I had no real proof of the Grendel's existence. Then I remembered something else: "The sea monster—"

He waved his hand dismissively. "Is the sort of creature Vikings deal with all the time, which you would know if your mother—"

"Mr. Lodbrok!" Professor Roth said angrily, enunciating each syllable. "I'd hoped we could do this with more civility." She sighed and turned back toward me. "Abby, I'm sure you understand the way this looks. Absent any hard evidence, all we have to go on is the word of three children, one of whom was unconscious during the alleged encounter with the Grendel, and the other who can only corroborate parts of your story. Meaning you are the only one who witnessed all the supposed events. Which I hope you can see is not sufficient in such a weighty matter to prove the veracity of your story."

"But the janitor, Glen—"

"Is currently away visiting family," she said.

Wait. He was still . . . alive? Feeling suddenly very cold and alone, I cast my eyes around the other faces in the room looking for help. I thought I could at least count on Doc, but frustratingly he had his head bowed and hadn't yet said a thing. Chase's smug look spoke volumes.

"Hold on," I said to him. "What you said earlier. About my imaginary quest. You knew about all this?"

He sneered. "Like mother like daughter."

Mr. Lodbrok said, "Precisely my—"

"Enough." The word had been spoken at barely above a whisper, but it seemed to echo through the room. All eyes turned toward Doc, who was now standing, his palms pressed flat against the surface of the table, a mischievous glint in his eyes. "I was afraid things might come to this. Fortunately, I arranged for a bit of, ah, supporting evidence."

A knock sounded at the door. As all eyes turned in that direction, Doc said, "And it looks like it's right on time."

Without another word, he strode across the room. Mr. Lodbrok and the headmaster exchanged a confused look that echoed how I felt. What was happening?

Doc pulled the door open and stood aside. The figure who entered was temporarily silhouetted against the light of the hall. Then the firelight caught her features.

I gasped.

A tumble of blazing red hair framed a face with fierce green eyes and a mouth turned up at one corner in a slight smile.

"M-Mom?" For a split second, my world seemed to collapse

around me, then just as quickly it re-formed as realization hit me. Heart thundering, I dashed across the room and collided with the woman, wrapping her in a fierce hug as tears sprang to my eyes.

"Aunt Jess!"

She folded me into her arms, laughing. "How's my favorite niece? Doc said you might need a little backup."

"But I thought—" I broke off as I leaned back, drinking in her features that so closely mirrored my mom's.

"What? That a Grendel got the best of me? Not a chance." She smiled down at me. Then she turned to Doc. "Thanks to your teacher here. He was able to warn me just in time. I'm sorry I wasn't able to get here sooner."

Her eyes shifted to the rest of the Grey Council as her voice turned grave. "But I saw it. The thing that's been hunting the Aesir." She nodded. "There's no mistaking it. It's a Grendel."

"Welcome, Ms. Thorne," said Professor Roth, smoothly recovering from her surprise. "It would appear that we have much to discuss." She turned toward me. "Perhaps Abby and Chase could leave us to debrief in private?"

I looked at Aunt Jess, unwilling to let her go so soon. "I . . . I guess so. Where are you going to be staying?"

She winked at me. "I was hoping I could bunk with you and your dad for now."

I smiled. "That would be perfect. I'll see you soon, then."

Chase stalked out of the door ahead of me, not even looking in my direction as he left. With a last glance over my shoulder at my aunt standing next to Doc, I turned to go too and heard the head-master's door swing closed behind me.

My brain hurt from the shock of everything that had just happened. Mr. Lodbrok's and Professor Roth's refusal to open their eyes to the great danger we'd just narrowly escaped. My aunt's sudden reappearance as if from the dead. Even if they didn't believe me, they couldn't ignore her, a real Aesir.

*They could find no trace of a Grendel.* And finally, the possibility that a Grendel still lurked somewhere in the shadows.

I pushed through a pair of doors leading out onto a snow-covered walkway behind Vale. A freezing wind temporarily tore my breath away, and I pulled my jacket tighter around myself. I started across the campus toward home, then heard a shout behind me.

"Abby!"

I spun around. Doc pushed through the doors and walked through the snow in my direction.

"Are they already done?" I said.

He looked back over his shoulder. "No, I'm afraid this could take quite some time. But I just wanted to let you know . . ." He turned back and looked me directly in the eyes. "I'm proud of you for standing up to them like you did back there. I know it wasn't easy."

I nodded. "Everything I told them. It all happened just like I said. You . . . believe me. Don't you?"

Some of the mischievous look from earlier still lingered in his eyes. "It's unfortunately not a matter of whether I believe you or not. There is a bigger picture that you're not aware of."

"What you said earlier in the hospital about the times you fear may be coming? Is that what you mean?"

He nodded. "Indeed. I feel something building. Events in motion that we don't understand yet. Almost daily the Vikings are alerted to new threats around the world. Supposed sightings of monstrous creatures that the world hasn't seen for centuries."

"Like sea monsters in the school pool?"

Doc shot me a sidelong look. "Abby, many feel that the idea of a Grendel living at Vale is simply preposterous. The truth is, we don't know what's going on, but it feels like we're under siege. And chasing after a supposed Grendel right here at our school is seen as an unnecessary distraction at present."

I stamped my foot in frustration. "But didn't you say Grendels basically run the show? Can't the others see that's what must be behind all of this?"

"Yes, but why now? Why after all this time? And why here at Vale?"

I cupped my hands over my mouth and blew into them as I considered. I couldn't answer any of these questions. Then, shivering from an internal chill deeper than the cold around us, I jerked my head toward him. "What Professor Roth said. About the janitor being away visiting relatives? Is that . . . ?"

Doc turned his head back toward the closed doors of Vale before replying. "That's the official story. But the truth is, he seems to have disappeared."

"So he's"—I could hardly bring myself to say it—"still alive?"

"All we know is there was no body found when the collapsed caverns were excavated."

I was suddenly finding it very hard to breathe. "But if he's . . . I mean, the only weapon we had that was any use at all against a Grendel is gone. That means if he's still alive, we're defenseless, right?"

He looked at me closely. "Not entirely, no."

Feeling strangely self-conscious, I said, "Why? What do you mean?"

"Abby, you remember the story of Beowulf's fight with the Grendel, don't you?"

"Sure," I said. "Why?"

"What weapon did he use to defeat it?"

I thought for a few seconds. "I guess he didn't use any weapon. He, well, tore off the Grendel's arm with his bare hands."

"Exactly. Beowulf's sheer strength allowed him to do what no weapon had been able to do up to that point."

"Okaaayyy . . ." I said. "But the only person with that kind of strength would be an Aesir. And Aunt Jess is the only one left. So it's all up to her?"

"Maybe not . . . the only one."

"Wh-what do you mean?"

Frowning, he extracted a small wooden ball from his pocket and held it up. "Abby, not long ago I witnessed you put this knat-tleikr ball through a five-inch-thick glass wall. I've never seen raw power like that in all my years of coaching. Added to that, you've foiled a dark Valkyrie, killed a sea monster, and defeated a Grendel—our most dangerous and ancient of enemies. It's hard not to be impressed by how you've accomplished in such a short time what even a seasoned warrior can rarely claim to do in a lifetime."

I blinked. "So . . . you're saying you think I really *am* an Aesir after all?"

He handed the ball to me. "I'm saying, don't give up hope. Not yet." And then he turned to walk away.

"Wait. So what am I supposed to do now?"

Without looking back, he said, "What the Vikings have always done. Hope for the best, but prepare for battle."

I watched his back as he walked away, disappearing through the same door we'd recently exited. Vale Hall loomed large and black against the late-afternoon sun, giving me the feeling that I'd only started to explore the secrets within its walls. Then I looked down at the knattleikr ball shining dully in my hand, wishing it was a crystal ball that could tell me the future. It was silent. But at least I knew that whatever the future held, I had my dad, my aunt, and new friends to help me find the answers.

# ACKNOWLEDGMENTS

More than a thousand years before Spider-Man or the Avengers appeared in comic books and on movie screens, the great story-tellers of old spun tales of Beowulf—the mighty champion of the north whose feats thrilled adults and kids alike, just as our modern superheroes do today. I fell in love with the epic of *Beowulf* when I first encountered it in college, but it wasn't until years later that the idea of adapting the poem into a more accessible, modern story for today's readers began to form. Finally, after many starts and stops, my story of the fierce young warrior Abby Beckett began to take shape. Readers of the original *Beowulf* will, I hope, note more than a few similarities, from my use of a Grendel as the villain of the story to the hero's battle with a sea monster (though my sea monster's wicked Ping-Pong skills were entirely my invention).

Though my name is on the cover, there are innumerable heroes who, like the anonymous author of *Beowulf*, might never receive due credit for their efforts, ideas, and encouragement in the creation of this book, but I would like to highlight some of those people here:

First, my agent, Maura Kye-Casella, who saw something in an early draft that convinced her to take a chance on a debut author. Without her excellent feedback on the book and guidance in navigating the children's publishing market, Abby's story may never have seen the light of day. I still recall the first time we spoke over the phone on a December day barely a week before Christmas, when she said about the manuscript, "I think this could be something really great," and, like that, I started to believe it myself.

Of course, a huge thank-you to my editor, Mallory Kass, whose enthusiasm for the story from the start was infectious. Your incredible insights into storytelling, relentless encouragement to push my book to the next level, and, I'm sure, countless hours of reading and rereading each draft and manuscript note down to the proper usage of the umlaut in Mjölnir have been invaluable in making the story what it is today.

Likewise, to the incredible team at Scholastic who made this book possible, including Baily Crawford, Josh Berlowitz, Melissa Schirmer, and Maya Marlette.

It's said that no man is an island, and this axiom certainly holds true for writers. I've found that it's impossible to write well without the regular support and feedback of other writers and readers. So I would be remiss not to thank the many critique partners and beta readers who helped shape this book: Eric Boyd, Angie Chan, Neal Chase, Trisha Clifford, Justin Colon, Deborah Drick, Liz Edelbrock, Andrew Edwards, Jen Jobart, Brad Johnson, Michael Lunsford, Margaret Mason, Joyce Masongsong-Ray, C. Lee McKenzie, Kate O'Shaughnessy, S. B. Porter, L. N. Russell, Melanie Savransky, Shari Schwarz, Shane Souther, Mike Wheeler, and Stephenie Wilson-Peterson.

A special thanks to the students and teachers of the fifth-, sixth-, and seventh-grade classes at San Jose Christian School.

Your feedback that my original story was "almost as good as Harry Potter" was super encouraging and helped me to keep writing and aspiring to achieve something worthy of the famous bespectacled wizard.

Mary Riley played an important role with her copious detailed sticky notes and insights throughout my early manuscript. And Beth Costa provided critical guidance regarding the workings of hospitals and the medical world in general.

Mom and Dad, you always surrounded me with books and love from an early age and supported my creative endeavors in whatever form they took, even if my earliest writing mediums were occasionally bedroom walls or my brothers. You were the models for the positive parent-child relationships that I tried to portray in this book and the inspiration for more than a few scenes throughout.

To my kids, who cheered me on the whole time, even when writing sometimes meant I had to miss out on playing *Super Smash Bros.* or throwing a Frisbee with you. I love that you regularly tell me that I'm the best writer in the world. You guys are seriously the best kids in the world. I hope my getting my book published shows you that you can accomplish your dreams too—even the big, scary ones.

And finally to my own Viking queen, my wife, Rebecca: You were a constant support through the entire process of writing this book, never failing to give me the time or space I needed to wrestle with a tough scene, be a sounding board for ideas, or quietly swoop in with a plate of snickerdoodles while I was writing and just as silently spirit away. This book would not have been possible without you. I love you with all my heart.

# ABOUT THE AUTHOR

Sam Subity loves writing stories that explore the magic and wonder of being a kid and is thrilled to share his debut novel with readers everywhere—both the young in age and the young at heart. When he's not writing, you might find him running the trails of Northern California, where the endless, winding miles past fog and ocean inspire stories of adventure and mystery. Or he might be mowing his lawn. Because that's what adults sometimes have to do. But in either case, he's very likely imagining himself fighting mythical creatures or at the prow of a Viking dragon ship, feeling the wind and sea spray on his face. His greatest hope is that in reading this book, you too were in some small way transported to another place where for a little while you could exchange the ordinary for the extraordinary.